About the Author

Born in Swindon, and after military service, Alan Paisey taught in secondary schools in Southwark and Lambeth, London and later Bulmershe College, University of Reading, retiring as Head of Administrative Studies. His other novels include:

Her Cell of Straw
Lyndsey

Elsa's Dangerous Games

Alan Paisey

Elsa's Dangerous Games

Olympia Publishers
London

www.olympiapublishers.com
OLYMPIA PAPERBACK EDITION

Copyright © Alan Paisey 2023

The right of Alan Paisey to be identified as author of
this work has been asserted in accordance with sections 77 and 78
of the Copyright, Designs and Patents Act 1988.

All Rights Reserved

No reproduction, copy or transmission of this publication
may be made without written permission.
No paragraph of this publication may be reproduced,
copied or transmitted save with the written permission of the
publisher, or in accordance with the provisions
of the Copyright Act 1956 (as amended).

Any person who commits any unauthorised act in relation to
this publication may be liable to criminal
prosecution and civil claims for damage.

A CIP catalogue record for this title is
available from the British Library.

ISBN: 978-1-80074-224-6

This book is a work of fiction and, except in the case of historical
fact, any resemblance to actual persons, living or dead, is purely
coincidental.

First Published in 2023

Olympia Publishers
Tallis House
2 Tallis Street
London
EC4Y 0AB

Printed in Great Britain

Dedication

To Alice and Amelia

Acknowledgements

I thank my wife, Sheila, for her indispensable support.

1

It had a charm of its own. Not many would have called it beautiful, but it was an exciting place for a visitor to spend a day. From a topographical point of view, it was greatly preferable to idling in a suburb of Manchester.

The man had driven very early that Saturday morning to the furthermost north-west tip of Anglesey, just to see the town. It was yet another day out during a visit to long-lost family members.

Holyhead was on the end of the land, but commanding the Irish Sea, northwards and southwards. On his way into the town, with its integral port, he passed the simple terminus of the railway station. Its platforms would soon be swarming with passengers from a ship he could see arriving and another already docked, towering over their surroundings on a high tide.

He drove along to the water's edge, where the true identity of the town could be clearly seen as a crossroads of sea and land, so evidently apparent when seen from the large ferry ships, with *Irish* or *Stella* company titles emblazoned on their sides.

People came or went on those ships in a steady stream, as had been the custom for at least a century and a half, on ships of cruder vintage, given the relative proximity of the island of Ireland.

On reaching the seafront, he turned the car left away from the railway station, and the port lying alongside it, to skirt nearer the centre of the little town. After a few hundred metres, with water alongside on his right, the car reached a long area of undulating, public-park greens, liberally served with wooden seats in ancient metal shelters, in fairly urgent need of maintenance attention.

He pulled in to a small parking area overlooking a rocky beach area. The tide seemed to be in two minds as to whether to come further in or not, lapping the end of a very long sloping ramp, enabling cars and larger vehicles to back their sluggishly towed boats down to the water where they truly belonged.

It seemed to be a useful spot to park that morning. His manner was unhurried. He was actually greeted by other men, some dressed in diving gear, when they saw his casual stance and interest in what they were doing.

'What's going on today?' he asked.

'We are here to rendezvous with an official examiner of the British Sub Aqua Club. He is coming to test the skills of several members of the local branch for their handling and management of boats used in diving operations.'

'That sounds like a worthwhile sight to see,' the man replied. 'I hope all goes well for you.'

He saw their trial boat standing nearby on its trailer, readied for taking down the ramp into the sea, but waiting to be crewed up for the simulated sea demonstrations to be conducted on board that day with the examiner.

It was a colourful boat, painted reminiscently of RNLI lifeboats distributed all around the coasts, with an orange superstructure and blue for the hull. When all the interested parties had clambered aboard, with others walking alongside, their fussing temporarily over, the boat was eased down the long ramp to the water backwards on its wheeled trailer behind a towing vehicle.

The hectic and noisy preparations that had filled the early morning air around the half-dozen parked cars—and disturbing the general peace of the environment—miraculously evaporated with the boat's departure. The emptiness created by its loss at the assembly point at the top of the ramp, left the visitor as an observer in a solitary state, wondering what he would do next, given the sudden transfer of the activity that had absorbed his attention.

He watched the scene with fascination. The boat's descent down the long ramp into the sea was delayed at the water's edge. The first official step to take in preparation for the day's activities was the usual introductions of the guest inspector to the personnel involved, followed by the briefing and mapping of the programme for the day.

The boat subsequently spent most of the day sailing endlessly up and down the enormous artificial bay, the centrepiece of Holyhead's maritime history. The construction of the breakwater, to the south side of the port, had provided what nature had not given gratuitously.

It was the longest of its kind to be seen in Britain. The curving wonder of man's genius—in days before the invention of modern engineering technology—with a length of close on two miles, had cost the deaths of forty men out of the several thousands, engaged over the long time building it.

The man, the sole person left, continued to lean on the barrier rail that prevented drunk or unsuspecting strollers from falling a half a metre onto the top of the sloping, rocky foreshore.

After a while, watching and musing, he turned to see another car arriving. It slowly drew into the rough ground containing the small car park for users seeking access to the ramp. Its driver was clearly disappointed to find the few spaces had been filled.

In addition to only six marked car park places, three or four other cars had squeezed in on other likely, but irregular slots, all at higgledy-piggledy angles, mostly against the hedge surrounding the small vegetable allotment area, which lay between the road and the top of the ramp and its nearby car-parking.

Seeing the lone man leaning on the steel fence, the driver lowered the car's window and called out.

'Good morning. Is there no other place to park?'

The man suggested a place a few feet away alongside the allotments. 'That's where I would park,' he said. 'There is just room for you to squeeze in. It would be protected enough. These other cars have enough space to back out.'

'I don't think I want to risk that,' the newcomer said.

Just then the man took a good look at the driver.

She was arrayed in the most bizarre adornments, far from everyday clothes. But her manner was so alive and forthcoming that her eccentric outfit was completely subordinated to it. The woman and her attire were not at one.

'You must be a visitor, like me,' he said.

'Quite right,' she replied. 'I don't know this town well, as I come from a place about a hundred miles away.'

'I am also a complete stranger. It's my very first visit to Holyhead, so I am sorry I can't be of much help to you,' he replied.

She switched off her car's engine.

It was an invitation for a few more exchanges.

'Why are you dressed like this? Are you going to a special event?' he asked. 'I must say you look rather stunning in all that gear, but it doesn't look quite normal to me.'

'I'm thankful you think it's not normal. If you did, I would have been judged the most eccentric woman in town. I belong to the Welsh Drummers' Sorority. We are leading the annual carnival here today. We have to look the part, you know,' she said, smiling, attractively.

She displayed a warm and responsive attitude that at first made him suspicious, but within a few seconds he had put it down to her firm character and not to superficiality. She was not a fly-by-night woman who had run into him.

'I have never heard of that. Are drummers' sororities common around the country now?' he asked.

'I think it's pretty common in most quarters of the country these days. It's part of the women's liberation thing. It was once assumed that only men could play the drums, so women just had to show that they could do it as well. It sounds as if you don't live in this country.'

'Yes, I do, but I have been living abroad for some time. I just haven't heard of it before. I have not been a devotee of carnivals. I'm looking forward to seeing your drumming in action. It must be my lucky day to come on the one day of the year when the carnival is on.

'Where will it be a good place to see it? And what time will it be running?'

'Right here, or just along the road. It's scheduled to start at eleven o'clock and will end up here just before twelve. The parade goes round the town and ends up along this part where there is no through traffic. The carnival and crowd watching it can disperse to enjoy the fair, already operating further along the greens, as you can see.'

'I didn't know about it,' he said, 'I have not moved away from this spot since I arrived. It sounds like a convenient way of rounding off the carnival.'

'I had better try to find another parking place for my car,' she said. At that moment she saw a car drive away from its slightly sloping slot, partly on a grass bank a few metres away against the hedge surrounding the allotments. 'What luck, I'll chance it there.'

Her temporary companion watched as she parked her car. When she climbed out of it, he was surprised to see how tall she was and well-moulded. He had assumed a drummer should be a short, thickset woman with stout arms. But he could see she had none of those particular assets.

Swiftly she removed her drum from the boot of the car with a bag, presumably full of drumsticks and other appendages.

The man complimented her on her outfit. 'My name is Vernon.' He introduced himself.

'That sounds like a Welsh name,' she responded. 'I'm Helga. I'm glad to have met you.'

'That sounds like a Germanic name. But you sound completely British if I may say so.'

'Yes, I am completely British, in the sense that I have never known any life other than my life in my family in Britain.'

'But it sounds as if your roots are somewhere totally different.'

'You could say that, as I expect your own roots are like that as well. We are all mixed up in one way or another. It makes life interesting, doesn't it?'

She hurried on her way.

Vernon walked the short distance to the road. Families were gathering, little children being hoisted up on anything to give them a clear vista over the heads of the grown-ups. Their vantage points included cars, statues, walls, and the shoulders of their fathers.

The town was small enough to allow the noises made by the carnival on the march to be heard from Vernon's location from eleven o'clock onwards. Eventually the sounds grew louder as the column approached the end of its run. Headed by the Welsh Sorority Drummers, it appeared at the top of the slight hill of a side road running at right angles to the small beach road.

The carnival consisted of a galaxy of dancing girls, lorries decorously dressed, and groups representing many local voluntary bodies, together with a sprinkling of extrovert local men and women dressed in the weirdest of costumes, representing spacemen, clowns, footballers, athletic belles, and bathing beauties.

The twenty-five women drummers, uniformly and attractively dressed, were in contrast to their bandmaster, who walked backwards in front of them for the purpose of conducting. He occasionally had difficulty with the backless bedroom slippers he seemed to be wearing. His makeshift clothes were in utter contrast to the spectacular outfits worn by the members of the band. When the column reached the small, cul-de-sac coastal road, the vehicles turned right towards the station, while all the marching people turned left on reaching the waterfront. The carnival participants gradually melted into the thin random crowds of the fair, helping to swell their numbers and increasing the noise.

Vernon returned to his vigil on the fence of the tiny car park, looking out to the vast harbour area to see how the British Sub Aqua Club's operation was going.

In a few minutes, he was accosted by a woman's voice.

'Were you able to see the carnival?'

It was Helga, carrying her drum, as lively as ever, but looking as if she had run half a marathon.

'Yes, of course. I saw it to the end. I thought the Welsh drummers stole the show. Their turnout, beat, rhythms, and compelling noise have riveted themselves on my mind forever,' he laughed.

'In that case, you deserve a drink to bring you back to earth. Can I invite you to come to my hotel where I am staying the night to have a knees-up evening with the rest of the girls? By the way, what time do you have to be setting off for home tonight?' she asked.

He was taken aback by her forwardness.

'I'm not really bound for time,' he replied, 'but I try to get back at a reasonable hour.'

'That should give us time for a drink or two to celebrate,' she said breezily, striding away to the car to change her outfit.

She called him over when she had changed her clothes. She drove him a short distance to the other side of the town towards a small hotel, with an old-world appearance from the outside and an inside-decor to match it.

On the way they exchanged basic information about each other. Her husband had died, and Vernon's wife had divorced him. He was forty-nine and she was forty-four. She was a programme executive in the British Broadcasting Corporation working in Manchester. He was a professor in a university in the south of Wales.

'I must say, I fancied you the very minute I set eyes on you,' she said, laughingly. 'But don't think I am given to picking up men on the drop of a hat. That would be grossly wrong.'

'I am not used to being picked up nor picking someone else up, either,' he stated, 'but I have no objection to being here with you, however you see it. Did you pick me up or did I pick you up?'

'Let's say we have married for convenience,' she concluded, relaxing both of them and making them laugh with pleasure.

'What are you thinking?' she asked provocatively.

'How the name Helga arose?' he replied. 'I have been wondering how you came to have Helga as your name. It's the first time I have met the name in Britain, although I know the name is Germanic. It has occupied my imagination since you introduced yourself this morning.'

'If I told you, it would be a long story…but entertaining.'

She added the appendage at the last second. In that moment of time, she thought of tempting him. She was not so full of carnival frivolity that her judgements were impaired, but she sensed it was an opportunity worth taking.

'Now you are persuading me that the story is worth hearing,' he said. 'But you have to have fun with the girls, so there will not be time for me to hear it.'

'It's now nearly two o'clock. You will have some time to kill while I have lunch with the girls. Let us meet up again at six o'clock.'

'I shall be able to have a sleep after I have savoured the hotel's lunch menu,' he said thankfully.

When she returned promptly as suggested at six, she wasted no time. 'Let's compromise,' she said firmly. 'I will join the girls for two hours. But at eight o'clock I will tell them that I have an appointment. Would you be able to stand the strain in between, waiting and doing nothing? You could watch the show!'

'If the high-jinks are worth watching, the time will fly by, but if not, I shall probably be tempted to take off,' he said.

'If the show is worth watching, it will have nothing on what will follow it,' she laughed. 'If it bores you to tears, what comes after it will lift you to heaven.'

'That sounds like a win-win offer I can't refuse. Your story now will have something to live up to. Or perhaps it will depend on how you tell it. You do not seem like a person who needs a couple of glasses of wine to loosen your memory and oil your tongue, so I'm hoping for the best. It sounds like a fitting end to the carnival day.'

'It will be,' she said. 'The best stories always include a surprise.'

'How do you know enough of the story to make an occasion for telling it?' he asked.

'I have researched it over the years and have had the benefit of first-hand surviving family members to tell me everything,' she answered.

When the drummers had assembled for their celebrations, Vernon helped himself to a glass of wine at the bar. He found a solitary seat hidden away in a corner of the dining room, obscuring his own presence but giving him a good view of the proceedings expected from the Welsh Drummers' Sorority band members.

He could see that half of them were already in a tipsy state.

Most of them were helplessly giggling at everything being said. He wondered how long they would last out. The time of eight o'clock, as Helga had elected, might have to be revised.

The majority of the drummers stormed through the meal with a boundless appetite. Their laughter dominated the dining room, making it difficult for casual couples to hear each other speak at other tables.

All the drummers but Helga had retained their decorous attire. The scene created by the large single table—prepared for them en masse in the middle of the restaurant—had the appearance of a medieval feast exuding riotous jollity after a day of jousting.

The meal never seemed to be over, but the management had arranged for dancing music to start before the end of it. Under dimmed lights the drummers danced successively in pairs, in fours and sometimes in long lines of women in various stages of inebriation.

Vernon could see Helga taking her part enthusiastically. She was evidently oblivious of his whereabouts. Perhaps she didn't care any more. The sudden thought of that introduced a note of regret in his enjoyment, which until that moment had been untarnished.

He need not have worried. The time passed quickly enough.

It was with a shock that he realised it was already eight o'clock. He wondered if Helga would keep her word or would the conviviality of the evening take her avowed intentions away to the moon.

He had no reason to doubt her word. Soon, she approached, fortified by holding two glasses of wine, when she found where he had been hiding.

'Was it worth watching or worth being somewhere else?' she asked.

'It was a celebration the like of which I had not seen before, so I found it fascinating,' he replied. 'How well did you enjoy it?'

'I have done it before. We always end up like this on our trips out and about. It gives us a release from our worries and something to keep us happy on the job.'

They sipped their wine, the time slipping away.

'Now, I have a story to tell you. But not here. Would you be willing to sit comfortably in my room while I tell it? I will bring another bottle.'

'Would that be in accordance with protocol for the band on a night like this?'

'You should see what some of them get up to on these nights away. They can be very naughty.'

'Let's see how constructive we can be, then,' he concluded.

They went to her room. She wasted not a single minute. She would tell the full story. It would have to include intermissions, as part of the ulterior motive that had crossed her mind during the day. It had registered itself in her heart.

2

Towing a wagon loaded to the heavens with hay, the tractor wended its way along a bumpy farm track. The year was 1936.

By a later standard, its primitive design would look farcical to modern minds. Lacking the benefit of weather resistant paints, subsequently obtainable at a later age, it was consequently a very rusty tractor. But it worked. Proof was in the enormous load it pulled behind it that day.

More surprising than the state of the vehicle's appearance and condition was its driver.

It was the days of labour-intensive farming.

Horses were generally the tractors of their age, before those machines became universally owned. They hauled the wagons, pulled the ploughs, and gave personal transport to the farmer himself on large farms, if not to any other farm workers—usually all men.

Women everywhere joined the farming force at harvest time, especially those from the large farming families that were the order of the day. The annual, scenic panorama in hot sun displayed fields studded with women in colourful dress, among the men and boys, gathering the cereal crops by hand and stacking them in methodologically spaced stooks across the field, to be collected by horse and cart. It was a lengthy and back-breaking operation, far from the mechanisation that took away the pain at a later date.

This farm was lucky to have a tractor. The driver of it that day was a young woman by the name of Elsa. She was female in every sense, in as much sense in one as in another.

She was her farming father's first born. He had returned invalided before the end of the Great War—promised to end all wars—to inherit the farm from his father in 1918, the year when Elsa was born. Four other children joined the family during the 1920s...two boys and two further girls.

Elsa was no ordinary girl. But she was no tomboy. Nevertheless, she had mastered the art of starting the old tractor on the days she used it. It was a stubborn and unyielding beast.

First, she had to pour paraffin into a small heater made for the job. She lit it with a match and took the safety guard off when it was burning fiercely. Then she placed it on a large brick under the engine of the tractor and opened the air vent, to increase the fire directed at the cold innards of the tractor. While the lamp warmed up the sleeping mechanical horse, she filled its tank with either good petrol, or old petrol, old oil, or even paraffin. It had a reputation for being able to run on anything that could make a spark.

The one item the engine needed for its own good was a drop of clean oil for its functional needs.

She then unwound the steering wheel, which she unscrewed with about three feet of steering column fixed to it. Jumping down onto the ground, she inserted the end of the steering column into an aperture and turned the handle sharply. It was just an unusual form of ignition contraption for the Lanz Bulldog's engine, in fitting with the eccentric engineering of the machine.

She climbed back into the driver's seat, restoring her steering wheel to its needed place, while gently revving the stuttering engine that was newly springing into life.

Once running, the engine would perform all day as a mechanical horse, never yielding to the fatigue that its animal rival would suffer sooner or later in a long day's work.

The haymaking took place late in June of that year in the middle of a glorious summer. The hot sunshine was the more acceptable half of the weather pattern under which continental Europe was annually assailed or nourished—a choice depending on a person's preferences, age, health, and occupation.

The farm was thirty-five miles inland from the Baltic Sea in the extreme north-east of Pomerania, the very last point of Germany before the Polish frontier. It may have been the relative proximity to the sea and the flattish land on the Baltic coast—exposing the farm to northerly winds—that had accounted for and encouraged, if not exaggerated, the rusty appearance of the farm's tractor.

'Careful with it, Elsa,' her father called to her, as he heard the tractor stalling in a rut. 'If that lot falls off, the track will be blocked and will put us behind with the work.'

'Have no fear of that, Dad,' she called back. 'I can handle it.'

She let the clutch in slowly and inched her way to the farm compound and a huge open-sided barn, where she neatly parked the load. Several men removed the bales manually. They had been strung by hand and loaded on the tractor's trailer by other virile young men. They were carried or thrown into the barn, where they were expertly stacked for the winter, ready for use in the usually harsh and snowbound conditions prevailing each year.

'I shall miss you pulling more than your weight while you

are at university,' her father added.

'No, you won't miss me that much, Dad,' she quickly replied. 'I shall be able to come home for the long summer vacations, at the very time of the year when you need me most. The rest of the family will be a year older, anyway.'

'I hope you will be able to get away from university life to keep your promise, darling,' her father replied. 'But there are so many distractions that will take you away once you get into the swing of your studies.'

He knew that her good intentions at that moment were sincere, but could be easily swept away, as her intellectual outlook and social connections were rapidly enlarged in the higher-pressure atmosphere, and infinitely more attractive form they would take from her normal farm life.

The experience she had previously had on the farm and her local schooling had been more parochial, in keeping with her childhood. She was as yet unaware of the changes she would face and have to cope with.

She in turn knew that her father had underestimated her resolve. She would surprise him. She wondered if he had overlooked the level of maturity she had reached.

At the age of seventeen, close to eighteen, you still think of me as a girl. The thought went through her mind, but she said nothing.

In a country where women were commonly regarded as subordinate, she had already become aware of the rising dissatisfaction with the assumptions made about men's and women's respective involvements in commerce, politics, and society in many other countries. She was determined not to fit in with the stereotypes currently in vogue in her own country, but she had no notion how that might be done.

The first shot I shall make is in the subject I shall choose at university. It will be an unprecedented choice of subject for a woman to take, but I shall enjoy the challenge, she thought to herself.

In common with most people, she was ignorant of the events that would overtake her. On the one hand, they would enable her to fulfil her desire to be one of the blue-stocking women as the British called them, but, on the other, they would throw her life into the melting pot of life's utmost turbulence.

Her home quarters of Pomerania had an air of historic tradition and continuation about it, in common with many other rural areas of Germany. The majority of the local population accepted and lived easily with the ownership of large areas of land firmly in the hands of aristocratic families.

The continuity had brought stability and steady prosperity over the centuries. Her contemporary resistant attitude to some of the changes enveloping her country and threatening to put them on a different footing, must have sprung from that fact.

The recent developments in domestic politics had grown in spite of the aristocratic traditions of Germany. They often generated the opposition of the landed classes.

The factor that saved the day was the latter's historical roots in the military. The developing revival and encouragement of their traditional commitment to the army and navy was becoming predominant. It won their cooperation, if not their respect.

For the moment, her life seemed stable. The plans she had made for herself were assumed to be fulfillable. Her immediate concern was to help her father through harvest, before she went away from home for the first time.

Her friend of a similar age on the neighbouring farm came

over that evening. She got on very well with Astrid. They were two of a kind. They argued over this and that, but essentially, they admired each other that stretched to a deep affection.

At first, they did not go into Elsa's farmhouse. The weather was just too nice to abandon such a lovely evening and remaining active out of doors. They made the most of the loose gatherings of hay strewn around outside the great barn, which Elsa had been filling up with bales that she had cleared from the fields during the day.

'Are you into the harvest yet?' Elsa asked her.

'Not quite, but any day now,' Astrid replied.

'Are you itching to have a go at it this year?' Elsa queried.

'Not really, dad doesn't like me doing a man's work. He thinks I should remain painted up and impotent, helping to make the sandwiches for the men. You know, his decorative daughter is supposed to please the men who slave away at the harvesting.'

'He's not so different from most of the fathers around here,' Elsa commented. 'They treat their daughters with untouchable deference but allow their own wives to work out their guts just like the men. Well, some sort of men, it seems.

'Did you read how much Germany's leader objected to the success of Jessie Owens, an American black runner, who won the hundred metres race in the Olympics at Nuremburg this week? I think he is still in the stage of having all black people back on the land working the crops, rather than winning celebrated races.'

'No, I missed that,' said Astrid, 'but I do know about the disturbances down south between the communists and police. Even my father is upset about the victimisation of the unwanted minorities of people in the cities. It looks like an ominous sign.'

'At least, keeping away from harvesting must be good for your hands. Your hands are still beautiful,' Elsa said. 'A bit different from mine.'

Elsa showed Astrid her hands, cut in one or two places and with rough skin on her fingers and thumbs. 'And that's in spite of wearing gloves while I work,' she explained.

'I'm not sure whether you are envious or just plain glad to be you,' Astrid rejoined. 'At least my hands are still human.'

'Let's hope they stay like that, then,' Elsa concluded. 'The way things are going, according to some people, it will not be long before we shall all be soiling our hands doing unimaginable tasks.'

'Why do you say that in such a veiled way? It isn't like you to be so pessimistic. Are you expecting the world to come to an end soon?' Astrid retorted.

'It's only eighteen years since the war and we all know how disillusioned Germany is with the peace settlement,' Elsa said. 'We re-occupied the Rhineland only this year and we know how rearmament is going apace, secretly but wilfully. It may not be long before the countries come to blows again. And it will be worse this time.'

'Oh, it's not worth bothering about that sort of thing. It will all probably blow over sooner or later.' Astrid passed her verdict, with a smile. 'Let's live for the present. It's much more exciting.'

'Are you looking forward to going to university?' Elsa was prompted to ask by Astrid's last remark.

'Yes, of course, it will be much more stimulating than being here. Life can be so slow. Have you ever been to Breslau?'

'No,' Elsa replied. 'I shall miss this place. City life doesn't attract me that much. I love the farm, the fresh air and being free to get on with my own life.'

'But even here we are being gradually included in the net of the government party. Urban ills are creeping into the provinces. They are getting very active. You have to watch what you say and where you go these days,' Astrid volunteered.

'True enough,' Elsa commented. 'It's the young men who fall for it. They love the authority that goes with telling other people what to do. They seem to have no prohibitions about reporting people for what they think they see as wrongdoing.'

'Wrong and right doing these days are entirely according to the interests of the government party,' Astrid added. 'I wonder how far it will all go before there is a reaction.'

'There won't be one.' Elsa said with conviction. 'Hitler has got the majority of the population in his pocket. They see him as the saviour of all things German. He's on to a winning streak, mark my words.'

Having talked themselves to the edge of depression, they suddenly threw their conversation overboard, leaping up and throwing their arms around each other. They tried to dance around the hay-strewn ground.

Finding the choreography they tried to execute impossible, owing to the random lumpiness of the hay, they were forced into adopting an alternative to hide their ineptitude.

They began by defending their inexpert performance with giggles that developed into helpless laughter, as a response to the futility of their efforts. There could only be one possible outcome.

Their hilarity outweighed the dexterity of their feet.

They crashed over onto a larger heap of hay, where they gladly expended their laughter and terminated their footwork.

For a long time, they clutched each other, lying prostrate where they fell. Soft hands and working hands combined to hold each other in place.

Carrying no reflection of their working preferences, their tender lips met passionately, interchanging, and lasting the distance until approaching darkness overtook them.

3

After a few years of more open access to their numbers as undergraduates, the trend turned down again as women were increasingly excluded from university education. By the time of Elsa's entry, female students numbered about five thousand a year, down from eighteen thousand.

The difference was a function of the new government which had come to power three years before, reflecting the regime's belief that a woman's prime role in society was to be the home keeper and to rear children for the fatherland.

It was made more difficult for girls to obtain the abitur, the examination qualifying its holder to enter a university.

The emphasis on completing the compulsory Labour Service for young people was a further deterrent to women to enter a university career.

Elsa and Astrid were two of the lucky ones. Being on a farm and working in vacation time counted as a substitute for the compulsory service. Elsa had discharged farm work as an enjoyment and did it for the love of her family. In contrast, Astrid was a reluctant farmer at best.

They happened to be both very clever. Furthermore, the aristocratic families who owned the estates on which their farms were located had a lot of influence with the powers that controlled the flow of young people to the university in Breslau. Their influence, however, did not extend to the kind of subject they would be able to take as their study course.

At the beginning of the university year, several weeks slipped by before Elsa and Astrid had the chance to meet again at leisure. Their paths had been so divergent, they despaired of finding common ground again to share their lives.

'What did you go for in the end?' Elsa asked Astrid on their meeting that day.

'You will never guess!' she replied. 'My abitur was strong enough on the science side that they insisted I took advantage of it. But I rather believed they really meant that they would like to take advantage of it.

'I found out afterwards that this sort of thing is going on everywhere. It seems to be part of the secret rearmament steps being taken in all sorts of ways.'

'What have they put you in?' Elsa asked.

'Aeronautical engineering,' Astrid replied.

'Didn't you protest?'

'Yes, of course I did, but it was no use. They said the country needed it. To tell the truth, I was a bit frightened to resist,' Astrid said. 'I had thought university life was to give people freedom to choose. The man responsible was wearing a government party armband. He seemed to be elbowing his way into what normally happened.'

'I can understand that,' said Elsa. 'I found the same thing myself. They seemed to be telling people what they had to do. I didn't expect they would be so dictatorial as I found. I have ended up taking metallurgical studies. I had chosen it for my own reasons, but it happened to be coincident with the interests of those you are talking about.'

'Life in the city is not like our rural enclave in Pomerania,' Astrid added, pensively. 'It makes me want to go back there.'

Elsa was surprised to hear Astrid's lack of resolve. It was

she who wanted to leave rural farming life behind her.

'Astrid,' Elsa said tenderly, 'you've got to see that life for all of us is on the change. It has been a great shock to me.

'It puts a different slant on the activities of the government party youth leaders back home in the last year or so. Remember the interference they were exerting in our locality. They were a confounded nuisance, upsetting the local habits and ways of doing things that we were used to.'

Just at that moment, a knock on the door of her tiny student's bedsitter sent Elsa across the floor. She guardedly opened the door and addressed the caller.

'Kurt, what can I do for you?' she asked.

'Nothing you can do while you have a visitor,' he said.

'Don't be cheeky with me, Kurt. Come and meet Astrid. She and I come from the same village on the Baltic.'

'Two country girls. You are a long way from home. I only came to see if you were up to a night on the town.'

'Astrid, this is Kurt. He is a third-year student. I have to suffer seeing him as a neighbour. He is also a member of the department doing metallurgy. So, I keep running into him.'

'Make sure you look after my friend, then, Kurt. Can't you find another chap to come with us?' Astrid challenged.

'Of course, I can now that you have asked me. I will only be a few minutes,' he said, rushing off.

'He fancies me, but I don't like his attitude one little bit,' Elsa informed Astrid while he had gone. 'He's too much government party minded for my taste.'

'There's a lot of it around, I've found in these few weeks,' Astrid replied. 'It won't do us much good in the long run.'

Kurt was soon back, dragging Georg, a friend of his, who seemed to have imbibed too much alcohol already for early evening. Both young men were handsome and lively, Kurt with dark hair and Georg with a blond head.

Georg pulled himself together when he saw Elsa and Astrid. His fair hair seemed to go with Astrid as a brunette. Elsa's blond head sharply contrasted with Kurt's dark brown hair.

Objectively, in their physical appearance, the four of them represented the best of the nation's young adults. In their intellect, outlook, and degree of sympathetic understanding, they were diversified reflecting the contradictory, turbulent, and irreconcilable suasions that tormented their country.

Two of the four, city-bred and already imbued with government party ideology, contrasted with two from rural Germany, dyed-in-the-wool with traditional aristocratic social structure and practices. But they were all in the prime of their youth, energetic, passionate, and tolerant with each other.

'Let's head for the Market Square,' Kurt suggested. 'It's where most of the fun is in Breslau, especially on a Saturday night.'

'We haven't spent any time there yet, but we've heard a lot about it,' said Elsa. 'It's the historic place where cloth merchants, who belonged to the Hanseatic League, transacted their business on a large scale.'

'They've all gone now,' Kurt laughed. 'They are all coffee-mongers and beer drinkers in the square now.'

Breslau stood on the river Oder, one of Europe's longest rivers, wending its tortuous way to the Baltic Sea. The four young people crossed the river by one of the more than a hundred bridges over waterways in the city.

Elsa recalled that such a convenient mode of conveyance by water from shore to shore had justified and facilitated the city's inclusion in the defensive, commercial Hanseatic League. It was a big organisation, variously consisting of many of the largest and dozens of smaller cities in the north medieval German states, the Baltic, and Scandinavian countries.

The streets of Breslau were wide and lined with the beautiful houses built by the Hanseatic merchants. The architecture of the public buildings reflected the wealth of the city of six hundred and fifty thousand people. They had inherited the fine buildings from their predecessors of previous centuries—those who had grown prosperous from trading in wool and cloth, augmented in the nineteenth and twentieth centuries by the rampant coal industry of Silesia.

The long trek from the university buildings to the Market Square was thronged with people, all walking the town on a weekend night, shrugging off their worries and looking for an hour's excitement. Cars were few and far between, but the tram service was at its best for transporting the city's population about their domestic, business, and leisure activities, seven days a week.

Before that night, neither Elsa nor Astrid had been as far as the Market Square in the centre of the city. Consequently, when the four people burst into one corner of it, the two women stopped dead in their tracks, overcome by the immensity and beauty of the vista before them.

The square was truly impressive, a city in itself. All four sides, each side stretching for around a fifth of a mile, had a continuous row of side-by-side buildings, all reflecting one architectural age or another from the past.

Many were sky-lined with various Flemish and Germanic architectural finishing at the top of the façades of the properties, many reaching up to five or six storeys and all generously lit, adding up to a seductive scene.

Probably sixty percent of all the buildings were given over to drinking establishments, restaurants, cafés, ice-cream bars, confectionary and food shops, and the rest devoted to women's and men's selective apparel.

Very few were committed to business offices, and therefore unlit by that time of evening. The widely spaced intermittent absence of light did little to diminish the splendour of the luminosity of the square as a whole, with its wide cobbled roadway on four sides, and thousands of people indulging one delight after another.

The multi-coloured painted properties around the square gave the place a warmth and stimulating feel, which could soon be augmented by the huge jars of beer readily available at almost every step of the way.

In the warmth of late summer, dozens of premises provided their sales gladly outside as well as inside their walls. As well as immediately in front of the premises, sales were extended further by spilling tables onto the cobbles, the owners taking advantage of their respective shares of the square's space on their frontages. The extension of their business protruding into the Market Square replicated faithfully the items of their main inside attraction. It was just cooler outside than in.

But when the weather changed from hot to cool, so the number of people sitting outside diminished, leaving only the stubbornly hardy to sit it out for yet another night, while those inside gradually filled all the accommodation to overflowing.

All around the square, handcarts and motorised vendors were selling easy-to-eat food, ice-cream, and a dozen other enticements to eat or wear.

It was a sight for sore eyes for the two women from the country. They saw people having a quiet drink alongside people who were already drunk, or private couples out for sober entertainment, alongside men and women anxious to mate, and plenty of casual males and females, all milling around the pedestrian-only cobbles.

Stately in posture and position, looking beautiful in its Gothic style, the Town Hall provided a spectacular centrepiece in the middle of the square. Its construction had begun in the thirteenth century in common with some of the surrounding buildings in the square.

In daylight, the colour of its stonework and exploratory shapes and profiles were breath-taking.

Later in the day, the building modestly withdrew itself, internally plunged into darkness, but externally illuminated by the scores of street-lights and its own selective and revealing lighting. The soaring heights of its spires, architectural devices, and intricately finished designs, made it one of the finest examples of its kind throughout the world.

'What an amazing sight!' Elsa was the first to give voice to what lay before them.

'Come on, let's get in and have a good time,' said Kurt.

'I shall have to spend all tomorrow in bed,' Georg complained.

'I shall have to spend all my time tomorrow catching up on my studies. I wasn't expecting to come out like this tonight,' Astrid said, trying to throw cold water on the burst of enthusiasm that had suddenly overtaken the men.

'Don't you ever have a good time?' Kurt chided her, not expecting an answer.

'Not if I have more important things to do,' Astrid replied.

'Let's give it a go, then,' Elsa said. 'We ought to combine duty with pleasure. Isn't that what the party stands for?'

'There's no answer to that,' Kurt said.

'I believe, I believe, I believe,' Georg added his few words, sniggering.

'Thanks for that,' Kurt laughed. 'I can tell you are not doing linguistics.'

'What do you mean?' Astrid asked Georg. 'You sound as if you are going to a religious meeting.'

'I suppose I am in a funny sort of way,' Georg replied, 'but I don't want to talk about it now when there's all this fun staring us in the face, and we are standing here talking.'

Astrid missed the ominous meaning of his words.

They strolled along but shortly saw several fellow students they recognised, who called them over.

'This is one of the university hives in the market place. Best prices in the square.'

A woman student called out, accosting them as they approached. 'And the proprietor is a good man. He supports the party like a good man should. The food's excellent and the Dortmunder beer is exceptional.'

The two men joined the crowd of students enthusiastically, the two women hesitantly. The latter could see that all kinds of students were more or less joining in the bonhomie. They quickly latched on to several women of the quieter sort.

'You look a bit lost. Are you at the university?' one of the women asked.

'Yes, we are both first year—and you?'

'I'm second year. These others are third year, old hands.'

'What are you going to drink?' another woman asked.

'I'm not used to drinking alcohol,' Elsa announced.

'Nor me,' said Astrid.

'It's an old German custom here,' the women declared, 'you have to drink a Dortmunder or two.'

'In that case we had better give it a go,' said Astrid.

The beer came in a standard German jug. The size of it looked formidable to both Astrid and Elsa.

'Better take it easy at first,' the most helpful woman student said.

It could have been the underlying excitement of the unexpected evening out on the town, or the intense atmosphere amid the gathered students at that particular venue, or just their native thirst, but they both found the taste of Dortmunder to their liking. It gave them release from their worries.

Elsa and Astrid were not able to complete their circuit of the square on that first night. They were soon in the middle of conversations the like of which neither had previously experienced.

It was dominated by the looming policies of the government party and what they might mean for Germany.

The discussion was mostly new to Elsa and Astrid, who remained somewhat silent throughout, but taking it all in. They suddenly came alive when the subject of a policy called Strength through Joy cropped up.

'What's all that about?' Elsa asked no one in particular.

'Haven't you heard about it?' one of the second-year students responded.

'It's new to me,' Elsa rejoined.

'And me, too,' added Astrid.

'Where have you two been lately, not to have caught up

on the latest rumours going around.'

It sounded like a reprimand.

'Tell us about it, then,' Elsa instructed the speaker. 'By the way, what is your name?'

'It's Isolde, and yours?'

'I'm Elsa.'

'And I'm Astrid. Can't wait to hear your story. There seems to be a hush-hush feel about it, or are you just being excited about it?'

'Well, it depends on how you look at it. Wait until you have heard it, then you can judge for yourselves,' Isolde laughed, indicating that what she was about to tell them could be interpreted as being something worth knowing.

Isolde first drew the attention of two others of her pals.

'Can you believe that these two have never heard about the Strength through Joy programme in the offing. You had better help me with the details.'

She began her story with the air of someone disclosing facts that would not be made public but had currency among certain citizens of a prescribed age group.

'Earlier this year, in February, the government party leader and representative of German interests—looking after expatriate Germans—in Switzerland, based in Davos, was murdered by a foreign enemy of the state for his political views.'

'That doesn't sound much like an overture for something that might be of interest to us,' Astrid interrupted.

'But wait a minute,' Isolde told her. 'The government was so upset that it has laid down a new liner in Hamburg that will be named after the man.'

'We are building ships all the time,' Elsa said, adding to

Astrid's doubt, 'unless you are going to spring a surprise on us in the end. It doesn't affect us.'

'You could be wrong,' Isolde declared triumphantly. 'The ship will be launched next year with over four hundred and eighty private cabins. But wait for the best bit of all. The ship will sail to the Mediterranean Sea with only nine hundred passengers, although the ship is designed to carry many more than that number.'

'So, what, none of us could afford to pay for that kind of cruise,' Astrid said.

'Hurry up, Isolde,' her friends encouraged her, 'tell them the best bit of all.'

'You can take over now,' Isolde retorted. 'I know you are enthusiastic about it.' The others clambered to complete the story, brimming over with their secret.

'Of the nine hundred passengers, half will be girls, the other half boys,' they said.

'Oh, it sounds like the government is planning to promote the best school trip ever devised,' Elsa said.

The others all laughed, aided by the Dortmunder they had liberally been drinking.

'Not that kind of trip. It means big boys and big girls,' they chorused. 'You have to be over eighteen to be eligible.'

'What else?' Astrid put in the obvious query.

'Both parents and grandparents on both sides of the family of any passenger must have been born in Germany, of German stock, and all seven free from criminal convictions,' they said.

'There must be a snag in it somewhere,' Elsa concluded.

'Yes, there is,' Isolde replied. 'You have to join the government party faithfuls, but many people will do that anyway, not from conviction, but for the opportunity.'

'But what's the idea behind it all?' Elsa asked, 'it makes your mind boggle at the possibilities of what they could get up to, what with the leisure, the sun, good food, and plenty to drink.'

'That's just the point,' Isolde replied, 'it's to have babies for the fatherland. It will be possible for a couple to keep their own baby, but it is expected that most babies will ultimately be taken into care as part of the scheme.'

'I can see a difficulty or two coming up,' Astrid commented. 'More than one partner might be seduced during the voyage. Or do the authorities intend to register their chosen partner and have complete surveillance over what goes on?' she asked.

'They would have to allow a degree of licence or spoil the fun,' Elsa observed. 'What would be the point of going to all that trouble if you couldn't please yourselves. At least the state would get a baby out of it. Isn't that what they want?'

The rhetorical question added by Elsa, now roused her into an investigative mode. She continued. 'You could ask all passengers, before they leave, to sign a declaration form disclaiming any liability on the management for any disputes between couples over partner liaisons or the subsequent ownership of any pregnancy.'

Another first-year student, called Kirsten, who had not yet spoken on the subject interrupted at that moment.

'There's no doubt in my mind that the whole project turns on the loyalty to the state issue. Those chosen as passengers would have to be certified as undyingly dedicated to their country, the party, and the ideology which is increasingly getting a grip on the German population.'

'Yes, I think you are right there, Kirsten,' Astrid supported her view. 'I think it will be a matter of feeling specially chosen for an allegedly noble purpose. I am sure the passengers will be left to themselves—a sort of free for all. There will be so much choice of partners.'

'It's time we were going, Astrid,' Elsa said, looking at her watch.

'That goes for all of us,' someone else said. 'If we don't set off soon, we shall not make it back before the appointed time, when all women students are expected to be inside the walls of the university, unless they have a pass for overnight absence. It's such a bother to go through the rigmarole if you have to report late.'

Elsa said, 'Glad you mentioned it. We haven't been here long enough yet to have tested the system.'

Elsa and Astrid looked around for Kurt and Georg. They were nowhere to be seen. In fact, the large group of men they had joined on arrival in the square had eroded to only a dozen.

They gave up the search and returned to the group of women. About fourteen of them set off at a stroll, continuing around the giant square to get a last-minute glimpse of the Saturday night proceedings, before retiring to their university lodgings.

The dwindling number of women students in the university had suffered the indignity of being discriminated against in the degree of freedom they enjoyed as undergraduates.

Among the handicaps they endured was the curfew. They had to check into their lodgings by ten o'clock each night. It wasn't quite clear what purpose the inhibition served. It prevented any high jinks out in the city in bars and restaurants.

It smacked of prudish attitudes — when men's and

women's residences were side by side. But there were always ways to get round the frustrations for those with the determination and the courage to defy the authorities.

On the way several women couldn't resist indulging a further jug of beer. The tongues of half the group had already been loosened to the point of giving vent to their vocal cords. They chanted traditional folk songs. Before long, the welcome arm of a friend around the waist of three young women became a necessity.

As the group turned from one side of the square to another, they were strung out, larking about, as they ambled or staggered in some cases. Their collective attention was greeted with a cacophony of random noise, including the shattering of glass and many men shouting.

Momentarily sobered, they moved on with a firmer step towards the source of the commotion, then visibly located, since by then its site had been surrounded by a host of onlookers.

Many were joining in on the disfigurement of a shop frontage that was well on its way to being completely destroyed. The damage was spreading into its ground floor.

The main glass windows had already been smashed. The area in front of the premises had been spread with tables and chairs for customers to eat outside in the warm evening air. They could see young men hurling the items of furniture into the holes made in the frontage.

No restaurant staff members were in sight. No one was protesting, no one was resisting.

'What in hell is going on here?' Elsa asked.

'It looks like another minority-owned business is going to the scrap heap,' said Isolde. 'You can see some of the men have arm-bands and are dressed in black. They have evidently discovered the ownership of the business. It goes on intermittently.'

Astrid pulled on Elsa's arm.

'Look, there's Kurt throwing a chair into the chaos, and Georg is in it, too.'

Elsa quickly recognised Kurt and Georg and others from the group of students they had been with in the Dortmunder beer centre earlier in the evening.

'They are making an awful mess of that shop frontage. I'm going to try to stop them,' Elsa said. 'In God's name why are they doing this. If the police catch them, they will all be in jail before the night is out.'

'It's no use and you might get hurt if you interfere,' Kirsten told her. 'This is something we have to live with at the moment.'

Ignoring her injunction, Elsa plunged into the mêlée and threw her arms around Kurt just as he was about to hurl another chair into the chaotic mess that had replaced the beautiful restaurant frontage.

'Stop it! Stop it! Why are you doing this? You will be in prison in next to no time if the police come and catch you doing it,' she shouted at him.

'Let go of me,' he shouted back. He was surprised at the strength of her arms that made him drop the chair. 'No, they won't interfere. It's OK to rough up some shopkeepers, who are considered harmful to German interests and are not wanted. It's not official, but it's condoned.'

'Leave it now,' she cried at him, 'come away from it. You are drunk and don't know what you are doing.'

Elsa dragged on his jacket, preventing him from picking

up a chair again, but taking advantage of his inebriated state to drag him away and then propel him away from the scene.

She dumped him in the safe hands of Astrid, returning to the fray to find Georg tottering around in a worse state than Kurt. Putting her arms around him she half carried him, stumbling away from the frightful incident to catch up with the others who had begun to move on.

4

The lurid event in the Market Square passed without any repercussions, either for those perpetrating the violence or for any neighbours or bystanders who witnessed it.

The mess was cleared away and the frontage boarded up.

Within days, another proprietor secured the use of the premises for business as usual.

Elsa and Astrid, in common with all the university students who had visited the square that night, were soon preoccupied with their studies, too busy to worry about the politics of their country.

Their only concern was born of the pressure in the university on them to embrace formally one of the many official and semi-official organisations, which had sprung up all over the country, especially those of a military nature.

Elsa and Astrid successfully completed their first year of studies, but Astrid confessed to her friend that she had become disillusioned with her commitment to the course and was looking for a way out.

'I thought you were never quite happy with it from the start. But it's too late now to switch subjects,' Elsa said.

'Yes, I know that well enough,' Astrid replied. 'I can only honourably retreat by joining one of the service or semi-service organisations for the government.'

They had met up in the students' common room, where the atmosphere was determined by the large number of third year students, who raised the excitement of the place to an unusually heightened state by the farewells they were enjoying, before they took their wings into the big world beyond the university.

Some of them raised the strange phenomenon of the ship, destined to be a Strength through Joy means of enriching the fatherland with children of their finest young people.

'The ship was duly launched as predicted in May this year,' one student in the know declared. She was among a small group of students who had evidently intended to take advantage of the opportunity to apply for a place, among the over four hundred women passengers who would do their enjoyable duty for their country.

Another student contributed to the hubbub of conversation.

'The ship is expected to be fitted out and ready for sea in September and has already been named as the *Hans Frayling,* after the national representative in Switzerland, murdered on political grounds. Apparently, there's a lot of interest in the project in the northern ports and states.'

Elsa reacted with lukewarm interest to the news, but Astrid pricked up her ears when she perceived that a number of the ex-third year students looked as if they were intending to apply for a place.

She remarked her interest to Elsa when they had a quiet moment to themselves.

'I think the men passengers will include a good number of the most promising young officers from the three services.'

'So, third year students at twenty-one or twenty-two years of age should be well away with them, then,' Elsa said. 'It will be a nice break before they get a job. In fact, I wouldn't mind betting that some of them have already calculated that going on the cruise could be a means of getting a better job from a passenger or two, rather than hunting for one from scratch.'

Astrid sniggered in reply.

'I think half the men will end up being recruited into the armed services, probably many of the women, too. But I agree that many young men and women without jobs before embarking on the ship are likely to pick up the promise of employment for one reason or another by the time they disembark.'

They soon abandoned the subject. Elsa was preparing to return to her farmstead home to help her family to gather another cereal crop. Astrid stayed around for a few more days until the end of term, growing steadily disillusioned with her predicament.

In the closing days of term, the usual clutch of agents put in an appearance, fishing in the sea of third year graduates for good employee prospects. Not least were government military agents bidding for recruits to the navy, army, and air force.

Astrid had a casual look around the jamboree of offers held for the agents in a large hall. She was distracted by a disproportionately large crowd gathered around one stand at the far end of the hall.

Pushing her way in, she found the attraction was in the hands of the merchant navy representatives, holding forth about the vacancies—of some substance—on offer to men and women in the leading maritime companies.

She couldn't conjure up any enthusiasm for the sort of jobs being advertised and wondered why so many people were standing around maintaining their interest.

'What's it all about?' she asked a third-year male student

she knew by sight. 'Most of these jobs being offered are not really suitable for graduates, are they?'

'Oh, I think a lot of men may want to find out what is going on as an opportunity to go into officer training. It's a great career if you like the sea,' he replied. 'But I think most people are waiting to hear from the agent for the *Hans Frayling*. Do you know about the Strength through Joy project that the ship will sail on soon?'

'Yes, I've heard of it,' Astrid replied.

A new speaker just at that moment appeared, somewhat rattled, apologising for being late. He addressed the waiting students about the *Hans Frayling* project, outlining the terms and conditions for those applying to be passengers on the ship, stressing the overall justification of the project in sober terms. Only men and women loyal to the fatherland and government regime, struggling to restore the greatness of their country, would be considered.

Astrid was mildly deterred from any interest in the cruise. She didn't consider herself in that category. She considered herself, however, as a loyal and good citizen of her country, but not to the extent of exhibiting the heterosexual conduct necessary for the purpose—only because her own predilections were in another direction.

After the main speaker had finished, another maritime agent continued to advertise the vacancies for crew members on ships. Astrid was surprised to hear of those wanted for the crew of the *Hans Frayling*.

Most of the small crowd had drifted away once the information about the passengers required had been given.

Some had been directed to a nearby desk where application forms were available.

She listened, while the agent listed a number of jobs, she had never imagined could have been part of the crew of such a ship.

They included medical people, doctors and nurses, psychologists, beauty specialists, hairdressing staff, entertainers, and shop assistants, as well as, of course, the full range of catering staff—not to mention the officers and crew to run the ship.

However, it was just the one appointment that struck a note in Astrid, changing her attitude in an instant. She even felt a slight electrification in her body as the reality of the possibility made its presence felt.

He mentioned a speech and deportment specialist.

Astrid had always been brought up to speak nicely, with the right cadences, and all the right voice strength and tones to match the purpose of what was said.

Deportment concerns had run in the family, her father having served as an officer in the Kaiser's army as a professional soldier. She had taken speech classes while she had attended high school and continued to study the subject during her first year at university, as a hobby and distraction from her main subject.

Impulsively, but not without justification, she put her name down as an applicant for the post.

Several weeks later, having tired of hoping to get the job, she was called to Hamburg, the home of Blohm and Voss shipyards, where the ship was built.

She was ushered into an office of Hamburg Süd, a company operating the ship.

'We are sorry for the delay in contacting you. But we were impressed with your qualifications for the job and can tell you that you are offered an appointment.

'We had to enquire about your family background and general credentials. At the age of twenty-one we think you will have a better rapport with the passengers than other older competitors who applied.'

She left the offices for a tour of the completed ship, finally being prepared for its maiden voyage. She was shown her office and workroom and had a half-day talking with other specialist staff. Her job was unprecedented, but she had arrived with prepared notes and plans for responding to what she expected to be the reasons for calls on her services.

With a fortnight interim before the deadline for reporting to sign on as a crew member, Astrid went home to her family.

Elsa was top of her list of contacts.

'What on earth have you been doing?' was Elsa's first word to her. 'Have you given up university?'

'Yes,' she replied, 'aeronautics wasn't really my thing. I have signed on for the *Hans Frayling.*'

'Oh, no,' Elsa cried in despair. 'I shall lose you, now.'

'Not as a passenger, but as a crew member,' Astrid enjoyed clarifying her commitment, knowing the hidden thoughts going through Elsa's mind.

'What will you be doing as a crew member?' Elsa was eager to know. Sinister and untoward thoughts had crossed her mind, as she inferred that Astrid and she would be parted.

'There will be plenty of on-board entertainment, a few shops, and other personal services such as hairdressing, manicure, and beauty salons to occupy the passengers—that is, for when they have nothing else to do. I shall be contributing a small addition to the list by offering speech and deportment advice and training,' she said.

'I shall have to run little classes on both subjects and offer private consultations for those interested.'

'Well, I'll be damned, that's a far cry from aeronautics, but it does make sense to me,' Elsa said candidly.

'I have to admit you always speak so well, and so commandingly. No one could fault your deportment, so I reckon you are the right girl for the job. I shall have to come aboard one day and get some treatment from you.'

'Oh, there's nothing I could teach you, Elsa,' Astrid countered. 'I've always had the highest admiration for your physical posture, as you well know, and you speak with the clarity of the tradition for our part of the country. But you would still be welcome aboard, while I'm there.'

'Let's make it a date, then,' Elsa laughingly said. 'I look forward to it.'

Astrid had to part from Elsa, when she returned to Hamburg late in September in 1937 to embark on the *Hans Frayling* for its maiden voyage. It was bound for the Mediterranean Sea with a full complement of special passengers, male and female. They numbered nine hundred as planned, only half of its full capacity as a public passenger liner.

Regretting the departure of Astrid, Elsa resumed her degree course, with unabated enthusiasm. She missed Astrid but admired her initiative in joining the merchant navy and envied her search for something challenging to do.

It reminded her of her own decisions lying ahead, torn between capitalising on her degree, remaining faithful to her family farming, and coping with any developments her country might force on her—that might be unavoidable owing to the circumstances of the time.

Astrid was away for about four weeks until late October. Elsa couldn't wait for her return. Her impatience to hear about the cruise was as telling as Astrid's eagerness to relate it.

The ship would be in port for three weeks, enabling Astrid to take some leave, including a visit to Breslau to renew her lasting relationship with Elsa.

'What was it like?' was Elsa's first question after they had embraced and before Astrid could take off her coat.

'In short, wonderful,' was the partly unexpected answer.

'Conduct was free from the licentious behaviour many people might have imagined would be going on. The decorum was impressive for the whole trip, well organised, and well run.'

'But did you get any babies out of it?' Elsa quipped.

'How did they manage that crucial element of the voyage?'

'That remains to be seen. It was just not obtrusive,' Astrid explained. 'Liaisons naturally developed, some quickly, some taking a week or two, some not at all, although, since the purpose of the cruise had been made patently clear, there was an expectation on everyone to play his or her part.

'We shall have to wait to see how productive the voyage turned out to be. It will be a means for comparing one cruise with another. In the end people will be asking if there were any factors that altered the numbers of successful births for different voyages.'

'That sounds like a new field for economists and sociologists to mull over in future,' Elsa said, both women laughing. 'Anyway, how did it all happen in the end?'

'You don't really want to know the answer to that, do you?' Astrid asked, sending them both into hysterics.

'It was all very ordinary. At meals, in the bars, and just through casual contact in games and various other activities during the day, men and women made contact.

'Sooner or later as they felt inclined, they paired off and retreated to his or her cabin. It was, after all, a twenty-four-hour opportunity. It seemed a bit too mechanical for my taste.'

'What did you expect, a torrid struggle of the sexes? Two women running along the decks after the same man, and that sort of thing?' Elsa asked, laughing. 'I never thought of your being a voyeur on a ship.'

'Oh, you are naughty,' Astrid retorted. 'Perhaps I expected some explicit signs of wooing and yielding, but it never happened.'

'What took place when the ship called at the various ports?' Elsa interrupted.

'Many passengers went ashore. I noticed that some went off in small groups, but some, who had formed strong liaisons, kept together in pairs,' Astrid said.

'Was there really no profligate behaviour at all?' Elsa asked.

'I noticed that some men and women changed partners during the trip. I think they were indulging the loose conduct they had dreamed about but could never practise at home,' Astrid replied.

'Or could they have been those who wanted to make sure that the purpose of the voyage would be fulfilled as far as they were concerned,' Elsa commented.

'There speaks the biologist. But the identity of the father would be a problem for them later on,' Astrid concluded.

'How did your own job go? Did you have any takers? Or were they all well-spoken and with deportment beyond reproach?'

Elsa fired her questions, anxious to prove that her friend had accounted for herself with a satisfactory performance, if not with distinction.

'There wasn't much business at first,' Astrid explained. 'The group classes were poorly attended. I think many people were trying to overcome their shyness among all the strangers and novelty of the purpose of the voyage.

'As time passed the classes increased in size, and a flood of private consultations resulted after the message circulated about what I could offer.'

'Perhaps that was after some people had tried their luck and wanted to improve their potential,' Elsa commented. 'There's nothing like a bit of competition to force you into making an effort.'

'Yes, I agree,' Astrid said. 'I think that some of that did come into it. Individuals were inevitably measuring themselves against others, especially any rivals for identified partners.'

'Did you like doing it enough to do it again?' was Elsa's next question. 'I never thought you would ever have left the farm for a life at sea.'

'Of course, like you, being brought up near the Baltic coast, the sea was not too much of an alien medium for spending my life. I am a regular crew member, not one of the passengers. Note was taken of the clientele who asked for my services, so I am assuming I shall have a job in the future.'

'Did you not miss your university studies?'

'To tell the truth, I was so busy I had no time to spend regretting my decision. I found myself enjoying my new job. I was completely preoccupied designing the class talks and accumulating notes from individual consultations for future use.

'If any regrets resurface in future, it will be over the possibility I could have been taking university studies in speech and deportment studies. It would have suited me more than aeronautics.'

'Do you think I ought to join the passengers one day, Astrid?' Elsa asked playfully, knowing her friend would play the game.

'How would you cope with the opportunities? You wouldn't know what to do. You haven't had enough practice to make your mark,' Astrid questioned, with a challenge.

'We could go on the rampage, with you going your way and I'm going mine,' Elsa said, making Astrid blench, but playing her part.

'I would much rather we went our own way, straight into my cabin,' Astrid said, in mock disgust.

'That wouldn't help the production statistics for the ship,' Elsa countered.

'But it would do a lot of good for the workers,' Astrid said decisively, 'or at least one worker and the one passenger who could be spared to assist the crew member for her comfort.'

'How about after my second year ending in June? Could you put in a good word for me?' Elsa asked, pursuing her suggestion.

'Of course, I could, but, of course, you don't need it. You will have to be one of the most eligible applicants for passenger status the *Hans Frayling* will ever carry.'

'It's a date,' Elsa said.

5

Astrid made five further trips after her inaugural voyage, two before Christmas, the rest between January and June in the following year. With her accumulating experience, she built up a reputation for her expertise. Women in particular passed on to their friends taking future cruises, that it was worthwhile having a consultation with Astrid.

The months of study for Elsa's second year passed quickly for her. She missed seeing Astrid. They met only once during that time, while Elsa's enthusiasm mounted.

She looked forward to her cruise in June as had been planned. They would misspend the purpose of the ship but use the opportunity to be together.

She duly travelled by train to Hamburg to take her treasured voyage. Although a passenger under false pretences, in the sense that she had every intention of bypassing the vaunted objectives of the ship, Elsa was nevertheless enamoured of her status as a passenger on the ship.

She played up to a number of overtures. Over the first week she resisted the approaches of several young men, said to be officers in élite armoured units, who found that at nearly twenty-one years of age, she was no pushover, even for the confident young men of the best units in the army.

With the arrival of each night, when Astrid's job responsibilities for the day had drawn to a close, Elsa repaired to Astrid's cabin, glad to relax, and to share the hours of darkness with her, reviving the relationship with the woman she loved.

'We don't have to bother about us,' Astrid said one night. 'I happen to know from my consultancies on previous trips, that a number of passengers made single sex relationships on board, some actually in between having heterosexual partners.'

'Have you had any figures about the success of the venture for previous voyages?'

'Only for two, the first and second,' Astrid stated. 'There were one hundred and twelve live births from the inaugural cruise, and one hundred and fifty-six from the second.'

'So, a lot of passengers had a glorious cruise without payment, but perhaps disappointment.'

'That's the luck of the draw,' Astrid commented. 'I don't know how those figures would compare with a control group from the regular population over the same period.

'Of course, it's not merely a matter of numbers. The supposed standard of the parents who have produced the births is the inspiration determining the purpose of the ship. Undertaking this venture is the government party's idea of quality production.'

The cruise was over too quickly for Elsa. She and Astrid had to part again, when Elsa returned to the university at Breslau for her third year and the completion of her degree, while Astrid continued with the same pattern of cruising into the next year.

By the summer of that year, most citizens had become aware of the international resistance to their country's policy of subjecting neighbouring countries to their peaceful occupation by a forced or agreed but negotiated settlement from Berlin.

With those rapid geopolitical developments, and widespread expectation that war was inevitable, Elsa was persuaded to join the Women's Naval Service. Unforeseen pressures on students were simply a symptom of the inevitable approach of conflict.

It rapidly became clear that it was the thing for her to do, with the completion of her degree in metallurgy. On leaving the university, she went immediately to Hamburg for an initial course at the navy's training school for women.

The importance of the job she was taking up and her own bearing and personality made her one of the trainees earmarked to hold the rank of officer. It led to a second training course, also in Hamburg.

The prolonged training courses enabled her to meet up with Astrid whenever the *Hans Frayling* put into port. It was a regular and delightful experience for both women to have the frequent pleasure of getting together so conveniently.

With her degree in metallurgy, Elsa was directed to join the Blohm and Voss design offices in Hamburg to be trained in the field of naval architecture, with particular reference to U-boat construction. The constraints on the numbers of submarines that the Kriegsmarine, the German navy, could acquire—imposed by the treaty arrangements made after the First World War—had by then fallen into desuetude.

She found herself working on U-boat developments that would rival and surpass those of all other navies. She was particularly absorbed in the design of the Type XXI, a spectacular initiative in its infancy that would take several years to come to fruition.

While on the training course one day, she heard that all

German ships at sea had been ordered to return to their home-ports. She assumed the *Hans Frayling* would not be made an exception to the order. In fact, she found it was due to dock only two days later.

Astrid on board the vessel was as surprised as anyone else to see their ship suddenly turn around in mid-ocean, accompanied by the captain's message over the loudspeaker to all crew and passengers.

'*This is the captain speaking. I am surprised, as you will be, that the ship has received an order to return immediately to its home-port, in common with all German ships at sea. For the passengers it will come as a disappointment to arrest the cruise in only its eighth day. No reason has been given, but we all know that international political tensions have reached an advanced and complicated stage. This is unfortunately an irreversible order, which I am now executing.*'

Astrid found the mood on the ship changed dramatically. The crew were mainly indifferent, although in the crew mess room the talk turned on what might happen to the ship if the nation was ushered into war. Strangely, the fate of the ship took precedence over the individual destinies that crew members might have to confront personally.

The passengers reacted differently. Some who had committed themselves to partnerships made the most of the opportunity, which was about to be withdrawn from them before they had fully exploited it.

Others were thrown back on themselves, reading various inferences into their premature return. Men from the army, navy, and air force speculated freely about the possible developments on the military front, if the politicians failed to find an answer to the pending impasse. The women passengers thought about returning home or joining the women's services if war was declared.

Astrid herself suddenly had a rush on her expertise from the female half of the passengers, keen to use the short time left to the best advantage. They were full of excitement.

'This is the only chance I have ever had of a free opportunity to help my country and to help myself as well,' one woman told her.

'Have you had the chance yet to help your country?' Astrid asked her, with an understanding, but quiet and restrained laugh.

'Not yet,' she replied. 'I'm in with a chance, but I suppose it's too late to make much of it. Many of the men have suddenly become distracted.'

'Oh, don't despair,' Astrid egged her on, 'you know what can happen on a one-night stand. There must be plenty of chaps who are only interested in what is happening at the moment. Be positive.'

Hours after the captain's announcement, the mood changed again. Among some sections of the passengers, the reversal of their expectations and the shortage of time left at their disposal, turned many towards desperate behaviour.

Risks of denial or refusal were freely run, and more open invitations became common as many clamoured to fulfil their personal mission for the cruise.

On arrival in Hamburg, Astrid, like many other crew members who were not responsible for the actual operation of the ship, was expecting to be paid off. For two days company representatives came aboard to interview crew members and to establish their performance records from their officers.

A company official who interviewed Astrid remarked that

she had become a veteran.

'I believe you have made nine trips altogether,' he told her.

'You know the ship well and are respected by the senior staff. As you will appreciate, the ship will have to be used for different purposes in future. The nature of the political situation overhanging the return of the ship is now proving an important factor in any transaction.

'We would like to invite you to follow up your success as a crew member by remaining with the ship. If you decide to accept our offer and stay on the ship, you will need to have an appropriate job and the status to go with it.'

'I have been thinking about that,' Astrid said. 'I would like to join the Women's Naval Service if there is any chance of keeping an appointment in the crew of the ship.'

His reply was encouraging.

'Staff are now being increasingly directed to positions and jobs. It's the pending seriousness of the situation that is compelling the trend. If you joined the Women's Naval Service, it would accord with our directives, anyway. We have a job for you that would be well filled by you, if you did volunteer for the service you mentioned.'

She went into initial training immediately in nearby Hamburg naval barracks for two months, while the ship was converted from her previous usage into a vessel for non-military transport purposes. Her speaking voice, fluency of speech, and impeccable deportment made her stand out among the recruits for the naval service.

As a result, having passed out from the initial course, she was seconded to training as a junior officer for several weeks, before returning to an appointment briefing at the offices of Blohm and Voss, where representatives from Hamburg Süd, the ship's operators, were dealing with crew appointments.

She was appointed as director of accommodation for military and non-military passengers on the *Hans Frayling*.

When she next met her, Elsa wanted to know what such an august title meant. She congratulated Astrid on her promotion.

'Now we are back on the same level again. I wonder if it will stay that way. You will go higher in your job, but I shall stay in the doldrums in mine.'

'Oh, it sounds grander than the job actually is, darling. It's simply getting the appropriate person or persons into the right one of the nearly five hundred cabins on the ship.'

'What do you expect to do next? The prospects of war seem overwhelming. I've heard that we are about to launch an invasion against Poland soon. Are you likely to be mixed up in that?' Elsa asked.

'I don't know about that, but we are sailing in two days to Spain, to a port on the east coast called Cartagena, to pick up the airman and soldiers of the Condor Legion who have been helping Franco to achieve his victory in the Spanish civil war.'

'Back to the sunny Mediterranean, so soon! It will keep up your nice suntan.'

'If things go the way they look like going, it will be the last sun I shall see for a long time,' Astrid rejoined.

'On return from Spain, the ship will be converted into a hospital ship. It looks as if someone or other is anticipating a few casualties in the near future. I wonder where they will be coming from.'

Returning to Hamburg, the ship was berthed in the shipyards to have the refit as a hospital ship.

'What on earth will you be doing on a hospital ship?' Elsa

asked Astrid.

'Remember, I'm now an officer in the Women's Naval Service,' she replied. 'I am going for more intensive training for the next few weeks. They will be medically oriented, but I expect to be still in charge of accommodation in some way. It looks as if they have got me there and intend to keep me.'

'And you? What have you been doing?' she asked Elsa.

'I've been learning a bit about the metallurgic characteristics of the outer casings of submarines. I shall soon be working exclusively on the Type XX1. It will be several years before it can be put into production. But it will have the capacity to attack shipping while submerged.'

'Is that something new?' Astrid asked.

'Of course. They will be the first submarines to engage enemy ships while submerged,' Elsa said.

'It will save them from sailing on the surface and having to submerge to escape attack. It will mean fitting many more batteries to spend the extra time under water for a day or two. They would be able to surface to periscope depth for recharging with a snorkel. It's a long way off yet.'

'But that's enough of submarines,' she continued, suddenly reminded of the *Feind hort mit* notices—the enemy is listening—as if by a sixth sense, which had sprung up everywhere. 'I can't say any more.'

'Quite right,' Astrid said. 'I have a suggestion.'

'Here we are in Hamburg. The downtown is not a long way off, so how about painting the town red to celebrate.'

'That's a good one. Let's do that. We could walk down the Reeperbahn to Spielbudenplatz and book a theatre ticket before we go and eat somewhere.'

'I think I would prefer to leave the Reeperbahn to the rest

of the crew from the ship,' Astrid said, 'they'll be itching to try their luck.'

'We might get ourselves picked up down there,' Elsa said.

'No chance in our uniforms,' Astrid quickly retorted.

'What are we saying? That's the last thing we would want. Who would welcome it?' Elsa remarked in disgust.

'Touché,' Astrid said. 'We are already taken in.'

Trying to find a theatre in the Spielbudenplatz was no easy task on a busy night. After two failures, they were ultimately successful at one of the film theatres.

'What are you showing tonight?' Elsa asked the ticket clerk at the first cinema they tried.

'An all-American double bill,' she replied. 'A Charlie Chaplin comedy and the sinking of the Titanic.'

'I like Charlie Chaplin, but I'm not sure about the other film. We are trying to get away from our jobs, not indulging them.' Elsa poured cold water on the offer.

'Yes, I agree,' Astrid assented. 'I'm going to sea and don't want to be reminded of the ominous possibilities.'

'No, sorry, but we will pass it up,' Elsa told the ticket clerk.

There was a queue at another cinema.

'This looks popular,' Elsa commented to Astrid as they approached. 'I will join the queue if you go and see what films are being shown.'

Astrid returned.

'You will never guess. We have joined the queue for a blue cinema.'

'The film titles mean nothing to me. What do we do?' Elsa was in two minds.

'If we go on like this our evening will disappear. Shall we

give it a try? We can always walk out. Let's get tickets for a later show and go to a restaurant first,' she decided.

They found an up-market restaurant, preparing to indulge themselves.

The menu, although the war had already started, was still vibrant and varied. They mulled over the dishes on offer, thinking that they may have already disappeared from lower class restaurants.

'They are still bringing in the fish. There's a good choice,' Astrid concluded, after searching the menu.

Their choice decided, they ordered drinks and sat back, surveying the venue and the rather select people in it, several senior navy and army officers included. The place was filling up.

After their main meal, they debated over eating a dessert. While doing so, a waiter came to their table.

'Excuse me, but as you see we are very full. Would you be averse if two men joined you, now that you have nearly finished?'

A bit taken aback, they assented. Astrid remarked they were only behaving like obedient German women. They would be absenting themselves shortly, in any case.

The two men were shown to their table, profusely apologising for the imposition.

'It's wartime,' Elsa said, 'we have to face such adjustments with aplomb. If nothing worse happens to us today, we shall be lucky.'

'You can say that again,' one of the men said. 'We might be lucky. We might be unlucky. Who knows! I'm Heinz, by the way.'

'And I'm Gunter,' the other man spoke for the first time, joining his companion with a warm smile of greeting.

'I'm Elsa.'

'I'm Astrid.'

'We can see you are in the navy,' said Elsa. 'Are you on the same ship? And both oberleutnants zur see, senior lieutenants.'

'Unfortunately, no,' Heinz replied. 'I'm on the *Deutschland.*'

'And I am on the *Prinz Eugen*,' Gunter added.

'But we can see you are both in the Women's Naval Service, and have both qualified as officers, as well. How did that come about?' Heinz asked.

'You look like two peas in the same pod,' Gunter added, laughing, 'you must have a lot in common.'

In relating their personal stories, including the circumstances that demanded their joining the Women's Naval Service, the two women hinted at the relationship that had drawn them together.

The two men had come from the same town in the north of Germany. Elsa correctly deduced the nature of their relationship. It turned out that a close sexual affinity had brought the two men together as well.

She glanced the information to Astrid.

Once the women had established the men's liaison, it relieved them of trying to avoid any thought the men might have of picking them up for the night. It also provided the women with a converse reason to refer to their own particular relationship.

After a few minutes of general discussion, the question of interest to all of them came back into circulation. Sitting in the Reeperbahn, it was natural to start talking about sex and sexual relationships.

Elsa brought the interchange first into focus.

'The country we have known has not forbidden relationships between men and men nor between women and women, but there is a hint around that we seem to be heading into some sort of prohibition.'

'You are right,' Heinz said. 'Between women in any case has always been considered as unimportant since it did not preclude the possibility of their producing children, but the stringent morality of the government party is rumoured to be acting towards disapproval in future.'

'Of course, they have a more plausible charge to make in the case of men. It takes men away from fathering children,' Gunter added.

Astrid was quick to point out the flaw in the state's argument.

'In both cases the men and women involved could be strictly abstinent regarding producing children, or they could break their allegiance and produce them.'

Elsa eagerly added her own opinion on the question. 'I think there is another factor involved. A vast prudishness in the religious tradition in Europe governs so many considerations, interests, policies, and practical behaviour. I think one day it will all be regarded as less relevant and more a matter of the choice of individuals.'

'A noble thought. But in the start of a war, with a dominant party to steer thought and practice, it doesn't look very hopeful,' Gunter said.

It was soon time for the women to finish their coffee and take their leave.

'It was a very odd experience to run into those two by chance. You could say that our guardian angel had engineered the meeting as a warning of persecutions to come,' Astrid said on reaching the street.

'Oh, the bureaucrats can think and do what they want, but they can never prevent the preferences nature has determined for a particular person,' Elsa responded.

'After all, they themselves are subject to the same influences. We suspect there are many practitioners among them.'

They strode out briskly for the cinema, but had scarcely left the restaurant when, with a blood-curdling sound, air raid warnings filled the air over Hamburg. If it wasn't the first, it was certainly one of the very earliest warnings of the war for the city, a token of the horrendous days ahead.

'That puts paid to our blue film,' Elsa said. 'What shall we do, go to a public shelter, or try to return to our hotel room?'

'I think we had better do the shelter. We don't know what evacuation procedures they have in the hotel. Guests might have to go to special shelters in the basement or even retreat outside the hotel,' Astrid said quickly.

Being relative strangers to Hamburg, they were forced into joining the flow of people apparently heading for a public shelter.

They found themselves plunging down steps into the underground railway system, called the U-bahn. It was crowded and distinctly an uncomfortable experience, but the all-clear sirens went one and a half hours later. Nothing had been heard, no bombs had been dropped. It appeared that a German aircraft had mistakenly strayed into the warning area and triggered the sirens.

'I bet the pilot will get his knuckles rapped over that,' Astrid commented.

'But the authorities presumably welcomed the mistake as a dress rehearsal for the real thing, if it ever comes,' Elsa said.

They made tracks for their hotel, in mixed minds as to whether their evening in Hamburg had been a success or not.

'Our evening could be regarded as a flop,' Elsa said. 'But spending it as a flop is still exciting for me when I spend it with you.'

'That goes for me, too,' Astrid agreed. 'It was quite fun meeting those two officers from the navy ships. They were really nice people, even though they carried an air of gloom with them over their relationship.'

'I didn't mind losing the cinema show,' Elsa added. 'It might have been entertaining, but I didn't expect it would have told us something we didn't know. If we find we missed a treat, we can go another night. I spotted a girl in the queue from my course. She came to work at the same offices where I work. I will ask her if it merited the effort.'

'We shall have a week or two to spend together before I have to return to the ship,' Astrid mentioned. 'By the way, I expect to go for interviews next week about the changes in my job if I stay in the crew.'

'Do you want to do that, I mean to stay in the crew?' Elsa asked. 'It's a rather long hop from offering speech and deportment to the passengers on the Strength through Joy sailings.'

'Yes, I do. I feel attached to the ship. Most of the crew I know are pleasant and treat me well. I feel I belong.'

'There were plenty of women on the ship for the cruises. There will be plenty of women there when it's a hospital ship,' Elsa pointed out. 'No fear of being molested by drunken sailors.'

6

Astrid duly met the crew assignment officer on the day appointed. He began by reiterating the respect Astrid had attracted by her performance of her job in the recently transformed ship.

'Your officers have given good reports of your efficiency in doing your job and also your manner and influence in the mess and in general. But we are here to discuss your job when the ship has been refitted as a hospital ship.'

'I really want to remain in the crew just the same,' Astrid said.

'In that case, let me outline the changes that will now have to be introduced. The alterations to the ship will entail reducing the number of separate cabins back to three hundred. Room has to be found for wards, operating theatres, and the many supporting spaces to run a hospital on a ship.'

'Will the remaining cabins be kept for personnel use?' Astrid asked. 'And will they stay in use for single or double beds?'

'Some will stay single, some as double, but some will have four beds in bunks,' he said. 'There will be senior military medical officers and nursing staff to accommodate, as well as younger male and female hospital staff, not forgetting any walking wounded or recovering patients. It would be a tricky daily job for you if you were the accommodation officer.'

'I still look forward to being appointed. But I expect there is some competition,' Astrid said.

'Yes, there is. But you have the advantage of having done the job, and well. As an officer in the Women's Naval Service, you will have the authority to support your decisions and solve any disputes.

'It will be the first time you will have encountered military people on operational duty, so it will be a different kettle of fish from the cruises. We are at war now. You, too, will be doing your bit for the war effort.'

She was informed that she had been appointed with a promotion from oberfähnrich zur see, the highest officer training rank, to leutnant zur see, lieutenant.

By Christmas, the ship was ready for its transformed purpose. Its one outstanding voyage, was sailing to Africa in the early weeks of 1940 to rescue civilian refugees from German territories taken over by the allies after war was declared.

In April of the new year, it took part in the invasion of Norway and the Lofoten Islands, subsequently repatriating Germans wounded and captured enemy casualties as prisoners of war.

It was grossly supplemented by a service of mercy, carried on through the series of conquests westwards, conducted by the army and air force in the whole of May, and into the first part of June. The ship evacuated exceptional cases back home from the campaigns. Its usefulness as a hospital ship ended with the occupation of France and the retreat of British and French forces from Dunkirk to England.

Consequently, later in 1940, all the medical contents of the ship and its outward livery and appearances as a protected hospital vessel were removed, as it went through yet another dramatic change of usage.

The hospital ship colours of white with a green stripe were repainted to the standard naval grey, as the *Hans Frayling* assumed its last appointment as a navy training ship for the 2nd Submarine Training Division in Gotenhaven in the Baltic.

In becoming a navy ship, all its merchant navy crew members were paid off, with the exception of the captain, who retained a formal command, with his first officer, and two engineering officers.

They constituted a skeleton crew who were familiar with the vessel and could keep it in a basic condition of seaworthiness. Necessary repair work on the ship was discharged by staff imported from the ship's builders.

Once again, Astrid, although a naval officer, expected to see the end of her varied career on the *Hans Frayling*. It was with heightened expectation that she responded with renewed enthusiasm when the naval officer responsible for staff disposal and relocations sent for her.

'You were appointed as the officer in charge of the distribution of accommodation during the period when the ship was in its hospital colours. The ship has now been permanently allocated to the training programme at Gotenhaven. It will be moored but will take on board during a typical day scores of men for eating, sleeping, instruction, and respite.'

'Is there a job managing the accommodation for me this time?' Astrid asked.

'Many more of the individual cabins will be surrendered to make large spaces for barrack accommodation. Some of the large spaces left over from the hospital ship modifications will be useful for lecture rooms. But there will still be over a hundred of the original cabins left for the use of senior officers and visiting specialists.'

'Are you saying there's no need for me any more?' she asked. 'The ship will be navy run and I'm a naval officer.'

'No, I am not. You will be appointed to manage the cabins and barrack rooms, mostly using two-tier bunk beds.'

'It sounds as if my job is being reduced,' she queried.

'We are also taking part in the training of Women Naval Service officers. You ran speech and deportment instruction on the ship for its cruises at first. We want you to do the same for the women selected for officer training.

'As you probably know, the war is likely to engulf the entire population. More women are being recruited into the services to relieve men for combat duty. So, you would have two jobs instead of one.'

Secretly, Astrid was thrilled to hear what he had just said. It added a pleasurable exercise of her skills as well as doing the routine duty, which tended to be mindlessly automatic and gave no personal job satisfaction.

'Can you tell me a bit about the commitment the ship will discharge in Gotenhaven?'

'Gotenhaven in the Bay of Danzig has become a major training facility for U-boat crews. It is as removed from air attack from the west as it is possible to achieve.

'As early as January this year, a tactical training programme was established. It will be re-designated the twenty-seventh flotilla about now and will remain like that for the rest of the war. It is expected that in about six months' time it will be followed to the training arm by the twenty-second flotilla, again as a permanent arrangement.

'Crews have been trained elsewhere with the twenty-second flotilla, before being exposed to practising simulated attacks on a convoy lasting eight to fifteen days. They do this in their newly completed or repaired U-boat to prove themselves combat ready. But in future they will be doing that here.'

'So, how many men would be involved at any one time?' she asked. 'It's upwards to fifty men in a submarine crew, isn't it? Perhaps even a little over fifty, would it be?'

'Yes. That is right. This year there are two hundred and fifty crews passing through the final training phase before becoming operational. Next year it will be greatly augmented to three hundred and fifty crews. It will remain at that figure in each year after that.

'Consequently, an average of between seven and fourteen U-boats and their crews at a time will be on an up to fifteen days training attachment.'

'The variable training time required and the overlapping of arriving and departure of crews, must present a complex logistical operation,' Astrid remarked.

'It has been solved with the foresight of the decommissioning of the *Hans Frayling* and its conversion into a military transport. As you already well know, large numbers of its nearly five hundred separate cabins have already been combined into larger spaces to enable the vessel to be used as a hospital ship.

'The further adaptation I have indicated to you will make way for large numbers of military men in large dining rooms and sleeping quarters.

'In addition, the ship makes an ideal headquarters for the submarine training operations. It's very convenient to have it all concentrated in one place.

'It can be calculated that up to two thousand trainees from both resident flotillas in their various phases and purposes of training, together with the administration and training staff, will be able to live an accessible and convenient way of life on and by means of using the *Hans Frayling*, at any one time. It will be tied up at a wharf in Gotenhaven, and not going to sea.'

'It looks as if I will have a job for as long as the war lasts,' Astrid said. 'Who knows how long that will be?'

'It's a good question. I wish I could answer it. But Britain has successfully resisted us so far. There's no knowing what will happen next,' the officer said.

'But as far as we are concerned, the ship will be berthed in Gotenhaven, and that's where you will be.'

And that was exactly where Astrid spent the next four years of her life, years that would see the war pass her by with the invasion of Russia and see it revisit her with the retreat of German forces in 1944.

She played her own part in the war by helping to run the *Hans Frayling* with efficiency as the headquarters and temporary homestead for hundreds of U-boat crews in training, so many of whom never returned from their missions.

Occasionally she and Elsa were able to meet, but official leave time was almost non-existent. Being able to arrange a convenient rendezvous proved prohibitive.

As time went by, the air attacks by allied aircraft dictated their lives, curtailing their interests, and putting their first priority on escaping from being caught in an air raid.

Train travel was never less than restrictive and became physically a torment that had to be endured. Eventually, it practically ceased to exist as a tireless, reliable, and direct mode of transport.

7

Elsa had become used to being separated from her friend during the time they had both left home for the university. The precious hours they had enjoyed, when they occasionally met, were subsequently once again stripped from them when Astrid finally left for Gotenhaven, leaving Elsa in Hamburg.

For the present, U-boat design and construction were unthinkably continuing in the Hamburg shipyards, which had the reputation of being their natural place of origin. Her present employment tied Elsa to that famous powerhouse of the sea and centre of the historic Hanseatic League in past centuries.

She spent long hours in the office as a member of a design team of over twenty specialists, many of whom were exclusively concerned with the Type XX1 project.

Talking while you worked was not Elsa's preferential mode of behaviour and was discouraged anyway by the supervisor. Some matters in the job, however, needed to be talked about. She needed to adapt to talking over a knotty problem from time to time.

'You can talk to me any time you wish,' a colleague said to her one day. 'My name's Lance.'

'I'll remember that if I run into problems.' She dismissed his remark with a little contempt. She thought he was inclined to be a little too pushing for her taste.

The day he once mentioned materialised when she wanted

some advice on a technical hang-up she had run into.

'Lance, I would be glad of your assistance on a matter that baffles me,' she told him.

'Glad to help,' he responded.

Talking with him, she found him a more amenable and likeable person than she had expected him to be.

'By the way,' she questioned him, 'what does your name mean? I must say I have not come across it before.'

He refused to oblige. Instead, he seized his opportunity. 'It's canteen time. Let's go down there now, and I will tell you the answer to that question.'

They ordered some ersatz coffee and found an unoccupied table for two, where he imparted the surprising meaning of his name.

'It means I am a man of all trades. The name means a ruler and servant of the people.'

'Well, how can you be those two things at the same time?' she asked. 'On the face of it they seem contradictory.'

'You must not think of a ruler in absolute terms as one who presides over others and expects people slavishly to carry out his wishes,' he said.

'You are not then a fuehrer in the ordinary sense of the word.'

'You'd better not say that word. If it carries an implicit criticism of our esteemed leader, you will be getting yourself into trouble.'

'Oh, you are referring to our own exalted leader,' Elsa replied. 'That was the furthest thought in my mind.'

She had learnt to watch her back.

Elsa said those words with the straightest of faces. Lance could detect nothing other than the formal meaning of her statement. There was not the slightest hint of a sneer, sarcasm, or disbelieving humour about them.

'Well, what else did you mean, then?' he asked her.

'I was toying with the two seemingly contradictory definitions of your name. Most people would see being a ruler as a form of directing other people's lives, while being a servant as a form of waiting obediently for those directions to reach you and then carrying them out faithfully and to the letter.'

'I must say I have never given too much thought to such niceties. In the end it's all a matter of words. I have always been persuaded by what I can draw and calculate and make, to bother about it,' Lance said, hoping to move on to another topic of conversation.

Elsa was too fired up by then to let that happen. She really wanted to test out Lance's sympathies. Was he a loyal servant of the Reich, happy to discharge his duties? He seemed to keep his own mouth shut in line with his protestation about not being bothered about words.

'There's a good explanation for the juxtaposition of the two concepts attaching to your name, Lance,' she said, renewing the dialogue.

'I have a feeling you are going to say something that has not occurred to me before,' he intervened, 'or might upset me.'

'I don't think that would be possible,' she said, 'but I promise I am not trying to wind you up or compromise you. Just giving my view.'

'You haven't said it yet. When you do, I shall be the best judge of what you are trying to do.'

'If you are ruler, you have the potential or actual power at your fingertips to make things happen,' she said.

'Well, of course, that's what being ruler means,' he confirmed. 'I like the inclusion of the potential of power. Sometimes a ruler has never quite grasped it, or it slips from his fingers if he has achieved only half a grip.'

'Exactly,' said Elsa, 'and if that happens, a ruler loses the ability to be the servant. But being a servant can be so plausible if you have the power to go with it. You can please the people and consolidate your position at the same time.'

'You sound as if you are writing an apology for our national leader. He is pleasing the population by our conquests, and restoring full employment, but at the same time tightening the noose of his power.'

'That's something you have said openly,' Elsa commented, testing him. 'Do you have a prejudice, by chance?'

'I am a loyal and hardworking citizen,' Lance quickly replied, mindful of the fact that although they were colleagues at work, betrayers were in every walk of life.

'How long have you been working for Blohm and Voss? You seem to have become part of the office, knowing everything, the whys and wherefores, and everyone around the place.'

'I joined the company in 1934, when I was twenty-two,' Lance declared. 'They were the days when any work on design had to be totally hush-hush under the prevailing treaty conditions that had inhibited Germany from pursuing preparations for rearmament. They were expectations that could easily be circumvented in a dozen ways. I played my small part in that subterfuge.'

'I knew nothing of that,' Elsa said. 'So, you really are an old hand in this game. What did you do before that?'

'I was at school, not in Germany, but in Poland.'

'Why were you there? You must have spent some of your years between the wars in a foreign country.'

'Some of it. My father is Polish, my mother German. I went to university in Hamburg, where, as you might have guessed, there was a strong emphasis on maritime studies, seafaring, shipbuilding engineering, and—at the time—secret design and construction engineering for the Kriegsmarine, the emerging navy, which had such a sparse beginning.'

'Oh, what has happened to you since the takeover of Poland? More than eighteen months have slipped by. It must have been a confusing and anxious time for you when we invaded that country.'

'That is an understatement. My parents were living in Poland at the time of the invasion. Their house was badly damaged by bombing. In the confusion of the eventual Polish collapse, they were driven onto the streets.

'German police were arresting able-bodied men, presumably for compulsory war work. My father was taken away. We never knew where. We never heard from him again. It was nearly two years ago. We have never known what happened to him, or where he was taken.'

'But you used the present tense about your father when you said, "is Polish",' Elsa disarmingly said, quoting the fragment from his conversation.

'That must have been a slip of the tongue. We assumed he had been killed or had died a natural death.'

'What did you and your mother do when he was taken from you? You must have lost your income immediately and most of your possessions?' Elsa pressed him, realising it had become a sensitive subject of discussion.

'It was a tortuous experience for mother and me. To be wasted like that,' Lance said.

'How do you feel about it now?' she asked.

'Time is a great healer, of course. The German police sent my mother back to Germany. She came to Hamburg. They provided housing for her. I went to live with her. She just had to adjust as quickly as she could and get on with her life.'

'Were you not bitter about the loss of your father?' Elsa asked. 'It was not as if he was recognized as the husband of a German woman.'

'That's a question I cannot answer,' Lance replied.

Or won't, Elsa said to herself.

'I am a German national with a responsible job. Perhaps I am lucky to have escaped being taken into custody, being half Polish. My half German status must have been sufficient to save me. It was evidently regarded as the dominant and telling half of me.'

'Well, I hope it stays that way,' Elsa said, thinking it was time to break off this conversational engagement. 'But in any case, you have made a strong contribution to the regime and have a lot of potential for meeting the demands that will confront us in the near future.'

Lance frustrated her move by suddenly asking her, 'But how about you? You are an officer in the Women's Naval Service and in a protected job. You ought to regard your situation as privileged.'

'I don't think of myself like that. Being here is the natural outcome of doing a degree in metallurgy. I was a farm girl. My father is a farmer, growing food for the Reich in the estates of Pomerania. I went to Breslau University, where I chose a science subject, partly I must admit, to secure a university place as a woman.'

'They have been squeezing women out of going to university,' Lance interjected. 'Mostly on account of the pretentions women have been attaching to that ambition.'

'You mean it could upset the status quo, spoiling the man's world as we have known it,' Elsa said, laughing.

'Good for you,' Lance agreed. 'You know how it is. Behind it all in our country, there is a tradition of the man's being head of the house. Nothing much happens without his say-so. Then they thought the men of Germany could be the master race. But woman certainly had to have their place. A woman was respected, but essentially as a mother to give birth to a member of the master race and become the manager of the family home.'

'Yes,' Elsa stated with conviction. 'They have put a brake on the movement of women's determination to adopt a profession, to specialise in an occupational subject, to run the show as they are able to do in industry, commerce, politics, education, and just about everything else. The composition of the pyramid of talent and application ought to be composed of men and women, according to their individual propensities and demonstrable abilities.'

'You seem to have pronounced views for a woman sitting here in the canteen of a famous shipyard, sounding off your beliefs while busily engaged in design work for future submarine warfare.

'You can't afford to be known for extreme views, especially if they are contrary to the government's line. I wouldn't like to see you carted away. You might end up like my father and never be seen again.' Lance seemed genuinely anxious.

'Your own views surprised me, too. I would not express my views to anyone else. You seem to be a reliable colleague to have. I have always wondered if you could be trusted.

'One of the handicaps being in uniform for me is that I have to button my lip, but not to inhibit my thoughts passing through my mind that would conflict with protocol, if I gave them voice that would land me in real trouble.'

Elsa was touched by his concern. She had another thought. Sitting opposite her was a man who had a genuine grievance against his own country. She wondered if a time would ever come when he would turn it into revenge.

It was idle dreaming on her part. On reflection, she saw that it owed its origin to the circumstances of the moment, when the war was in its infancy and any steps to injure national interests could not be effectively taken.

On reflection, she thought that so many people like Lance had cause to be vengeful towards those who had engendered the war and caused such hardship. Their numbers were always considerable, but war was a great leveller. In totalitarian warfare, everyone had to play his part, overcoming his private prejudices in favour of the greater good.

8

Elsa did not see Lance again for over two months. She heard he had been moved to another office. She had lost Astrid to the navy in Gotenhaven, and now she had lost her recent confidant, Lance, although she was reluctant to ascribe such a self-sacrificial title to him.

Elsa's attraction had always been to Astrid, but she had never mentioned her to Lance. Not that she had anything to hide.

Her relationship with Astrid was so prominent in her life that she regarded all other acquaintances as irrelevant to the mainspring of her existence.

It was not that there never could be someone else in her vista, it was simply a matter of there being no need for it to happen.

Another complicating factor for living in Hamburg was the repetition, regularity and growing threat from allied bombing. It had not yet become inhibitive to the citizens of the city, but the future had a bleak look about it.

A total of eight raids by various forces of bombers, usually about one hundred strong, had begun to inflict damage and cause casualties so far in 1941. Oil refineries had been the early targets in and around the city, but they gave way to attacks on the Blohm and Voss shipyards and residential areas.

It was during a daylight alert in June 1941 that Elsa clapped eyes on Lance again. The staff from several buildings had been ordered to the underground shelters during working hours.

It was an unusual event, since raids were inevitably delivered at night, rudely interrupting the workers' sleep and spoiling their working concentration at work the next day.

On this occasion it was a false alarm. They were incarcerated in the shelters for about an hour before the all-clear sirens went, sending them back to work.

Elsa spent that futile hour idly wandering around the spacious air raid shelters underground. It was just something to while away the time. She didn't really attach much effort in her search. She thought she might bump into him if he had had the same idea.

But it was not to be. There were hundreds of employees from Blohm and Voss but also those from other companies.

Being released again into the open air and bright sunshine by the all-clear sirens, Elsa set off on her trail back to the design office.

It was when she had almost reached the entrance of the building, that a slightly winded Lance caught up with her, having hurried a distance and dodged a lot of people, after sighting her from afar.

'Elsa, you are still around, then.'

'Yes, of course, but where have you been?'

'I have been away for most of the time, but I can't explain where I have been, while we are standing here. I shall not be coming back to the same office where we were. If you like we could meet in the Reeperbahn for a meal, and I could tell you all about it.'

They promptly fixed a meeting point and a time for the same evening.

The next week or even the coming weekend might be too late.

Elsa tried to tell herself that she was pretty indifferent to the rendezvous she had arranged with Lance. She kept shrugging it off as something of little consequence. And then she realised how many times she was telling herself the same thing. At last, she finally gave in to her own cogitations.

I'm looking forward to meeting him tonight, she admitted to herself. *I have been so busy. I have not had a chat to anyone lately, so it must be the opportunity of a lifetime that is turning me on.*

She did not have the chance to return to her flat after work. Her hurried preparations for her night out, just had to be a matter of a visit to the ladies' room and making the most of her hair and face, before arriving punctually at the appointed time and place in town.

On approaching the chosen spot, she saw Lance talking to an older man. When he saw her, he said something to the man, who then turned and walked away in the opposite direction from hers.

'This is a glorious surprise, Elsa. I thought you had probably been sent to another office or had asked to be taken off your commitment.'

'There's no chance of throwing in the towel, Lance. They will keep me at this job until the way ahead becomes clear, or until they want me to do another thing, but in that case, it will have to be something of a tall order in importance, I have to say.'

'Let's not worry about it. We have to get a meal. The best there is. We have to celebrate.'

'What have you done, then, been promoted to a more

senior job or been dragooned into the army?'

'Neither, as it happens. But you could have hit the nail on its head with your last remark. Did you know our forces invaded Russia yesterday?'

'Have they really! No, I have missed that news. That should set all the families of soldiers on edge. Did you know what happened to Napoleon, who was the last man to try that trick? It's a different kettle of fish from invading the Low Countries and France.'

'It remains to be seen if your implied fears are realised,' Lance said, as he ushered her into the restaurant.

Being early, they soon found a table for two.

Elsa was eager to hear Lance's other news, although it seemed to be dwarfed by his declaration of the invasion of Russia.

'You were supposed to be answering my question. If you keep me waiting any longer, I shall think you have little to tell.'

'What I am about to tell you is not an open secret like the invasion of Russia. It's only for your ears. Promise me you will never disclose it to another soul.'

'I promise, I promise,' Elsa said laughing. 'Please take me out of my misery. You have been away from work for a number of weeks. Now, what's it all about?'

'I have been to Peenemünde,' Lance began.

'Not for a seaside holiday, I hope,' Elsa interrupted him.

'It's the place on the Baltic where secret aerial weapons are being developed. They should reinforce Germany's triumphs and make ultimate victory absolute.'

'What were you doing there, may I ask?'

'Blohm and Voss are making an input to the projects. I was one of several staff who had to be briefed about the work to be done.'

'Where will you do it, in Peenemünde or in Hamburg?' Elsa queried.

She suddenly had the realisation that he might be posted away and become another loss to her intimate, or potentially intimate, friends.

'In Hamburg, I'm pleased to say. Peenemünde is a very cold place. It could also be the target for air attacks, except that one of the reasons for choosing that place apparently, five years ago before the war, was the extreme distance away from British bombers.'

'But nearer Russian ones, I fear,' Elsa interjected.

'True, that is now the question,' Lance agreed.

'I saw you talking to a man when I arrived tonight. Is he another employee involved in the project?'

'No, he's a friend I happened to bump into.'

Elsa had sprung the question out of the blue. Lance had taken it calmly. But she suspected he had told a lie.

'Haven't we talked about business more than enough?'

Elsa thought that indeed they had been in a reserved frame of mind, in keeping with their discussion.

She surprised herself by hoping the man opposite her might have more strings to his bow than making the Blohm and Voss contribution to the Baltic project. She hoped that his last remark might be an invitation to tell her something more interesting, perhaps even provocative.

'How is your mother faring these days?' Elsa thought she had changed the subject.

'Unfortunately, she was killed in one of the recent air attacks on the city,' Lance said, pouring chilly water on the conversation. 'It was while I was away. The house was badly damaged. I've had to move out. They gave me a flat, quite a superior one, but of course, it is no recompense for losing her.'

'How ghastly!' Elsa said to him, catching her breath, and regretting her previous wandering thoughts that now seemed so irrelevant.

'So, I am alone in the world. Without family, with a flat, but no house. It's all a matter of being at war.'

Lance was evidently determined to put a brave face on his grief.

'I'm impressed with your indefatigable spirit,' Elsa said in a subdued and respectful voice. For the first time in her life, she had just heard a close family survivor's account of the loss of a close and dear relative. It was not to be the last.

'You mentioned being alone. That implies you have no brothers or sisters and no girlfriends. Is that the size of it?'

'Yes, my mother could have no more children after my birth, owing to complications.'

'She made a good job of producing you,' Elsa ventured, lightening the conversation with gentle laughter. 'I suppose you have had girlfriends who have come and gone.'

'Now that would be telling,' Lance said. 'It's true there have been several along the way, but they have tended to become fed up with my irregular working hours.'

'You mean they didn't fancy becoming married to the job,' Elsa quipped, once again raising a smile from Lance. 'They could not have been professional women of any sort themselves.'

'They were the usual office-hours or shop-hours women, who wanted regular evenings and weekends free, some of them only to paint their faces and the town red.'

'You must have given up some attractive finds in your

time, then, and all for the job,' Elsa said.

'That's stretching things a bit far, I suppose, but you could say that.'

'It's a pity you are out of luck just at the moment when you could do with a woman to support you through a trying time,' Elsa ventured.

'There has been a woman in my world for the last six months who could fill the bill in my estimation, but I think she is too far out of my reach.' Lance suddenly let the comment slip, after first deciding not to say it.

'There's hope then. You will have to give up some of the attention you have given to work and redirect it towards her. You could be lucky. You are an attractive man with a good job. Go to it,' Elsa said.

'Talking of going to it,' she added, 'I must be on my way soon, and they have not brought the meals we ordered yet.'

The meals had indeed been a long time coming, but not that exceptionally long. Elsa had been so engrossed in the conversation that she had exaggerated the time they had waited for their meal. She did not really need to get away.

The waiter was polite, which pleased her. She deplored waiters of the silent sort, the gruff ones, and the abrupt individuals of the species. Mostly they were men she reflected.

At last, they were served a wartime meal, consisting of white meat balls that had less substitute meat content than should have been the case, but as much as the war demanded. Green beans, boiled potatoes, and cucumber salad, without dressing, completed the menu. Dessert was simply cheese of two kinds with slices of pumpernickel bread.

'These particular meatballs originated in Prussia, in Königsberg. That's not so far away from your place of birth,'

Lance informed Elsa.

It was an item of knowledge she did not know but did not regret that fact. She had always protested that she regarded such obscure items of fact, despised by some people, should be respected by an educated person.

'Do you mean these meat balls have been hanging around since Bismarck's time when the name Prussia was changed to Germany, or when the colour and ingredients were devised?' Elsa asked, as a comment on his statement, laughing.

'No, they haven't had refrigeration around for that long. I meant centuries ago when Prussia was a large and powerful state,' he corrected her, perpetuating the humour.

'And this pumpernickel bread originated in Germany,' Elsa informed Lance, slipping into a mock advertiser's speech. 'They perfected the art of producing these slender and beautifully finished slices, making the eating so much more enjoyable.'

That was an item Lance did know already, but he saw the funny side of her remark, the two of them sharing the moment of humour with the most liberated laugh of the meal, aided by a bottle of wine.

They were relaxing after their meal over a cup of ersatz coffee, when their pleasantries and peace of mind were shattered by the sound of the air raid sirens. They had already paid their bill.

Joining the exodus from the restaurant, they hurried out into the Reeperbahn and headed for the nearest entry to the underground tunnel, fortunately near at hand. The celebrated thoroughfare sported its own U-bahn station.

The bombing had not yet reached the point of intensity and frequency to force the Hamburg population to abandon their city life. People clung to its continuation as far as it could be supported, in spite of the military recruitment of men, and the bombing disruptions.

Consequently, they had to mingle with hundreds of city people bent on filling the underground platforms. The operation of the train service, according to custom, was immediately suspended, creating more room underground.

Although it was a mid-year month, it was surprisingly cold underground. They walked as far on one of the platforms as was possible, just short of the train tunnel entrance. They expected the crowds coming along behind them to be large enough to spill over onto the lines, with the termination of the electric current.

Before long they could hear the sound of bombs exploding. It was a raid employing two hundred aircraft. They were arriving singly, serial style, each dropping eight to ten one-thousand-pound bombs.

For about an hour, they listened in silence. Around them the scores of people comforted themselves with constant chatter, some telling jokes, others playing cards. Yet others remained silent, perhaps concerned about their loved ones, praying that on a random basis the chances of their families would remain high, and they would escape destruction in such a big city.

With the passing of time, many servicemen among the refugees, predominantly from the army and navy, lost themselves with their girlfriends. Both men and women were anxious to make the most of the evening that otherwise would have been wasted.

They substituted the underground platform as the alternative to a more suitable place—whether on the street corner, in the park, or in a bed—where they would have chosen to spend the same amount of time.

Perhaps the sights and sounds of such indulgencies in the height of an allied air raid, in an underground city shelter, late at night, had an effect on Elsa and Lance.

Lance had done the manly thing. He had first given Elsa his coat. After a while, she rebelled against his sacrifice. He had no option but to cuddle her to him when he ultimately felt cold himself.

Both Elsa and Lance realised their relationship to date had been governed by reserve. Each had had no idea what the nature of the other's inhibition had been.

For Elsa, her reserve had been based on her love for Astrid, which had produced a general aversion to men, although she had no rooted objection to men as such. Lance was a handsome man with a good figure, a brain to match his physique, a good catch for any woman.

For Lance, he had held a secret attraction for Elsa since meeting her, but she was in the officer class and somewhat forbidding at times in manner and the expression of her sharp mind. That said, she was beautiful and attractive in all parts.

He wanted to tell her she was voluptuous, but his reservations about her forbade it. Besides that, she would say such a remark was a man's view, caused by his body juices.

The meal in the restaurant was behind them. They were lost for mutual protection in a dark corner in the bowels of the earth.

It was a chance that nature seized. Lips were involuntarily sealed.

They inevitably found their hands wandering.

If their thoughts could have been synchronised, they

would have expressed themselves variously in a manner of self-justification.

It's wartime. These things happen.

We might be obliterated while we lie here.

I've had a passion for you, but there was another contender in the offing.

You have been the woman I mentioned when I told you about my love life, who I always regarded as beyond my class.

We can live for the moment. It will be something to look back on as an aberrant indulgence we enjoyed but had to forget in the circumstances.

You might surprise me. I might surprise you.

This could be a trivial affair.

In wartime, you have to take your chances. This is a chance to be taken.

You may be killed tomorrow.

Without the war, we would never have met. What a way to end the evening!

Even you could not have had this in mind. The allies have done us a favour.

This could be the start of something big.

The reverie thrashing through their minds was eventually interrupted by the all-clear sirens. 'You see,' Elsa said, 'the all-clear sirens waited long enough to cover the arrival of the last bomber, and to give the chance for those on the ground to complete their business.'

'You are naughtier than I ever imagined,' Lance replied, 'I was not aware that anyone was discussing business. I should have thought that most people were too distraught to be able to concentrate on their business.'

'Depending on the nature of their business,' Elsa added.

Their comments made them continue laughing with the oblique references to the course of their own evening that had come to an unexpected climax.

9

The number of attacks on Hamburg and the weight of bombs dropped increased from that time onwards. It was the result of the introduction of the Short Stirling...the first of the three four-engine heavy bombers produced by the British in the third year of the war...and the arrival of the American air force in Britain.

In June and twice in July 1942, the Blohm and Voss buildings, installations, and shipyards were specifically targeted.

The Americans bombed their targets by day with the benefit of a fighter escort after early, costly reversals. The British continued bombing by night.

Blohm and Voss decided to take as many movable interests, tangible facilities, and staff eastwards, before it was too late. They excluded the small number of staffs contributing to the work on the rockets being developed at Peenemünde.

Elsa heard the news one day towards the end of 1942. She had been bombed out of her customary office and had been rehoused away from the dock area. She was of course pleased to hear that with her work, she would be posted away from Hamburg, but mortified to hear that Lance would be omitted from the move. The signs of increasing warfare being levelled at the city certainly justified the decision.

When she learned that the place of retreat chosen was Gotenhaven, her private life was thrown into confusion. Torn from Lance and with a renewed contact with Astrid, she would be faced with a turbulent time in her personal relationships in the near future.

She had been living with Lance and sharing the cost of renting his flat, his home being superior to her own flat. She continued on secondment to Blohm and Voss throughout that time, as an oberfähnrich zur see, a sub-lieutenant, the lowest rank in the Women's Naval Service, doing work of the utmost importance to the war effort.

Her work in conjunction with the other members of the design team had become so far advanced that she suspected that the move might recoil on her, leading to her transfer out of the commitment.

There had been talk that a number of women on secondment might be recalled to strictly naval duties, irrespective of their particular specialist commitments.

She had lost contact with Astrid but knew she was still in her job on board the *Hans Frayling*. However, the stark possibilities had to be faced. If orders came, then orders were orders, and she would have no choice.

The falling of the axe was delayed as long as possible, but time was running out. Part of the reason for the decision was the appearance of the Handley Page Halifax and Avro Lancaster, the second and third British four-engine bombers, each able to carry a huge bomb load.

They were rumoured to be introduced by the British to the bombing campaign in 1943. In fact, they duly fulfilled that expectation during the early weeks of the year.

The axe fell in the event mercifully, therefore, before the most severe raids of the bombing campaign, which came on those nights when well over seven hundred bombers inflicted severe damage to the city of Hamburg in terms of the destruction of property and the injury and death of its citizens.

Elsa and Lance spent their last night together before she left for Gotenhaven. It was more of a farewell than a till-we-meet-again event.

'It has been a while since we shared a platform slot in the U-bahn. I never thought we would have enjoyed our war so much in the meantime. We have each had a job and drawn our pay in relative comfort.' Elsa summed up their relationship. It had appeared out of the blue but lasted well.

'We've had a relatively comfortable life of it compared with our troops on the Russian fronts. Some people are murmuring that the great reversal at Stalingrad was the beginning of the end,' Lance added thoughtfully.

'I have to tell you that our being together was something I had never imagined, but always wondered about. It has been great for me,' Elsa said.

'And I have to tell you that you were my dream girl when I first met you and have proved every part of my dream. It all came true.'

They made no promises of meeting in the future. Their relationship had had the appearance of a temporary affair, with that underlying understanding of both. In the circumstances of the war at that point, life was seen to be short, and it seemed to be getting shorter.

Their actual parting was finally precipitate, just a hug, no tears, no kiss.

Elsa's actual passage to Gotenhaven was to be by train.

A navy truck took the Blohm and Voss party, including several of the seconded Women's Naval Service staff, to the main railway station in Hamburg.

But there was no station.

Remains of stone parts of the impressive former buildings, were totally open to the sky, shrapnel studded and hanging in a precarious manner.

Railway lines had been hastily repaired, but the hundreds of passengers, including a majority of army personnel returning eastwards for military duties, were waiting for their trains to pull in by standing or sitting on the former platforms.

Here and there parts of the platforms had escaped the bombing, retaining their original function of supporting passengers for easy embarkation at the height of train doors.

But mostly, the platforms had been gouged out in whole or part into piles of rubble. Naturally, all the facilities and services of a major railway station had been obliterated with the physical destruction.

It was a wasteland. Elsa could hardly take it in. Even the pigeons—the ubiquitous parasites of railway stations—were completely absent, either annihilated or had prudently fled to safer hunting grounds elsewhere.

The absence of the constant movement of pigeons, leaving only the steam and smoke of stationary railway engines, gave the whole scene a bizarre and mystifying stillness.

When their train arrived, the staff of Blohm and Voss was fortunate to inherit a crowded coach—but the empty reserved half of it.

All the rest of the passengers on the train, travelling under their own auspices, had soon filled the rest of the carriages, spilling over onto their roofs and even between the overcrowded carriages.

The journey was tortuous. Delays en route and diversions

made the journey twice as long as the normal time for a train travelling around five hundred miles.

On the way Elsa had heartaches for the passengers clinging to the roof of her coach. Two fell off with the train at speed.

One of them desperately clutched at the roof guttering to arrest his fall. He found either his grasp on it, or the protrusion itself, was insufficient to save him. He swung crazily at Elsa's window for a few seconds before being helplessly plucked away to his death by the slipstream.

Not a person could move inside the carriages carrying the generality of passengers. Elsa's company had thoughtfully provided water and food for their employees. Several of them used the toilet reserved ostensibly for their private use within minutes of leaving Hamburg. They were the privileged few.

Within the hour, the reserved lavatory for their use was besieged by the crowd in the unreserved half of their carriage.

'It's no use,' Elsa cried out. 'We shall never stop them. They are scarcely able to move to another carriage.'

'Then it's a good job our carriage is first behind the engine. If we had been in the middle of the train somewhere or other, we would have had dozens of people coming through here hoping to reach a heavenly spot further up or down the train,' one of their supervisors said.

'Some of them are saying that passengers are urinating and defecating in the luggage departments, the longer the journey goes on,' Elsa's neighbour told her.

'That is not a pretty sight,' another colleague said to Elsa. 'What on earth will it be like if this train is delayed and goes on overnight?'

It was a question no one ventured to answer.

'We just have to put up with it. At least we all have seats,' someone else interjected.

'But don't bank on keeping them,' another added.

'Let's hope we shall make it before night.'

'Even if it is midnight.'

Someone expressed the unspoken thoughts that were in everyone's mind.

After two hours of travel, an older, senior soldier came into their carriage, stopping at the first Blohm and Voss staff member.

'Can you point out your supervisor to me, please?'

'He's the man with the baldhead, asleep, at the other end of the carriage. He won't be pleased to be woken up. He's had a rough day.'

The soldier was not put off his mission in the least by the admonition. He strode down the carriage and shook the Blohm and Voss supervisor in charge of the party by the shoulder.

'Excuse me, sir, do you think you could share your half of the carriage with some of those people in the other half? Conditions there have become unbearable.'

'This is a reserved carriage for an important group of industrial people being transferred to resume their war work.'

'I appreciate that, sir. We all have an important job to do these days. Some of the boys in the next carriage are returning from leave to the Russian fronts. There are women standing up and approaching exhaustion point. If we could ease the congestion there a little, it would be appreciated.'

'All I feel I can offer is to let some of the people into our half of the carriage. They can stand in between the seats. If members of my party want to surrender their seats, that would be up to them. I think that's my best offer.'

'And I think that would be a great help, sir. Regard it as a special aid to the fatherland.' They both laughed.

Having accomplished his purpose, he returned to his half of the carriage and within minutes an overflow of people spilled into Elsa's half, voicing their thanks freely as they stepped forward, bringing their own relief and that of those left behind. An elderly woman and a young man in his early twenties stood near Elsa.

'You can sit down here for as long as you like,' Elsa told her.

'Thank you, my dear,' she said, 'I am so grateful for a seat. What with the early morning rise, and then all that standing at the Hamburg railway station for so long has just about exhausted me of all my energy.'

'How far are you going?'

'I'm going to Stettin or rather returning to Stettin after visiting family members near Hamburg. I was unlucky enough to be caught in some of the bombing while I was there.'

'We should be in Stettin shortly. I expect you will be glad to get your journey over at last. I understand that you had a raid in April this year.'

'Yes, we did, we were surprised they could come so far. It seems that nowhere is safe from heavy bombing any more.'

The swaying of the train took Elsa suddenly into the body space of the young man. She apologised and recovered her balance.

'Are you going all the way?' she asked him.

'Where would all the way be, then?' he asked her.

'In truth, I don't know. I'm going to Gotenhaven. And you?'

'That's where I am heading, too,' he replied. 'What will

you be doing there that you couldn't be doing in Hamburg? Or is it a secret?'

'You know you shouldn't be asking questions like that. If I put the same question to you, will you give me the same answer?'

'Yes and no,' he replied. 'I am going to join the navy. Or should I say that I am going to rejoin the navy.'

'How can you rejoin? Are you already in the navy?'

'Yes, I am, but I have volunteered for the U-boat service.'

'You must have a large patriotic streak in you.'

'Thank you, frau, the losses have begun to rise dramatically this year. The navy has asked for volunteers to fill the ranks.'

'Well, I hand it to you, and wish you well. By the way, I am not fräu. In fact, I am in the navy. I am an oberfähnrich zur see in the Women's Naval Service, but currently seconded to an industrial appointment. I hope we shall bump into each other in Gotenhaven. What is your name?'

'Oberfähnrich zur See Heinrich Prien,' he replied politely.

'That's the same name as the famous U-boat captain of U-47 from the early part of the war. He sank the *Royal Oak* battleship in Scapa Flow.'

'Quite right. He was my father. He has since been lost. I hope to step into his shoes.'

'In that case, I wish you all the best in the world.'

Before leaving Hamburg, the staff had been briefed about their arrival at Gotenhaven. They would be transported to the same hotel that was used as a transit accommodation for the substantial flow of personnel to and from the port in connection with the U-boat training programme.

Two free nights were provided. They would be charged for the third.

From there, they could either arrange their own digs or take advantage of hostel accommodation in the port. They were expected to report to the makeshift workshops, adapted expressly for the particular Blohm Voss submarine project team, on the morning of the next day but one.

It was very late at night when the train reached Gotenhaven. It had taken more than the anticipated time, but short of the midnight some people on the train had envisaged.

It had been thirteen hours since leaving Hamburg. That represented around thirty-seven miles per hour of travel or stoppages. As journeys went at the height of war, it could have been a lot less efficient than that, but it was all the same a tiring and boring journey.

A bus took them to the hotel, immersed in total blackout.

In the darkness of the night, Elsa had only a fleeting impression of the place. As far as she could see, there was little damage from bombing.

Wearily, the transferred employees of Blohm and Voss debussed and gratefully discharged themselves into the hotel, in the expectation of a good night's sleep.

The lighting in the foyer of the hotel was far less than a self-respecting establishment would wish to display, but times were hard. There was every encouragement to economise with the electricity supply and to reduce the power bill.

Elsa did not see her. She found Elsa.

Elsa had difficulty recognising Astrid dressed in her oberleutnant zur see's uniform, in the dim light. But she admitted to herself how attractive Astrid looked and impressive in her uniform.

'Astrid. It's you. How did you know I was coming here? How wonderful that you have given me this welcome.'

Unashamedly, they embraced.

In those few seconds of their bodily contact, Astrid whispered to Elsa. 'At last, we are together again. I'm so glad to see you. It's been a lifetime being apart. How cruel the war has been!'

Elsa felt electrified by seeing her. The realisation of her fulsome welcome embodied all the thoughts and passions that had formerly dominated their relationship but had lately lain dormant.

'What are you supposed to be doing in this hotel?' Astrid asked Elsa.

'We have accommodation for two nights, after which we could use a pad of our own private choice or join in the hostel life which has been prepared for us. On the day after next we have to report for work.'

'I can offer you a third option,' Astrid said.

'What would that be?' Elsa asked curiously.

'There is a spacious cabin aboard the *Hans Frayling,* one of those left for VIPs visiting the ship, and surviving after the wholesale redesign and refurbishment for the training of U-boat crews. It's mine. If you like, you are welcome to join me either immediately, or once you are settled back at work.'

'Do I really have a choice?' Elsa asked. 'The options you have given me will need thinking over for a few days,' she said, with a straight face.

She carefully scrutinised Astrid's face as she spoke. There was a pause. For just a few seconds.

She noted the momentary pain that passed over Astrid's face.

'I'm surprised you gave me those options,' she added.

'What will you do, then?'

'I shall come with you immediately...options are out. How could you think otherwise, darling Astrid?'

They both smiled knowingly. The many months of isolation from each other had generated growing fears that coolness had ultimately set in. They were both well over two years older, but it was a relief to find some things had never changed.

Astrid promptly hurried out to the entrance of the hotel, where some of the Blohm and Voss party were still disputing the identity of their respective belongings. She found the driver and had a few words with him.

'Have you just driven the party from the station?'

'Yes. What have I done...left someone behind?'

'No, not at all. I just wanted to ask a favour.'

His eyesight had been long adjusted to the night. He saw she was in the navy with officer rank.

'What can I do for you?' he asked.

'Would it be possible to take one of the party and me to the *Hans Frayling* on your way to the garage?'

'Yes, of course I can. It'll be a pleasure, ma'am.'

Astrid ran back into the hotel to fetch Elsa, the driver following her into the foyer.

'Leave her luggage for me to carry out,' he called out to her.

The bus was able to drive on the open quayside all the way to the gangway of the *Hans Frayling*. The ship was blacked out for the night, but shielded lights shed their dim light over the scene as Astrid and Elsa farewelled the driver with a warm and grateful, 'Good night.'

The sentry guarding the gangway was a member of the naval provost.

'I am Oberleutnant zur See Mayer, a member of the staff on the ship,' Astrid announced. 'This is Oberfähnrich zur See Bauer from Hamburg. She will be my guest on board.'

He saluted. They mounted the gangway onto the ship.

'This is like old times. I never thought I would see this ship again,' Elsa said. 'It must be a good luck sign. But we shall see.'

Astrid's cabin was one of the luxury suites from happier days. It was warm and well appointed.

She has been a lucky girl to fall on her feet like this, Elsa thought.

'And I see you have been promoted to oberleutnant zur see rank since I saw you last. You must have been doing a good job to deserve it.'

'It's been a busy life for me,' Astrid said. 'Sometimes I have been rushed off my feet. It has amazed me how many ramifications crop up with people coming and going, very often at odd times of the day or night, and at very inconvenient times.'

Elsa dumped her baggage on the floor.

They stood looking at each other for a full minute.

Why they did so could have been anybody's guess. It may have been to overcome the excitement of meeting each other again. Then it might have been simply to give Elsa time to breathe, having arrived safely. Or was it to invite those bodily functions to regenerate, enabling two persons to seal physically the mutual inner passions that they felt?

They slowly threw their arms around each other and hugged for minutes on end. The war had torn them apart. It had propitiously brought them together again.

They spent the next two precious hours, when they should have been sleeping, telling their respective experiences since their last meeting.

Elsa's story was brief enough. Ensconced in Hamburg, she had concentrated on her secret work at Blohm and Voss. The aerial attacks had disturbed her lifestyle.

She was a little embarrassed to dwell on her liaison with Lance, but the circumstances precipitating it were told with humour and incredulity.

Astrid, too, had had a man. He had been a newly appointed U-boat captain preparing a new crew to go to sea together for the first time. It was not, of course, his first mission by far in U-boats.

She had fallen for his charm and good looks, but rather more importantly for the stern character he displayed. It was a combination she had not previously prescribed for herself but led to her taking him to bed one night. It slipped into a habit she couldn't shake off until he finally went to sea. He never came back.

She described the change in mood and atmosphere in the U-boat base that descended during the time she had spent there.

From March of 1943, the allies were gradually reversing the fortunes of the fight in the Atlantic. The loss of U-boats had become relatively greater than the destruction of allied shipping.

The cause had been put down to the mass production of Liberty ships, the allied development of aerial and seaborne technology, and the improved convoy arrangements with more experienced escort expertise.

10

An instruction from the Women's Naval Service headquarters was awaiting Elsa when she arrived at the port. The headquarters had long since moved from Hamburg to Gotenhaven. It ordered her to report in on arrival.

The following morning Elsa donned the naval uniform she had grown out of the habit of wearing and reported into the headquarters.

The woman naval rating on duty at reception had a message for her. 'You have to see the chief at ten o'clock, ma'am. Better hang on here till then. I'll get you a cup of coffee if you like.'

'That's a good idea. Thank you. What's it all about? Do you have any information about it?'

'None at all. They don't share anything with the rank and file as you should know.'

'I should not have asked that question,' Elsa said. 'You are right. I've been too long in a civilian job and got used to a more general sharing of information. I've come back into the military now.'

'Keep your mouth shut and do as you are told,' the receptionist replied.

'And always obey the last order,' Elsa added.

Their combined cynicism made them both laugh.

Sharply at ten o'clock, she was ushered into the office of the commanding officer of the Women's Naval Service at the port of Gotenhaven.

'Oberfähnrich zur See Elsa Bauer reporting as ordered,' were the first words Elsa said, after saluting her superior officer.

'You've been away from us for a long time, Oberfähnrich zur See. But I am sure your secondment has been a worthwhile contribution to the war effort.'

'I hope so, too, ma'am.'

'I have two matters to put to you.'

'The first is a request from the Gestapo to interview you this afternoon. It can be done in our offices. I know nothing of the reasons for it, but you will have to arrange the appointment with reception.

'The second comes as an order but, as you know, in the case of women military personnel, any unusual commitment away from the routine jobs of their particular unit can be queried and might even be revised if their objections are strong enough.'

Elsa felt her heart beat raise its rhythm, taking a rush of blood to her head. She had been in a cushy number in the offices of Blohm and Voss, although the bombing which overtook them had turned the appointment into dross. Was the service going to extract their pound of flesh by asking her to compensate for an easy number by taking on something more nasty or dangerous?

'We are withdrawing your secondment to Blohm and Voss. It's convenient for them since we are told the project on which you were working is now almost complete.

'We are seconding you to the local naval intelligence unit. They have at times regretted not being able to run with a woman operator. You could meet their need. I know that you are billeted with Oberleutnant zur See Mayer. That can continue if she is willing. It will be a suitable cover for you in the job. If you are willing to take it on, you will be promoted to Leutnant zur See.'

'I regard it as an order, ma'am. I am pleased to undertake it. When do I start?'

'Immediately.'

Elsa saluted and left.

She met the Gestapo agent at half past one, as arranged.

The man was quite young and personable. He didn't mince his words.

'This concerns the man who was a colleague of yours at the Blohm and Voss design department, where you were seconded from your service unit. I believe you may have lived with him later.'

'That is correct.' Elsa confirmed.

'I have to tell you that he was killed in the bombing on the night of the fifth. Did you know he was engaged in secret work based in Peenemünde?'

'Yes, I did. He had to go there just before I started living with him. But he never mentioned what he did there nor any responsibilities he had as a result of it. Not in the least.'

'I'm sure what you say is true. But my main reason for talking with you is over the question of his parents.'

'He did tell me about them. His mother had already been killed in the bombing on Hamburg before I went to live with him. The family was living in Poland when we invaded it. He said his father had disappeared, avoiding being apprehended. He had no idea where his father went, or if he was still alive.'

'Did he ever express any sentiments that could be judged anti-German?'

'He stressed that he was German. He gave many years to the design work in Blohm and Voss. He made the usual quips that most of us make, but nothing that I felt was, or implied, a subversive attitude.'

'So, he was never absent or behaved in a suspicious way that made you feel that it defied normal explanation?'

'The only thing that didn't quite add up occurred on the night I was due to meet him for a meal before I went to live with him. As I approached the rendezvous point, I saw him talking with a man.

'When he saw me, he said something to the man, who turned and walked away. He told me it was a friend he happened to bump into that night. I have no recollection of the appearance or dress of the man, other than he was older than Lance and fairly tall.

'Otherwise, from time to time I wondered if the thought would ever cross his mind to take his revenge on his country. I dismissed it but could see that the news of his mother's death by bombing and the presumed incarceration or death of his father could have formed the possible fuel to generate a vengeful attitude.'

The Gestapo man thanked her for her assistance. She thought no more about it for some months, but then picked up the grapevine news that manufacturing plans and parts of the rockets had reached Britain, the latter surreptitiously collected by Polish patriots from experimental rockets that had crashed.

Perhaps, after all, Lance had had a hand in that unlikely achievement, particularly if his father had survived and remained in touch with his son.

Immediately after that interview, Elsa was inducted into her new job at the port naval intelligence service. It was a matter of meeting people and being shown her workplace in the offices, but without a specific project.

She was briefed on the background of the place where she was newly posted. Käpitanleutnant Heinz Weber, a Lieutenant Commander, her new boss, gave her a run down on the fates that had overtaken Gotenhaven.

'When we invaded Poland in 1939, the name Gotenhaven, after the ancient Goths who came from the area, was replaced for the town name and its port of Gdańsk. The Poles were expelled.'

'Were there any harbour installations of much worth?' Elsa asked.

'Such harbour as existed was transformed into a German naval base. The shipyard was expanded in 1940 and became a branch of the Kiel installations. Gotenhaven became an important base, owing to being a long way from the war theatre.'

'It probably made a safe hideaway for ships, like Scapa Flow, which the British have,' Elsa said. 'It was safe then. But less so, now, unless we can turn the Russians back.'

'It's beginning to seem there is no hope of that,' was the instantaneous comment of her commander. 'I dare not say that out loud. It is safe from aerial bombing, you might say. You are right, but not necessarily from submarines, as we proved with the sinking of the *Royal Oak*.'

'Talking of that, I believe the son of Prien has just joined the submarine training establishment here,' Elsa remarked. 'I met him on the train travelling to Gotenhaven.'

'He follows a distinguished father,' her boss stated.

'He has joined at the wrong time,' Elsa ventured.

'Perhaps,' he replied. 'Many large ships, battleships and

heavy cruisers, are anchored here, as you know. We have had several air raids this year, but not a lot of damage has been suffered. With the reversal of the German army in Russia, I think we shall have to expect that we will be in the thick of the evacuation of troops and refugees from this port area.'

'What sort of work will I be doing?' Elsa asked him.

'At this moment we have no project or mission for you to carry out, but rest assured they will come soon enough.

'But you need to get some training in. Your initial courses for the service are several years old. You have had a sedentary job since them. In other words, I want you fit. You must also get some gun practice in, particularly with the latest luger pistol and the heavy version of the Schmeisser sub-machine gun.

'And get some driving in, too, particularly large service vehicles. I will give you a pass to use, when requesting things you want to borrow.

'I would also like you to get familiar with being on the water. I do not mean on the deck of a liner. And do some swimming. Get yourself used to the rock of the waves. Take out a canoe and become adept at handling it in rough water.

'I can give you a month to be any use to me, and another month if you continue your training while you do some work. You have been posted with the best of recommendations, especially intellectual and determination. Now use them to prepare yourself. Report to me once a week.'

That night Elsa confessed to Astrid that she may have bitten off more than she could chew.

'But you have all day and every day for a month,' she observed. 'It's quite a list, but you can already do many of the items, so it will be a brush up for most of them.'

'He spoke as if he wanted to see a trained jack of all trades at the end of a month,' Elsa stated.

'Not that many,' Astrid said. 'He didn't mention parachute jumping, flying, or diving, so count yourself lucky.'

The weeks flew by while Elsa found her feet. She began by imposing something on herself that the kapitäleutnant did not mention. She attended the local navy physical education programme in the gymnasia for the U-boat crews in training.

As her physical strength and endurance grew, so did her mastery of the skills she had to acquire—including those for the first time and the renewal of those that had fallen into disuse.

She found learning how to handle the canoe and fire the Schmeisser to be the most exciting and satisfying new experiences. Acclimatising to the water at first in a canoe called for rather a different demand on her reflexes than being on a ship.

Being at sea in a canoe bore no relation to the sedate voyage she had made once in the *Hans Frayling* with Astrid.

In sloppy water she found the rolling movement in her lone craft churned up her stomach, but she soon adapted to the swirling turns and plunges the canoe enabled her to take during her lone forays into the night.

It was by night that she first found justification and personal satisfaction with her appointment.

Her boss had explained that the local naval intelligence unit, which she had joined, had become hard pressed to counter the growing pilfering in the Gotenhaven complex of town, docks, and shipyards.

Apparently, the discipline of the indigenous population, ever fortified by the strictness of the national regime and heavy punishment for criminal activities, had worn thin under the increasing privation imposed by wartime reversals, the shortage of some commodities, and local dislocation of supplies.

But worse.

Submarine and ship crews were suspected of light-fingered operations to make up shortfalls in supplies of equipment, food, weapons, and perhaps even ammunition.

Recently, cases of stealing had occurred. The only explanation was the proximity of the thefts to the departure of a ship or submarine.

An impartial observer could sympathise with any crew members engaging in such nefarious work. Crews wanted to go to sea and face the enemy fortified with as many resources as they could carry. But unless supplies increased, any pilfering of the reduced available food, guns, ammunition, or equipment would deprive another crew of its fair share.

In fact, if such stealing was allowed to continue it would only lead to the widespread, increasing misappropriation of resources, and the successive denial to future crews at a time when they too needed the best and most complete supplies they could lay their hands on.

The losses of U-boats were known to be mounting. Elsa put two and two together and came to an untoward conclusion she dared not disclose to anyone in authority.

The thought crossed Elsa's mind when she first heard about the latest trend, that the German navy might be deliberately starving departing U-boats of their complete supplies of some items of provisions, perhaps equipment and ammunition.

A statistical calculation must have been conducted on the

number of U-boats despatched – those with the standard full stock of supplies, those with a shortage of supplies, those that returned having completed the entire duration of their scheduled missions, those that returned before time because of the exhaustion of key supplies, and those lost at sea – to give average operational times if known or guessed.

Her suspicion was that a scheme had been introduced, adding up all the supplies to all the U-boats going to sea from the port, before deducting a small percentage from all of them, to ensure the stocks in reserve were adequate for other boats to be re-victualled after them.

One night as Elsa paddled her way around the vessels moored in the dockyard, she heard subdued distant voices that carried across the cold, calm water with unexpected clarity.

It was very dark, but her night vision had long since become adjusted to the absence of any lighting from ships, quaysides, or streets of the town.

Being low on the water and dressed in black waterproof clothing and helmet, with painted black face, Elsa silently made her way towards the location of the voices.

She espied that the activity was centred on a U-boat.

A rowing boat was moored to the offside of the submarine near the conning tower and gun platform. Two men in the boat were handing up something to two men on the casing of the submarine.

Whatever it was took both men to lift it and the others to stow it away. She noted that the goods were being lowered into the deck of the submarine quite near the gun platform.

Elsa deducted that she was watching an illegal operation.

Otherwise, the supplies would have arrived on the quayside by land and loaded with the aid of proper lifting gear.

It was her first discovery of malpractice. The thoughts in her head were both confusing and stimulating.

I could go in close and shout at them that they should stop what they were doing as it was against the law.

But that was only a childish fancy. She reminded herself how high the stakes were in what she was seeing. They could as easily have drowned her in the harbour waters. What was her life against the odds they faced?

She quietly withdrew and returned to base.

In the morning, tired but excited from limited sleep for the remainder of the night, Elsa reported in to Kapitäleutnant Weber.

'You haven't given me a specific task yet, but last night I took it into my own head to try out my canoeing in the dark.'

'That was enterprising of you. How did you get on?'

'A bit different in the blackness of the night, but I coped adequately. Concealment in the dark means not disturbing the water too much either by exposing it to sight or sound. You have to paddle softly and smoothly.'

'I hope you were not too late getting to bed,' he said. 'Perhaps you were. You look tired this morning.'

'It was worth it, sir. I have something to report.'

'Go ahead, then. It will be your first. I am listening, but not to hear that you don't want to go through with your secondment and would prefer to go back to your office job.'

'No, sir. No fear of that. I was finding my way around the dockyards in the dark. Fortunately, the port was not interrupted by allied bombers last night. I was just turning for home when I heard muffled voices in the distance. You know how they can travel over water.'

'Yes, of course I do. Just get on with the facts of your

report, or we shall be here all morning.'

'As it was half past one, I thought it might be unusual, though not impossible, for anything to be happening. I steered towards the sounds and eventually found they were coming from a submarine.

'A large rowing boat was moored on the seaward side of it. Two men I could not identify were hoisting up boxes of some sort to the deck of the submarine to two men on the deck. They were pretty heavy boxes, since they had to be handled successively by both pairs of men. The men on board then lowered them into an opening in the deck quite near the gun mounting.'

'What did you make of it, then?' he asked her.

'The weight of the boxes suggested ammunition of some kind.'

'Anything else?'

'It seemed to me that the men in the rowing boat were either civilians or navy or dockyard men. But the significant fact suggests that crews could be in liaison with shore-based help in what they are doing. I wondered if any backhanders were involved.'

'Well done, Leutnant,' he told her. 'I think you have earned your keep.'

It brought a begrudging smile to the kapitäleutnant zur see's face and a snap of adrenaline to Elsa's tired body.

'You have confirmed what we expected has been happening, but not that crews had enlisted or been offered help from the shore. That is additional information, which we can work on. What was the number on the U-boat?'

'U-361, a VIIC type.'

'Do you yourself see any leads from this incident to be

followed up?'

'I think there are two, sir. First, it would be good to know the identity of the helpers, whether they are serving men from other ships or shore stationed, or civilians. Second, it would be useful for the navy to find out if supplies of food, equipment, and ammunition are being systematically and deliberately curtailed to U-boats about to depart on seagoing missions. The loss rate is rising, sir, and I can see the temptation to give priority to the army and the air force.'

'Leutnant zur See Bauer, the first of your two lines of enquiry is valid. The second must be expunged from your mind. We never discussed it at all. You can have the job of trying to solve your first question. Perhaps you can let me have an outline proposal of how you think you should go about it. Do you want to take it on?'

'Yes, I do, and will let you have an idea of how I will tackle it, after I have looked into the problem.'

'Regard it as urgent. And thank you for coming in. Dismiss.'

'Sir.' She saluted and went.

11

Elsa left the office of her boss with a feeling of elation that she had been able to make a contribution to the work of the detachment of naval intelligence at Gotenhaven. The prohibition that he had put on her inference about the supply question simply amused her. Anyone suggesting such a matter would be judged a traitor and be rightly terrified of being indicted. But she was shielded by the task she had been seconded to discharge. The ramifications from it were hers to frame, but not to pursue. She had a premonition that it would return to her notice at a later date.

She discussed the first fulfilment she had achieved to justify her secondment with Astrid. There was no sense in withholding any details of the event when telling her.

'Your boss was right to put a stop on the question over supply policy. He should know that no less a person than the overall head of the Abwehr, the secret intelligence service, himself was dismissed from office towards the end of last year when he questioned policy preferences.'

'What does that mean, then? That participation in policy decision at the highest levels is not allowed, but at our level we are at the mercy of policy mistakes and indecision.'

'It does. You just have to observe and live with it. In this case it might imply that some of our U-boat men may be sacrificed to keep the submarine arm going strongly overall and for the sake of other branches of the forces.'

'Now that we have proof of what is going on, we may be able to pick up some evidence from the conversations around us,' Elsa said. 'Do you think you could keep your ears open?'

'Yes, I will. I had no idea this was happening in the port. But in future, if I hear the right conversation, I shall be able to put an interpretation on it that would have meant nothing to me before you told me all this.'

Elsa had her own plan to unravel the identity of those responsible. Perhaps the two men she saw were the only people involved in the trade. Maybe they were doing a favour for their mates in the submarine. Or it could have been the tip of the iceberg? If the matter were widespread, it would need a number of shore-based people to take part.

She dressed in casual and unbecoming clothes. She changed her lifestyle at Astrid's expense.

Every night for the next few weeks she intended to pass her time in the circuit of drinking dens frequented by the lower ranks of shore-based sailors, submarine crews on breaks between missions, and crew members in training.

She found every establishment, large or small, had its full complement of women, some related to the men, some looking for a likely husband, a fair sprinkling of loose women, and a range of prostitutes.

She began her search by finding out where the rank-and-file members of the Women's Naval Service tended to congregate. Having been seconded to Blohm and Voss for several years, she had remained unconnected with the unit stationed in Gotenhaven after her arrival. Elsa remained unknown to them.

Furthermore, she made sure of her anonymity. She disguised herself by the simple means of wearing a beret type hat, concealing her hair and daubing the heaviest of makeup on her face.

Her purpose was to study the behaviour of women used to chatting up men and generally acting in a seductive way. She herself was not backward in knowledge in that regard, but she faced the fact that she had not indulged much in the kind of tactics that she expected to have to employ.

The first act in her plan took her by surprise in practise. She had concentrated on what she had to do to get the opposite sex in a drinking den to talk freely. She found that by looking demure and sitting around in such places, sooner or later one or more of the extroverts of the opposite sex would come to her.

'Well, what have we got here? A girl all by herself. Are you waiting for someone, love?' a sailor asked. His two companions didn't wait for her answer. They threw themselves rather clumsily alongside her, one on each side, while the speaker still stood, looking sheepish. At last, he made the obvious remark.

'Oh, I see you do have someone to keep you company after all. Which one of you is going to buy her a drink?'

'What are you drinking, darling? You look like a doll who will put down a jug of beer while I'm looking at you,' one of the two sitting close to her asked her. 'Or is it a nice little schnapps that tickles your fancy with not too much water in it?'

Elsa ignored his question. She addressed the first man who had spoken to her and was still looking sheepish.

'Get off your feet,' Elsa ordered him. 'Start walking and get me that beer you never mentioned. I can do with it.'

She mentioned her order in such a manner that took the

standing man's words away from his mouth. His lips opened and shut several times, but nothing came out of them. His two confederates capsized in laughter at his discomfiture. But he dutifully backed away and eventually returned with a jug of beer for Elsa and one for himself.

'Hey, man what about us?'

'What about you,' he parried. 'I've come back to look after this lovely doll. One of you two should get the drinks and leave a seat for me.'

'What's your name?' he addressed Elsa.

'You tell me yours first. If I like the sound of it, I will tell you mine.'

His other friend shook with laughter.

'That's taken the wind out of your sales,' he said, when he could get his breath. 'This girl is not to be fooled with, I reckon.'

'My parents called me Manfred,' he said almost politely.

'And mine called me Ursula,' Elsa replied. 'They are two nice names.'

'Are you good in bed, Ursula?' Manfred asked her point blank.

'Only when I've had nothing to drink,' Elsa replied. 'So, I'll be no good for one man nor another tonight.'

She took a chance.

'I haven't seen you guys around before,' she said.

'We haven't just arrived,' Manfred said, 'but we are leaving tomorrow.'

'Where did you come from?' she asked.

'That would be t-telling,' he replied, slightly slurring a word. The additional drink, added to his previous celebrations, was beginning to have its effect.

Elsa was quick to pick up the cue. He was evidently used to drinking and carrying it comfortably.

'Not from the sea,' she stated, rather than putting it as a question.

'How did you know that? You are not supposed to know such things.'

They were precipitately joined by two other women. Elsa had seen them several seats away, sitting in a group of four. She did not know them, but thought they had the look of Women's Naval Service about them—no longer gauche, a little reserved, more alert than the usual layabout women that frequented the bars. They had been drinking but carried themselves with a certain amount of dignity.

One of them addressed Elsa. 'We thought it was a good idea to come to your rescue. Three men onto one woman can be rough. Especially if they are from the sea.'

'You know what they say about women going with sailors in port,' the other woman said.

'No, what do they say?' Elsa managed to get a word in.

'Well, if you sit on a fountain head by chance and someone turns the water on, the effect can be really surprising.'

'Only if you're naked! Otherwise, you are just wet,' Elsa quipped.

'But you could have a free trip to the sky!' the newly joined woman added, 'and a pleasure packet with it.'

'What's your name?' Elsa inquired.

'Renate, and yours?'

'Ursula,' Elsa said.

'Mine's Christa,' her friend chimed in.

'Do you live in Gotenhaven?' Elsa asked.

'No, we are both in the Women's Naval Service stationed here. And you?' Christa asked. 'You don't look like a local or a member of the forces.'

'I just had to get out of Hamburg. I like to pick up the odd man or two here and there. Just arrived. I seem to get along pretty well. But I could do with a job, if only a part-time one.'

'What are you girls talking about behind our backs?' asked one of the sailors, who butted into their conversation.

'Never you mind. Tell us your name,' Renate ordered him.

'Hey, y-you can't be ordering a boatman about like that. But I c-can't remember my name. It's something like those four-legged animals you see pulling carts around.'

Elsa noted his tongue had possibly left him for the evening. He would not be much good in bed, but he could be useful in other ways. He might spill information she wanted to hear sooner or later.

'You mean a horse,' Christa said.

'You, you, have g-got it in one shot,' he spluttered.

'Well, what is it then?' all three women asked in unison.

'I've f-forgotten already,' he stumbled, freely confessing his lapse.

'You mean your name is Horst.' Renate supplied his name.

'Of course, that's it. My name is Horst. I'm a torpedo man in 516. I w-would like to take you around my ship one day, but i-it would not b-be possible until the war is over,' he stuttered on, while drinking.

Meanwhile, Manfred and his other friend had broken out in song. It was a sea song that Elsa knew. She added her voice to the rather eloquent voices of the two singers. Manfred put his arm around her shoulders.

When the song came to an end, Elsa leaned forward to Renate. 'Where do you have to work when you are in the women's service?'

'Both of us are on the staff of the naval supplies depot.'

'Do you have to deal with explosives, then?'

'No, not at all. We store and issue long-lasting foodstuffs for the submarine crews. Some of the girls do work in the arms store. Mostly they have various calibres of shells and torpedoes.'

'Is it that exciting with the foodstuffs or do you get bored?'

'It's pretty busy every day. We get plagued by crews who want us to increase their supplies. Apparently, they find themselves short before the end of a mission and end up hungry.'

'That's a pity. Our warriors need to be well fed,' Elsa asserted.

'You would think so, wouldn't you? But we have been subject to trickle cutting the amounts for the last few months. We are getting complaints, but it is not our doing.'

'It sounds a macabre situation. If they are sunk before the end of their mission time, they will die well fed. If they go the distance and survive full mission time, their hunger will be growing by the day.'

'Yes, you can put it like that. But some of the crews have managed to get around the limitation.'

'How have they done that? Do they take their own food?'

Renate laughed. 'No, not quite. I can't tell you what's been happening, but it seems to be a self-help solution to their problem.'

'Let's have another song.' Manfred interrupted their brief

exchange.

'But I don't mind a chat,' his singing companion cut across him. 'We've been singing from time to time under the ocean. But never while talking with a woman.'

Christa cried out. 'Oh, you poor darling, you've been away so long without a woman.' She swiftly moved herself to drag him onto her lap and threw her arms around him.

He took her gesture as an invitation, planting a long kiss on her mouth.

When he paused for breath, she did the same to him.

'Now isn't that the right thing to do for our heroes under the sea. Welcome home,' Christa declared. 'And don't be long before you come back again.'

Elsa had actually enjoyed the evening, but reluctantly concluded that she had already exhausted the potential of the present company for information she was seeking.

She was thinking about excusing herself to go to the ladies' room, with no thought of returning. A twinge of treachery reared its ugly head in her mind. It would leave her table unbalanced. They would wonder why she had disappeared. Questions over her identity might arise.

Before she had settled the confusion in her mind—a creature of her own making—two more navy men, their arms around two tipsy-looking girls, joined them from across the huge room, which was full of sailors, women, cigarette smoke, and ribald laughter.

Manfred leaned towards Elsa. 'These are also from the 516. We've had to come to Gotenhaven for repairs and to form a new crew.'

'Why did you need to do that? Surely the ports are all in France for the Atlantic?'

'We were badly beaten up. The boat was seriously damaged and many of our mates were killed. But we managed to get into Brest for temporary repairs.'

'No wonder you want to live it up,' Elsa sympathised. 'You're lucky to be alive.'

'Part of our disaster was that we ran out of ammunition. When a British Liberator reconnaissance aircraft on submarine patrol forced us to the surface, we had to fight it out. It was our good luck that he dropped all his depth charges at the same time.'

'You will have to carry more ammunition in future,' Elsa suggested.

'You can bet we will. We've got it fixed. We are in touch with a chap onshore here who can top up our ammunition beyond what we are allowed.'

Elsa drew a quiet breath of surprise at his disclosure. It was amazing what a state of inebriation could do to a man, although she was quick to add to herself that a woman had just come into the reason as well.

'What do you have to do? Do you pay him for the extra?'

'No more than a bottle of schnapps.'

'Where does he get the extra goods from, then?'

'He and his associates simply fiddle the store numbers. He has to be careful since the allowances are strictly defined according to the number of crews, but their control can be tampered with, according to the lengths of mission, size of the boat, and the actual number of men a particular crew ultimately takes on board.'

Manfred's slightly drunken explanation made sense to Elsa. She could see that the illicit activity was being carried out with the strongest of personal considerations.

In the judgement of most people, the subterfuge was as justified as it was possible to be.

Perhaps the participants covered their tracks as slips in paperwork. It would be likely that they had the tacit support of the interim navy authorities on the base.

However, on turning over the information, amid the noise of the chatter, singing, drunken calling out, and ribald laughter of women, Elsa came to the conclusion that she had landed herself into a moral dilemma.

Could she report her findings? She had found that they resulted from what she had suspected.

The shortfall of supplies of equipment, food, ammunition, and medical supplies to departing U-boats was being surreptitiously made up, but illegally according to the top navy directives.

If she did so, she reasoned, her action would simply be accepted as the proper discharge of her responsibility in her job. The morality of it would rest with senior people.

She soon reflected that Kapitäleutnant zur See Weber had told her to forget her concern for the question of shortfalls and supply economics.

But he had allowed her to proceed to discover whether the supply of extra provisions, hardware, and ammunition was masterminded and executed by crew members or shore-based people.

Elsa thought it was out of the question that the culprits were crew members themselves. Clearly such activity would be treated as criminal and against the credo of the service.

But the fact that she had been made party to the practice by relative newcomers, as well as her own witness of the clandestine delivery of goods at night, simply added up to an entrenched system she had stumbled on. Her boss and other interested parties knew it went on, but kept their mouths shut, knowing the good intentions behind the actions taken.

On mulling over those thoughts, she decided to wait a few days and then to confront her boss with her view of the situation, trusting that he already knew about it and would take the matter no further.

She felt more relaxed after coming to that conclusion. She re-engaged her conversation with Manfred.

'I see you are an obermaat in the submarine service. What does a chief petty officer do on board?' she asked.

'Fancy you knowing that from my uniform,' he replied. 'I am the oberbootsmann, mostly responsible for the discipline of the crew under the captain.

'I spend some time in the control bridge of the submarine hearing the discharge of orders to the crew.

'I am one of four obermaats, the other three are respectively responsible for the diesels, the electric motors and batteries, and navigation. I am also in charge of the provisions for the boat.'

'And then you make a tour of the boat to make sure everyone is happy. The morale of the crew must be your concern.'

'A bit like that. My real job comes into its own when we are under attack, and especially if we are hit. When the boat is damaged and leaking, the strain on the crew is at the maximum. You can't afford any man to lose his nerve then. If anyone loses it, there would be hell to pay in the confines of a submarine under water.'

'I think I should be going soon, Manfred,' Elsa said.

'So soon? The night is still young.' He answered his own

question. 'If you have to go, may I walk you home?'

That offer came as a surprise. It threw her into another dilemma. Thoughts raced through her mind. 'How on earth can I take Manfred home? It would mean the foot of the gangway of the *Hans Frayling*. There could not be an easier way to give the game away.

She tried to put him off.

'Are you not too drunk to come with me just yet?'

'If I am, you could stay longer until I am soberer.'

'Or more drunk,' she added.

Clearly there was no deterring him.

She combed her brain to come up with a solution. An obvious idea came to her. It was a good old-fashioned solution to a thorny and awkward choice.

No, it was not to conjure up a headache. She was too proud to do that. In contrast, if she had to go the whole hog, she would do it. She hid behind the needs of her country, or rather, the interests of her particular job within it.

'OK, let's go, then,' she said.

She led the way out of the rowdy establishment.

It took them a few streets to cover the distance to the hotel, where she had stayed on first arriving in Gotenhaven.

If they were not drunk before leaving the dive, the air and physical effort of walking caused them both to exhibit the full effects of the alcohol they had consumed. They expertly supported each other.

Every few steps they took, they had to pause for a cuddle and a kiss, adjusting their mutual support sufficiently to move on another few steps. It was to be a long walk.

By the time they reached the hotel, it was midnight. For the last few hundred steps, Elsa had developed an inordinate sexual passion, made worse each time they stopped and embraced. She could sense and feel Manfred was long past ready for what awaited them.

Without thinking about it at all, they both registered into a room they were lucky to find vacant. They stripped, not hastily, but as fast as their fumbled fingers could cope with disrobing—sometimes their own clothes, sometimes that of each other—before they transported themselves into oblivion.

12

Elsa awoke to find a letter by her bedside. He had not run out on her. It just explained Manfred's absence. He had to report for duty and would be at sea when she first saw daylight. She knew they were due to depart that day—but not that early.

That thought had partly influenced her choice of accepting his invitation to walk her home. If he had still been around for a few days or even weeks, it would have been awkward to square her relationship with Astrid.

They had both acknowledged they had taken a man to bed during the interim of their relationship, but this would have raised a different question of simultaneous liaisons. Her reasons for dual commitments might have seemed unacceptable to Astrid.

This time she elected to tell Astrid that she had been on night duty. It was one night of duty that had brought Elsa profound pleasure. Manfred would not be normally returning to Gotenhaven anyway. His future was now in the lap of the gods. So, it was a matter of wait and see.

She saw Astrid the same day. They talked over the information she had gained from her pub excursion and the conclusion she had reached.

'I think it would be a good idea to report exactly what you have told me,' Astrid advised. 'The fact that no payment is involved justifies your own conclusion. They are, after all, trying to look after themselves in a dangerous game that is crucial to the war effort. I think Weber must know about it and probably approves of the practice.'

Armed with that sympathy and support, Elsa repaired to the office and requested an interview with her chief.

'What have you got for me, Leutnant zur See?' he asked brusquely.

'I struck lucky, eventually, on my first night in the drinking dens.'

She related the explanation Renate and Manfred had given her with the assurance that no one benefitted personally from the process.

Her boss seemed only mildly interested, confirming in Elsa's mind that he already knew about the practice going on in the port, if not being a party to it.

'Thank you for establishing the circumstances in the case of foodstuffs. Have a go now with regard to ammunition. There is no special hurry. Do not get yourself on the wrong side of anyone. It might be different from the foodstuffs. By the way, 361 has been sunk. It was attacked off Narvik by a Catalina flying boat. All hands were lost.'

She agreed, promising to be as discreet as possible.

The loss of that submarine made her appreciate the temptation the authorities had to undersupply all boats. The increasing expectation that some would not return from completing their full mission had made someone realise the extent of the loss of scarce and valuable supplies with every premature sinking.

Elsa continued her canvassing of the drinking dens for the next few weeks but failed to repeat her success of the first night. It was a tip from Astrid that alerted her to the possibility that there was still something to discover.

Until that moment, only Elsa's own witness of a nighttime transfer of gun ammunition to 361 from a rowing boat had been the sole evidence available for reference.

'I overheard two officers from a new crew now being put together, talking about the shortage of torpedoes due to be put on their submarine. Their boat, 399, a VIIC, has been here for training purposes and is now being prepared to resume active duties.'

'What should be their supply for a long ocean mission, then?' Elsa asked.

'They are allowed fourteen torpedoes altogether, twelve for the four tubes in the bows and two for the one tube in the stern. I believe they were talking about having been assigned only ten—fewer than normal. That meant two each for all five tubes. They were talking as if they fully expected to make up at least some of the shortfall.'

'That gives me an idea,' Elsa told her. 'If you can find out where their boat is moored, I will keep watch on it for the next night or two in the hope of seeing if an attempt to top up their supply is made.'

It was a time of the year when the weather was less settled. Elsa faced a choppy sea surface, whipped up by strong winds, when she took to the water in her canoe at the first opportunity. She froze in her craft but glad to drink from the flask of coffee she had secreted aboard. She had also brought some food, as nutritious as she could make it under stringent wartime conditions.

Her determination that night was soon put to the test. She stuck it out until the first streaks of dawn appeared, before putting into her private hideaway, where she pulled the canoe from the water and docked it on the shingle.

The second night yielded the same result. The third tested her resolve to the limit, again without seeing anything amiss.

It was the fourth night, soon after she had taken station, that she heard sounds of a motor boat. Just as soon as her ears had picked up the noise of its engine, it ceased.

The shielded light, which appeared on the moored U-399, gave faint light to the silhouette of the approaching motor boat between Elsa's little craft lying flat on the water and the submarine. Silently, the motor boat drifted to the submarine's side and was firmly secured to it.

Within minutes she heard the unmistakable rattle of chains, from which sound she deduced that lifting gear was being put into place. Gliding silently towards the unloading scene, Elsa watched the transfer of a torpedo into the bows of the submarine. She waited. Nothing further happened.

The clandestine nature of the delivery left nothing to be explained. She was confident enough to abandon her post and head for home and bed.

Astrid heard her come in. She stirred. 'You are back early. It's still only about eleven thirty. What happened?'

'Fourth time lucky. I'm frozen. One torpedo turned up on a motor boat.'

'Well, that's a success. How will you handle it?'

'I shall go back tomorrow night. It's a bit early yet to say what I could do. I need to talk with someone in the business about it.'

'Here's a hot whisky. You'll catch your death out there on the water at night in this weather.'

'Are you going to have one as well, Astrid?'

'Yes, and then we can share our warmth together and goodbye to the world. There's not a lot to shout about at the moment. Things are going against us and next year will be decisive.'

Elsa, never deterred, returned to her maritime patrol the next night. It was as if she was prepared for a repeat performance.

It wasn't. It was a bonanza.

The motor boat drifted up to the offside casing of the submarine, just as it did the previous night, but then loaded two torpedoes and seven small crates of something very heavy. The men used the loading crane to transfer the crates onto the casing. Evidently, they were a consignment above the official supply for the main gun, or, perhaps, for its two anti-aircraft weapons.

She woke up the following morning to learn that the 399 had left for sea. There was no chance that she could get a word of confirmation from any of the crew, who were now far away in pursuit of their mission.

She mused to herself. *My only chance is to find and identity the motor boat. That's my next task. And then I can talk with the men who either own it, if they are civilians, or are assigned to it if they are navy men.*

She wandered around the port on foot, paying close attention to the area around the ammunition storage depot. A motor boat recollected from a dim sighting in the night could not be identified with accuracy. In her memory, she realised she had noted the light sounds of its engine. Putting two and two together she concluded that its motor was too frail to be a navy craft. It must have been in civilian hands.

The next day she went specifically to the area where the few local people kept their fishing vessels. It was there she saw several motor boats with the unmistakable sound from the night. One was actually under way, with a middle-aged woman steering it. She didn't think a woman had been involved.

Elsa persisted in her search until she spotted two older men working on nets, near a boat that fitted the dimensions of the craft she had seen and had no sails. She was pretty certain it was the craft in question.

An original and unanticipated thought came into her head.

If I rely on finding sailors to betray their surreptitious intents with extra weapons and ammunition, I shall be looking for them for weeks—and probably never finding them. I'm going to have to tackle this head on.

Having provoked herself into doing a risky step that might be dangerous, she idled along towards the men and their boat, trying to look nonchalant, like an idle civilian.

When she reached an appropriate distance from the men, she took out an ersatz cigarette and asked one of them if he had a light.

He was pleased to oblige.

'Are you fishing today?' she asked them.

'No, we aren't into fishing much these days,' one of them said. 'We are not as enthusiastic as we used to be.'

'It's a job to get a living in some parts,' Elsa commented.

'What are you doing, then? You look as if you should be in the forces or some job to help the war effort.'

'As a matter of fact, I am doing just that. Helping the war effort.'

'Why aren't you at work now?' he asked.

'I am at work, right now,' Elsa answered.

'Doing what?' he asked sharply.

'I'm looking for a man to do business with him,' she said.

'Are you a prostitute? If so push off, we are not

interested.' Elsa could see by their age they were unlikely to be.

'No,' she replied, laughing, 'I'm looking for the man who can lay his hands on some extra supplies for a certain boat like they did for 399 recently.'

'You want to get over to the navy quarters for navy matters. This area, as you can see, is only for poor fisher folk.'

'You would say that. You have to disguise your activity. But what a wonderful thing you are doing, helping to top up the supplies for the submarine boys who have to face the enemy, as well as the ocean storms, and then have to run out of food or ammunition before their mission date of return is over.'

'What sort of nonsense are you talking about? If you have nothing better to do you ought to be helping to mend our nets. That would be helping the war effort. Otherwise leave us. We have work to do.'

Elsa stood her ground, persisting with her enquiry. She could see the men were getting impatient with her. She began to think they might try to protect their illegal activity by eliminating her from disturbing it.

Just then a young girl, about twelve, turned up on a bicycle. Without waiting, she threw down her bike on the ground and ran towards the two men calling out as she approached.

'Your trip has been cancelled for tonight. He wants you to go over straight away to make other arrangements.'

The girl's impromptu delivery of her message evidently caused them considerable discomfort. It had all happened in no time at all. They realised the message the girl had brought did not sound like one for delivery to poor fisher folk.

'Thank you, Anna. You can get off home now,' one of the men said.

She rescued her bike and set off on her way.

Elsa noticed that a broken pannier strap on her bicycle had allowed a small packet to escape on the ground among the stones. In her haste to get away, Anna had failed to notice it. She thought of drawing Anna's attention to the fact but checked her impulse.

'Did I prove wrong in my assumptions?' Elsa asked a rhetorical question, as they prepared to answer the call of a mysterious someone or other away on the other side of the port.

'This was a message about fishing. Sorry, we haven't time to talk with you about it any more. We have to catch the fish when they can be found.'

Elsa thought his statement could so easily make sense if the word ammunition replaced the word fish. She bid them farewell, but knew it was only for the time being.

She would be back to see them. In the meantime, she proposed to wait. Anna was bound to retrace her bike ride to find her little parcel.

It took twenty minutes of patient waiting until Anna appeared on her bicycle. Seeing Elsa, she called out to her.

'I must have dropped a small parcel on my way home, but so far, I have been unable to find it. Have you seen it by chance?'

'Your worries are over, Anna. I found it among the stones.'

'Oh, thank you,' she said. 'Are you a friend of Otto and Paul?'

'I have seen them a couple of times. We have the same interests. Are you family?' Elsa asked the girl.

'Yes, Otto is my grandfather.'

'They are doing good work,' Elsa said.

'You mean fishing?' she asked.

'No, the other thing.'

'What other thing?'

The young girl's face was such a giveaway picture of honesty that Elsa had to believe she was innocent of the other activity she believed the men were allegedly involved in. Or was it the cover story that they had imprinted on her that she should use, if a stranger ever asked her about their secret task?

'It doesn't matter Anna. You have recovered your parcel. Your mother will be waiting for you. And don't fall off your bike. You are a lovely girl. You can't afford to knock yourself about in an accident.'

Elsa decided to wait around for the men to return.

It was nearly three hours later that she heard the slow beat of their motor boat's engine. She hid behind their shed, awaiting them while they beached their craft.

It was a reflexive move that had unanticipated advantages. She could overhear them talking about their immediately preceding business.

'The shortfall in torpedoes is getting worse. If the stack falls too low, it will be too obvious than if one or two are missing,' one of the men said to the other.

'We shall have to concentrate on the ammunition. At least any shortfall in that supply we can make up for will be obscured by the large stack of shells they have in there. It's a good job they aren't packed in crates which are easy to count.'

Elsa stepped out from behind the shed.

The two men could have dropped dead. They were speechless.

'Welcome back,' Elsa said, smiling. 'I have spoken with your granddaughter, too, Otto, so I have the whole picture. There are one or two points I would like to raise with you two men.'

'Are you a spy?'

'No. As you know, the Gestapo doesn't employ women. I will come clean with you if you promise to come clean with me.'

They remained silent. The initiative was hers.

'I am with the port naval intelligence unit. I am Leutnant zur See Bauer in the Women's Naval Service. I want to assure you that so far, my investigations have convinced me that your motivation is honourable and the full details of your operation, once you tell me about them, will remain with me.'

She suddenly blenched inside herself. Here she was pledging to withhold information from the authorities that could result in her being stripped of her rank, imprisoned, or even shot for activity prejudicial to the war effort. But the degree of severity she would suffer would depend on the few points she still wanted to discuss with these men.

'First. Who are you? All that you pretend to be. Simple fishermen?'

'We are both ex-submarine crewmen from the First World War,' Otto replied. 'We came from these parts and shared the antipathy to the new regime that the old aristocracy in Pomerania have perpetuated.'

'Second. Have you, or do you receive any monetary payment from ship or shore for the activity that you have followed?'

'Do us a favour, fräulein. The answer is no. We have done it out of patriotism and love of the service. Being paid underhand for this work is quite out of the question. We see it as the work that two old men can do for the war effort.'

'Third. How long has this been going on?'

'It was an idea that occurred to us the year before last but only came to fruition this year when the loss rate of our boats rose sharply, and the bombing increased to the extent that it has disrupted our food supplies and ammunition production.'

'Four. How do you manage to secure the removal of the goods without anybody noticing?'

'We have civilian compatriots with the same mind in the food and ammunition depots. They fiddle the paperwork, if necessary. But once supplies are registered into the depot, a small reduction in the piles of various stocks can be done without suspicion.'

'Do they receive any payback for what they do?'

'Absolutely not. They, too, are ex-submariners and do it for the same reasons as us. It won't be necessary to alert them to being discovered, will it?'

'I think not,' Elsa said, putting them at their ease. 'Five. How do you think this can go on for?'

'Provided you don't shop us, for a few weeks. But the Russians are getting closer. If they break through, we shall all be lost in this area. It was once safe, but now it's in the line of fire. So, we expect to do it while we can. Wait and see, is our motto.'

Elsa thanked them and parted from Otto and Paul as the best of friends.

13

Elsa mentioned the encounter with the two men neither to her boss nor Astrid. Astrid was always too busy with her problems to enquire too deeply into what Elsa had been up to. Elsa's dilemma over Kapitäleutnant Weber was abruptly swept aside a week later, when he sent for her.

She went with a trifle of fear and trembling to the interview, wondering if she was going to be hauled over the coals for not reporting about the clandestine loading of ammunition.

But she had her answers ready. She made the assumption that her boss also knew about the matter but had other matters to think about.

It became very clear to Elsa that an urgent issue had arisen to justify her being summoned to the office. She sensed immediately that whatever had cropped up, it was now the predominant item occupying his mind. The entire office had an unusual atmosphere about it that cushioned her apprehension over the matter of the two men and ammunition supply.

The novel untold matter would dictate her interview because it dominated entirely the mind of her boss.

'We have had reports from the advancing Russian front of the rapacious behaviour of their ground forces when they crossed for the first time into the most extreme eastward German territory.

'The news has spread like wildfire westwards. It has triggered terror in the population of the small area involved, but news of it has quickly spread westwards in the path of the Russian advance. It is rumoured that a trickle of refugees has already started. That trickle could grow into an avalanche. And if so, they will be coming our way.'

'That's bad news, Kapitäleutnant,' Elsa volunteered. 'Just think of the horrendous pressure on food and water supplies, let alone shelter, as the winter closes in. What about medical services for so many people?'

'Quite,' he said. 'This town is not equipped to house thousands of extra people. From our point of view, we would have an enormous problem of security. We could be faced with dozens of spies, disguised as German refugees. How on earth could we identify them, if the numbers of refugees are as huge as they potentially seem to be?'

'It looks as if we have a few weeks to make some preparations. While we have the time, we should start earmarking empty or underused buildings. We could also stock up with long-life foodstuffs, reserved for the purpose.'

Elsa responded with enthusiasm, freely volunteering her suggestions, in great relief from being released from a confrontation with questions about her investigations in the port regarding illegal supplies to navy ships.

'The trouble is that we are in the dark. It's only hearsay at the moment. We shall have to wait for official information to come through,' he said. 'And now the winter is coming on fast and will add to our handicaps.'

As the end of the year came up, Gutenhaven celebrated a quiet but apprehensive Christmas. The training of U-boat crews went on apace, without respite.

The weather was typically wintry, heavy snow making movement on foot a cold and forbidding undertaking. Motor traffic defied the snowfall, but often at the risk of collisions, breakdowns, and frozen engines. A petrol shortage for military vehicles added its own inconvenience.

Elsa and Astrid were glad to have the shelter of the inside of their ship, the *Hans Frayling,* to escape the weather. But inevitably they both had to venture out on one purpose or another. Their dominant thought when they did so was escaping back into their customary inner sanctum. It offered a preferential place to be.

The focus of everyone in the town was directed eastwards, where the fighting on a huge scale persisted and was slowly moving towards them.

For a time, a winter's lull saved their army from crucifixion from the abysmally low temperatures, howling wind, and mountains of snow and ice. The merciless winter impeded movement, tying fighting men to isolated spots of ground, without any chance of changing their station for better shelter.

The severe winter lasted into the New Year, with life at a standstill for many people, civilian and military. Many spared a thought for their men at the front. The Russians were more used to the severe weather than German troops. It reminded those knowing about it, that Napoleon's retreat in the extreme weather had formed a precedent for the current repetition of retreat, bringing such chaos and reversal of fortune.

Eventually the winter gave up its most savage aspects, life gradually restoring itself. There came the day when Kapitäleutnant Weber seriously gave his mind to the possible looming presence of a refugee influx into Gotenhaven in the near future.

He sent for Elsa.

'We can't rely on the military to supply us with accurate information about the rate of the Russian advance or the effects it is having on the German population,' he declared.

'If you gave me a motorbike and some authorisation, I reckon I could make an assessment just behind our lines, together with observations of the numbers on the move,' Elsa suggested.

'It's only about two hundred miles to the leading Russian front from here. It would take refugees about twenty days at ten miles a day at best to walk to Gotenhaven. That's three week's grace. If we could substantiate the facts, it would establish the liability on us. It will develop fast.'

'I won't argue with you about the figures. But how long away would you need? You have to allow for any breakdown and time to interview some of the refugees you find, if any.'

'I should think a week would be ample,' Elsa replied. 'How about it?'

She had seen her suggestion as a relief from being bored with her appointment. There was nothing more to get her teeth into. And then the long winter months only added to her frustration, with its long nights and stormy days. She had become deskbound again, underemployed with paper work about regular inspections, the occasional misbehaviour of navy men, and the continuous reports on manpower and work, routinely sent to headquarters.

If she could undertake a front-line exploration like she suggested, it would save her sanity and give her an impetus for living in a wartime world. The circumstances in her immediate environment were growing worse by the day.

The penultimate year of the war had proved disastrous to her country. The Russian hordes were sweeping westwards. Resistance was ferocious in defence of their homeland, but German arms by then were no longer in the ascendant order.

There was promise of secret weapons that would turn the war once again in their favour, but few people believed they would succeed in that unbelievable and unlikely outcome.

To make matters worse, the systematic bombing offensive from the west was reaching unprecedented heights.

No city and no town of any size was immune any longer from attack. It was the year when allied landings in the west compelled her country to fight on two fronts. It would be squeezed to death between the giant amalgamations of enemy forces.

Kapitäleutnant Weber surprised himself as well as Elsa by making up his mind on the spot, without recourse to any other authority. His act was testimony to the potential urgency of the situation around the corner. It was exacerbated by the growing feeling of chaotic uncertainty that had overtaken a large percentage of the population. It was increasing every day.

Their conversation continued.

'Now it would not be a satisfactory solution for you to go alone. There would be the problem of getting around, interviewing some people, putting up with challenges from our side and perhaps meeting a hostile enemy.

'I agree it would be very useful information to have an inkling of what we can expect. A reconnoitre would go a long way to giving us a basis for managing the crisis and not ending up in confusion and disarray.'

'I would not like to be accompanied by someone who handicapped my style,' Elsa replied with a smile on her face.

'He or she would have to work with me. I would not stand for being a dogsbody.'

'There is the transport to think about. You would have to be away for a few days. You won't be able to waltz around Pomerania with a suitcase. And don't forget food. There is a universal shortage. No restaurants are open any more. It might even be difficult to find a place to stay overnight. Do you still want to take it on?'

'Yes, I do. It will be doing something for the country I love, in the part of it that I know well, where I was born, and where I grew up,' Elsa said firmly.

'Those facts will certainly be to your advantage,' he said.

'But do I choose who comes with me?' she asked hastily.

'Only if you choose me,' he replied quietly.

'Chance would be a fine thing,' Elsa remarked.

'I'm serious,' he said.

'You certainly look as if you are. I think you might be, too. But you have taken my breath away. That would be too much of an overkill for me to cope with,' she responded. 'I know you used to be a soldier before you transferred to the navy. Are you missing the front line?'

'Not exactly, but a sense of inactivity has swept over me lately. This is a job, as you have said, which could be an important contribution to the awful dilemma we are all in. I am happy to have you as my companion. Are you happy to have me coming along with you?'

Elsa didn't want to seem too enthusiastic. She was overjoyed by his willingness to go with her, but she hid it skilfully.

She had always felt a distance between herself and the kapitäleutnant. He carried his authority with that air of superiority and isolation that successfully discouraged any opening of the emotional barrier that might be implied.

He was a handsome man, with the carriage of the regular soldier he had once been. At thirty-four he was as lithe and active as any man could be.

'I could be of benefit to you, he continued. 'I can drive a motorcycle with a military sidecar. You could have a pleasant ride. It could carry our personal things and some standby food. I reckon we could do a tour and be back within a week.'

He had visibly softened his demeanour. Elsa wondered about how he would secure his absence from the office and absent himself from his family.

She expressed her fears and reservations about both matters.

'But what about your family and how can you be away from your office?'

'My wife was killed in a bombing raid on Krefeld. I will have to square the trip with my headquarters.'

As he spoke, he picked up the telephone and dialled his senior officer elsewhere.

'Is Fregattenkapitän Wagner there, please?'

'Fregattenkapitän Wagner speaking.'

'Good morning, sir, Kapitäleutnant Weber here. We are getting reports of the excesses of Russian troops on the first German territory they have invested. They are terrible. It beggars belief. Rumours are travelling westwards, alarming the population who face being overrun by the Russians.

'If their offensive proves unstoppable, we are likely to be deluged in Gotenhaven with our own refugees.

'The suggestion has been made that we undertake a reconnoitre eastwards to assess the potential of the exodus.

This would enable us to make preparations in the town for the worst possible situation based on the findings.

'I will be pleased to go with another officer to see what we can make of it and will report back to you.'

'Yes. You have said enough. Do it, and the best of luck. Your office can surely survive for a few days in your absence.'

'Sir.'

Dutifully ending his call, Weber put the telephone handpiece down. *His permission shows how desperate we are*, he thought, but did not put it into words for the enlightenment of Elsa.

'We have no time to lose. We should leave in the morning. Where do you think we should go first?'

'Towards eastern Pomerania and return in a clockwise direction through Silesia,' Elsa suggested. 'The roads may be choked too much to do more than that.'

They spent the next few days establishing that in the eastern areas of German territory, women and children were being subjected to widespread, uninhibited brutality, and rape.

Among their discoveries, they met refugees who related, at first, what they regarded as seemingly wildly exaggerated stories, but which gradually increased in credibility as they pursued their task.

When two drunken enemy soldiers entered a house, while one raped the mother, the other, waiting for his turn, pressed his burning cigarette on the tongue of her eight-year-old son to silence him. When he quite naturally screamed all the more loudly, the enemy soldier took out a penknife and slit the boy's throat.

In another village the population of over two hundred and sixty were executed, including entire families with small children.

In a neighbouring village, the bodies of village people, including children, were stacked on tables in the village inn, according to a witness of the killing, who survived, and gave them his evidence.

The two investigators found yet another village where entire families were wiped out while women and girls were repeatedly raped, including the sick, the old, the pregnant, and undeveloped girls. When a mother refused to surrender her daughter of thirteen years, a soldier indiscriminately fired off his sub-machine gun and, reloading, killed thirty-six people.

Schoolgirls in a small town were shot or burned after being repeatedly raped. On the same day in a neighbouring village, the women and girls were left alive after their ordeal of rape, but subsequently found to have been abused by soldiers infected with virulent sexual diseases. Over sixty women and girls were repeatedly raped and made pregnant, including schoolgirls of twelve.

These early incidents had driven fear into the German populations lying in the path of the advancing Red Armies.

They were exacerbated by the fact that successive waves of troops, coming along behind their vanguard units, took every opportunity to plunder, rape, and savage the German inhabitants as if it were their prerogative to do whatever they wanted to do—assuming their acts were precedents.

Each wave of newcomers showed no consideration for the ordeal that their own units in front of them might have meted out, acting as if their arrival was the signal for deserved, exploitative spoliation for the first time.

Sometimes unit officers kept their men under discipline, but it broke down as soon as the officers absented themselves from exercising immediate supervision. All too frequently, officers themselves led assaults on women and children or connived at the indulgencies of their men.

In a small town in January, a continuous stream of enemy soldiers had entered houses, raping women and young girls of all ages and conditions. A witness they spoke to saw a fourteen-year-old girl raped twice in succession. Children could be rounded up to make labour gangs to dig ditches and construct earthworks. Their work was so temporary. They were driven mercilessly.

In a neighbouring town, a large group of teenage boys and girls was kept in the same overnight accommodation, receiving scant food. Soldiers took advantage of the imprisonment of the children. They called out the girls at any time, subjecting them to serial rape. Twenty-eight men raped one girl. Many of the girls died from their treatment. Their bodies were hung upside down on fences with their legs spread wide apart.

Women of seventy and eighty and children of twelve were raped in another town. In a further town, two women and two small children were found hanged.

In a larger town, the corpses of four or five children, whose heads had been kicked in by military boots, were found among the bodies of many women and young girls, who had died from multiple raping. The youngest was twelve, the eldest seventy-eight.

One sixteen-year-old girl had been raped daily for four weeks by a total of over forty enemy soldiers, and in a town briefly recaptured by German troops, a girl had been assaulted by several soldiers in animal fashion, her death from which treatment led them to wipe the floor of the room with her body.

Such was the tenor of the report they prepared for the authorities in Gotenhaven, together with estimates of numbers they had found on the roads they travelled over.

Overnight some half-hearted attempts were made to identify spare storage and accommodation space, but time was against the town's officials.

The flood of ingressing refugees continued, quickly compelling the realisation that ultimately only by undertaking a massive evacuation could the problem be solved. The authorities devised a plan to ship the refugees and local, military non-combative units by ship to Kiel. The plan preoccupied everyone for the rest of January.

14

Hotfoot from their successful mission to the east, Elsa and Franz thought they deserved a day or two's rest. But as soon as Franz Weber accessed his office the following morning, expecting to catch up with his messages, he found an urgent order to contact his superior on the coded line. News of the order was promptly conveyed to him by his secretary, who greeted his return with warm regards.

'Good morning, sir. I hope you will find everything in order on your return. We missed you. It was a long time to be away from the action, or did you find more of it where you went? You have an urgent message from headquarters.'

'Thank you, Elsa. Ring them and put it through to my room.'

'This is navy headquarters, Leutnant Hoffmann speaking.'

'Fregattenkapitän Wagner? I am trying to contact him. He has left an order for me to do so immediately.'

'Who is speaking?'

'Kapitäleutnant Franz Weber in Gotenhaven.'

It didn't take long before the fregattenkapitän came on the telephone.

'Weber,' he said. 'I will be glad to have your report from your reconnoitre eastwards to assess the pressure that might develop on the Gutenhaven resources.

'But that is not why I asked you to get in touch with me immediately. So, listen carefully. Do you have a suitable member of staff who would be qualified to take a message to Breslau and to escort a wanted man back from there?'

'Why Breslau, sir?'

'The Russians are investing the city. They are trying to encircle it. Already they have secured half a pincer to the north and south. I have been in touch with the army intelligence officer on the staff of the garrison.

'It so happens that one of the top five aeronautical engineers involved in developing the V1 and V2, and other secret weapons at Peenemünde, was visiting his family for Christmas and was taken ill.

'He has partly recovered, but we just can't afford to let him fall into the hands of the Russians. You can imagine the consequences if that happened.'

'I assume you have devised a plan for such a project to be successfully accomplished,' Kapitäleutnant Weber respectfully stated.

'Yes, of course. Here's the plan if you can find the right operator to carry it out. A Junkers 52 will fly from Peenemünde to Gotenhaven to pick up your operative and fly to Liegnitz, which is forty miles west and slightly north of Breslau.

'An army truck will take the operative towards Breslau along the Oder River to not more than six miles of the city. The operative will have the responsibility of devising the means to get into the city and to rendezvous with the engineer in the custody of the army at some mutually agreed point. He will then have the task of withdrawing from the city to a point agreed by the army personnel from Liegnitz.'

'Do you mean the operative has to bring the engineer back along from Breslau to the rendezvous for six miles? Isn't that asking too much?'

'I don't think so. Access and withdraw could be done either on the western bank of the river, or on the river itself. If the river is used, you need to remember that the flow of the current to get to the rendezvous will be against you for access but in your favour for the withdrawal.

'It will be so much easier to return on the strong waters of the north flowing river. The army truck will wait for them at the same point from which the operative started and take them back to the airfield at Liegnitz, where the Junkers 52 will wait to fly them to safety.'

'It sounds a good plan, with the virtue of simplicity. But it will all depend on the weather, the army keeping two appointments, the skill of the operator, and not least the continued absence of the Russians from the corridor of access chosen.'

'Agreed, but it's our best chance. Can I hand over this responsibility to you? Is there anything else you can think of to prevent a successful outcome?'

'No, but I shall need the contacts you have used to confirm the actual dates for the operation, the places involved, and then to check that everything is in place.'

'They will be sent to you, person to person, by an officer from here, within twenty-four hours. Good luck.'

The kapitäleutnant sent for Elsa.

She noisily came into his office, bringing a cup of ersatz coffee in each hand. Their time away together had done wonders for their personal relationships.

'It seems the Russians are closing in,' he said to her.

'What makes you say that?' Elsa said.

'While everyone has faith in the German defences, at the same time we have to acknowledge the overwhelming weight of the teeming infantry and tank regiments the enemy is massing against us.

'The weeks are proving the display of a fateful and unstoppable opposition. It is clear that the Russian intention is to sweep across the German state in a massive avalanche of military might, destroying, killing, raping, and pillaging as they might choose.

'Some might now be hoping a reprieve would be if the western allies, making progress in western Europe, could cover enough ground to reach as much of the German homeland as possible before the Russian armies.

'Yet the irony of our situation is that German forces are resisting the western front for all they are worth, while civilian populations on the eastern front are being subjected to such savage and inhuman treatment.

'This year has been adversely compounded by the unprecedented number of raids and the tonnage of bombs delivered by the British and American air forces. Simultaneously, the losses of U-boats are exceeding the sinking of allied ships. Against this weight of adversity, three favourable factors are left in German hands.

'The first and second are the triumphal successes of the V1 flying bomb and V2 rocket, which are being invested in attacks on London and other British cities and those continental cities wrested from German control.

'The third is the introduction of the jet-propelled fighter, which can outfly allied bomber escort fighters, but are still in insufficient numbers to make much difference to the huge numbers of enemy aircraft deployed. They are handicapped as a secret weapon by the fact there has not yet been time for the perfection of the mechanical and operational know-how to handle them. Furthermore, production has been sorely interrupted by the aerial bomber onslaught on aircraft factories.'

'Why are you telling me all this?' Elsa asked. 'It sounds like a studied summary of defeat which we are not expected to think about and much less to talk about.'

'In spite of it all I enjoyed our survey of the population together. It was brief enough. But not enough time when it was so enjoyable. I have to tell you I considered absconding to Switzerland and abandoning the war forever,' he commented.

'Then you would have been shot for desertion. That would not look good on your curriculum vitae,' Elsa said, her humour raising a laugh. 'But would you have dumped me on the way?'

'Of course not. Without you, it would not have been worth dying for.'

'In that case, I would have been shot as well,' Elsa said. 'Or could we have had an excuse? Something like we turned south by accident rather than to the north?'

'It would have been a long way to play on our mistake. Or could we have pleaded we were looking for spies,' Franz added. 'Let's do it again sometime.'

The conversation ended in good-natured laughter.

'By the way, you sent for me.'

'To talk about going south,' he said, enigmatically.

'It sounds as if you are serious,' Elsa said.

'This is very serious,' Franz responded, calling her to accompany him to another office free from interruption and telephone calls.

'One of the top engineers on the rocket programme at Peenemünde chanced his arm at Christmas to visit his family in Breslau. At the time, the Russians were a good way from the city. Unfortunately, he fell ill while he was with the family, but now seems to have recovered. Over the Christmas period and the time of his illness, the enemy made dramatic progress.

'We have received news that they have established a half pincer movement against the city to its north and south. It is clear they are going to surround it, rather than directly invest in from the east. As you know, it is a large city and full of waterways that would make a direct assault an extremely dangerous undertaking.'

'I know the city so well. I was at university there,' Elsa commented.

'Yes, and that is why you are being ordered to take on a special operation to the city immediately.'

'What for is the only thought in my head,' Elsa interrupted.

'Taking a package of orders and information to the garrison commander. He will be ordered to withdraw to a defensible perimeter to delay and hold substantial Russian forces from their westward thrust. Certain units will be ordered to escape through the existing gap, as will many civilians who choose to leave the city. The latter will be advised to make their way due west to Dresden.

'But the crucial task you have to do is to rendezvous with the army to collect the rocket engineer and bring him safely out of the clutches of the Russians.'

'Now I suppose arrangements have been made for me to do all that?'

'Yes, a Junkers 52 will fly from Peenemünde to our local airfield to collect you. It will fly to Liegnitz, which is forty miles from Breslau, from which an army truck will take you along the bank of the Oder to within six miles of the city. The main question is how will you complete the rest of the way after the army drops you?'

'That's the easy part,' Elsa replied. 'I shall use a two-man canoe, like the one I have been using around the port.'

'But that will be a long way to paddle in the middle of the night and in the bitter mid-winter weather. I am reminded that you will have the current against you going into Breslau, but it will be in your favour on the return trip, although you will have an inert passenger. It could be tough.'

'Perhaps he will be fit enough to do some paddling,' Elsa suggested. 'Where will I be expected to pick up the engineer and deliver the written orders?'

'It will be at a point of your choosing,' Franz replied. 'Can you think of a prominent and unmistakeable point that would serve as a rendezvous in the north-west part of the city?' Franz asked.

'I would choose the Dombrücke, at the left-hand bank as you arrive. It is right in the old city and, I believe, the first bridge you meet soon after passing the first historic buildings. It's famed for its single mid-stream pillar and superstructure, resembling a cathedral. How will they know which night I will arrive?'

'The meteorologist has forecast the weather will be suitable the day after tomorrow, the twelfth of January. But it will be as cold as ever. I have been given contacts for the army in Liegnitz and in Breslau. They will be expecting my call before you leave here.

'The aircraft will, of course, wait for you on the airfield at Liegnitz and the truck will wait at the point where it puts you down on the river bank. They will help you to launch the canoe in the river. How long do you think you need to reach the bridge and return in the dark?'

'Fortunately, the Dombrücke is on the Oder on the north side of the city. I know it so well. It is also called Lovers' Bridge. Thousands of partners have pledged themselves to each other on that bridge. They take a padlock and two keys with them when they do so. They select a place on the railings of the bridge to deposit their lock, which they close together and throw their keys into the Oder, sealing their love forever.

'I should think an hour and a half on the upstream half, and one hour on the downstream—faster, if the man has any strength and canoeing experience.'

'What time shall we fix your arrival at the bridge?' he asked.

'Shall we say midnight,' Elsa said. 'No one can forget that time.'

'I shall need time today to do more practice in the two-man canoe, which I have used quite a lot, as well as the single canoe,' she added.

'And put the equivalent weight of a man in it to give you the right experience in your training time. Let me know if, after a training run on the water, the times you have estimated are still suitable. You have told me you would enter the water at half past ten with a view to arriving at midnight, and one hour for the return trip, arriving back at one o'clock.'

'A pity you aren't a canoe expert, Franz. We could go together instead of on a motorbike...'

'...and sidecar,' added Franz.'

'Yes, that wonderful sidecar,' Elsa said. 'It was so comfortable. And carried all the things we needed. We really were an independent couple on the road. But it would be far too noisy for this venture, I'm afraid.

'Silence, surprise and secrecy are the watchwords for this job.'

They enjoyed a few minutes of reminiscence before Elsa prepared to go to her training ritual and Franz to alert the local authorities on his assessment of the advent of refugees from eastern Germany, driven out by Russian excesses.

As they turned to go, Elsa suddenly remembered something she had forgotten to mention.

'Apart from the two parties who have to keep the rendezvous points, I think the biggest hazard will be if Russian patrols have already infiltrated to the Oder bank in the north of the city. I shall carry an MP3008 maschinenpistole with me in case there is any argument.'

'We can confirm that the Russians have not crossed the Oder in the north, at least. But make sure you carry that MP around your neck at all times on its sling.'

Franz was nothing if not anxious for her safety.

'That's good to know. I shall of course have the weapon close to my trigger finger. I have been practicing with it for weeks, so I am a pretty good shot. A single, selected shot is my speciality. A short burst would take down two men, but I am not disposed to fire long bursts in the hope of hitting something. I shall keep the safety catch off once I am on the water.'

'There is something I forgot to mention to you, as well. I plan to fly with you to Liegnitz and will go without my sleep until you show up again. But the military reason for going is to ring through a final confirmation to the army in Breslau.'

'That's the best booster I could have wished for. I won't thank you for it, but I might find ways of showing my appreciation in other ways later.'

She fetched a two-man canoe, secreting enough bricks to equal a man's weight under the second seat. Far from having illusions about the extra passenger, she put her skills and experiences to the test on the waters of the port, where the choppy waters added to the handicap of the inert extra load.

The bricks simulated a man who was not quite fit and would not be earning his ride by helping to paddle the canoe.

The artificial extra loading made a considerable difference. She discounted or added, as appropriate, to her reckoning, the absence of choppy water, paddling with the flow of the river, the hope that the man would be lighter than the substantial number of bricks she had loaded with a few more in addition to a normal man's weight, and her own heightened adrenalin that would give her the extra energy to escape from Russian detection.

Concluding her canoe training in the morning, she promised herself to try it again after darkness had fallen that night. She oiled her chosen weapon and tested it on the navy ranges in the afternoon, returning to the port pleased with her own performance.

She joined Astrid for an early night, determined to repeat the day's training again on the following day.

'You are doing what!' Astrid exploded, on hearing the news of her mission. I cannot conceive of anything foolhardier than what you have described. Paddling in a canoe into Breslau in the dark. You may miss your way, the army may not turn up, or make a mistake in identifying the rendezvous point.'

'No. You have to see the plan in the light of the actual circumstances. The Russians are encircling the city. It is not exactly known where the limits of their incursion have reached.

'The engineer cannot join the refugees on foot leaving the city. For one thing, he has been ill. For another, it cannot be left to chance that he could be captured during his long escape on foot by the Russians or killed from the air by marauding Russian aircraft.

'The river is an unknown to the enemy, but to use any motorised transport on the river would be impossible.'

'You will be taking your life in your hands if you go ahead with it.'

'I don't really have a choice. Remember I'm a member of the naval intelligence service in Gotenhaven. And orders are orders. I have been given quite a lot of latitude over several months to train. There now appears to be the occasional demand for my services, which may not have come up, but in fact one has come up. I have to respond with a certain amount of professional conduct.'

'Yes, you do. I am proud of you. I shall not sleep while you are away.'

'You are the second person to say that.'

'Who else would say such a thing?'

'My boss. He will be flying with me to confirm the army rendezvous times, to help launch the canoe, and wait with the truck for me to return.'

'I wish I could come with you, but it is a secret trip, so it would not be allowed. But I shall be waiting at the airstrip when you return.'

The Junkers 52 tri-motor aircraft was due to pick up the passengers at Gotenhaven at three o'clock on the twelfth of January for a two-and-a-half-hour flight to Liegnitz, where it would arrive in the dark.

The passengers would then be able to have a rest and a

meal, before leaving in the army truck to drive to the launch spot chosen at half past ten.

In the meanwhile, Kapitäleutnant Weber would have enough time to confirm finally the arrangement with the army to meet Elsa at midnight at the Dombrücke, the time having already been provisionally fixed.

Elsa was well clad entirely in black, face blackened, her naval uniform, worn underneath specially thick layers of fatigues, with her hair cropped to a man's length.

Under her fatigues and uniform, strapped to her skin, was a waterproof package with the orders for the garrison commander. She carried iron rations and a small bottle of water, which she stowed in a waterproof leather container under her seat in the canoe.

The Junkers could be heard approaching the airfield before it could be seen. Elsa felt her heart pump a little faster and the adrenaline rise in her body. She exercised the self-control mechanism she had cultivated in the service, wanting to be cool and collected for the entire mission.

The aircraft made a perfect landing, drawing up to the hard pavement in front of the control tower, keeping its three engines running. A door opened on the left-hand, port side of the fuselage, through which a metal ladder was dropped out with its end attached to the floor of the aircraft.

Kapitäleutnant Weber and Leutnant Bauer said farewell to the members of the ground staff, who then loaded Elsa's canoe after the two had climbed aboard.

Once they were in the cabin for the passengers, Elsa was astounded to see six men dressed in unusual military clothing and carrying lethal equipment and weapons.

'Franz, what on earth are these men here for?'

She noticed that one of them had the rank of hauptmann, a captain. They were all silent.

'They are shock troops. They will be coming with us in the truck to the launch site. You didn't suppose we would let you come without the best protection we could provide? It just leaves you with the canoe passage in secret and silence to your rendezvous.'

It put as much heart into Elsa as was possible. Without the accompanying troops, there was the possibility of the launch site's being ambushed for her return. They would be able to carry out patrols around the area to ensure that no Russian forces approached during her absence.

Elsa was settled into her seat by a member of the ground staff, who then checked that Franz was also safely harnessed.

He left by swinging down the steps of the access ladder to the tarmac and sliding it back into the aircraft.

The aircraft increased the revs of its three engines. It raced across the airfield and took off, leaving doubts and reservations behind it, with no one to own them.

15

It was Elsa's first time in the air. She had sometimes wondered what had driven her compatriots to want to join the air force. A mixture of fear and ecstasy came over her. It lasted only for a few seconds. It was quickly overshadowed by her reason for being in the air. She had concentrated for several weeks on canoeing around the port. For the previous two days, she had been preoccupied with her looming responsibility as a canoeist with an inert man as a passenger on a large river, at night, in a mid-winter's temperature, but had given no thought to the experience of being off the ground.

The reality of it finally hit her. She was in a military aircraft with a group of armed soldiers on the way to a risky mission for which she alone would be the arbiter of its success.

Once airborne, Elsa and Franz tried to raise a conversation. It was futile. It was too much of an effort simply to hear each other speak. Elsa gave up trying to hold up her half of the conversation, leaving Franz to revel in the flight. He managed to tell Elsa one thing from his reminiscences, which she could understand.

'The last time I was in one of these aircraft was in 1941 when I was in the parachute regiment attacking Crete. That was where I was wounded. It led to my being invalided out of the army, but I volunteered for the navy.'

'Can't keep a good man down,' Elsa shouted at him.

By the time they landed at Liegnitz, it was dark, as

planned.

Elsa managed a sleep in a soft armchair, before rejoining the whole group in the army barracks for a welcome meal that would need to last them for the night's activity, although everyone's backpacks contained a supplement of cold, but nourishing, packaged food.

At half past eight, two army trucks turned up to take the party to the launch site for the canoe.

'We ordered two trucks,' Franz said to Elsa. 'There is always the chance that one will break down. It pays to have a truck in front to find the way. It will be driven by the officer who has supervised this mission.'

'Just as well,' she said, 'it would be an unexpected thing like that to ruin the mission. I hope we have prepared for every eventuality.'

The oberleutnant, the senior lieutenant, from the local army garrison in charge of the launch, spoke briefly to Elsa.

'We did not leave anything to chance. Yesterday we had a good look at the bank all the way to the city, keeping in mind that you had to be at your rendezvous at midnight. We have found an ideal spot about five miles short of the Dombrücke.

'Unfortunately, we heard some small arms firing in the distance. We think the Ruskies could be on the eastern bank, somewhere along there. But in the dark and with soft paddling, we think you will be able to cope with it from our chosen point of departure.'

'Thank you, Oberleutnant. You have prepared for me well. It's now up to me. I hope to be back at the launching point by one o'clock.'

The two trucks set off on a journey already pre-reconnoitred in the dark, with half a minute's interval between them. The first truck had only the oberleutnant, who was driving, and Kapitäleutnant Weber on board.

The two trucks covered about three quarters of the distance to the designated spot without difficulty, including some very rough ground inter-mixed with roads and paths that had been identified as the best route to the chosen site.

With only about one mile to go, the rest of the party in the second truck, still travelling in silence, was rudely shaken from being lost in their thoughts or dozing, when the night was shattered by a volley of small arms fire.

In the short time that ensued, their truck soon closed the distance between itself and the truck in front by a considerable amount.

It braked to a standstill. Without an order, the six shock troops disappeared without a word. The firing stopped as suddenly as it had begun.

Within minutes, the rapid fire of Schmeisser sub-machine guns opened a brief cacophony of gunfire. And then there was silence once again.

The feldwebel, a sergeant, from the Liegnitz garrison, acting as escort to Elsa, had meantime jumped down with Elsa from the truck. They concealed themselves in the bush.

The silence persisted until one of the shock troops came back to them. Elsa noticed that he was the soldier carrying the rank of hauptmann, the captain commanding the escorting shock troops.

'Bad news, I'm afraid. Both men in the front truck have been killed. A small patrol of Russian infantry has evidently crossed the river. They attacked the first truck and waited for the second to reach them. They could hear its engine. Eight of them. They are all dead. We quickly surprised them from behind.'

It was an unexpected catastrophe.

It was the blow no one believed would happen but had known it was always a possibility. The other shock troops returned and assembled around the truck.

The hauptmann called them all to order.

'Everyone must push the impact of this to the back of his mind. We have to press on immediately to keep the timing of the project right. Everyone aboard. We have survived and have a job to do.'

'Who knows where the launch point is now that the oberleutnant is dead?' asked Elsa.

'Don't worry, ma'am, I know exactly where it is,' the feldwebel assured her. 'Let's get on with it.'

The short distance to the drop point was soon covered.

Two of the shock troops manhandled the canoe into the water. Elsa said a quiet farewell and moved the canoe out into mid-stream in only a minute or two.

She spoke aloud to the group left on the bank. 'This has got to be done. I will do it now for Franz, the oberleutnant, and all of you.'

There was no time for grief. It was the first time someone had been killed alongside her. The fact that Franz was someone special for the moment had no impact on her.

Her own life had now been put in danger. She was alone.

Elsa struck out against the river current, slowly at first until her eyes had become night sensitive. Even the darkest of nights seemed to have its own glow of luminosity. That particular night was a good example. The sky was starlit. The temperature was exceptionally low.

Her body was a little rusty at first, but she soon shrugged

off her inactivity over the past few hours, finding the energy and drive that she knew she could call on. The thought brought her comfort. Within minutes she established a rhythmic bodily action that promised the few miles to the bridge would soon be a past hazard overcome.

She had no easy opportunity to glance at her luminous watch. Her hands were wrapped warmly in woollen gloves.

Her only thought was to erase the distance between her present position and the Dombrücke. The easy movements of the canoeist warmed her body with the exertion, protecting her from the bitter temperature.

After about an hour's hard paddling, she faintly heard intermittent small arms firing away to her left, the eastern bank of the river. Even on the coldest of nights some soldiers were not resting. Russian patrols were taking advantage of the night and climate to test out the resolve and strength of the defending troops of the Wehrmacht, at the perimeter to the north of Breslau.

She had reached the extreme periphery of the city. Elsa could see houses and other buildings on both banks of the river, all without their own lights, but lying ghostlike in the moonlight. The periodically passing cloud gave her interrupted snapshots of the east side bank. She thought it was time to check her watch and assess her schedule.

She paddled to the left from the centre of the very wide river towards a small wooden jetty, jutting out about eight metres from her left-hand bank. It lay flat, only a few inches above the surface of the water.

When reaching the end of the jetty, she was silently startled to hear muffled voices and saw at least four burning cigarettes in the dark on the shore, but away from the water's edge.

Her watch told her it was twenty minutes to twelve. She had not yet reached the Dombrücke but knew that it could only be a short distance away, perhaps less than a mile.

Remaining still, silent, and unseen against the blackness of the river, she was shaken to the core when a voice called out.

'Wer geht dahin?'—who goes there? It was the customary challenge to friend and foe in no man's land.

Instinctively, her first physical reaction was to raise her sub-machine gun to a firing position.

Her first mental reaction was to be pleased to hear a German voice. Her second, coming instantaneously on the heels of the first, was to doubt the authenticity of the pronunciation of the challenge.

Without thinking, but suspecting a trap, she answered.

'Freund,' she called. Friend it was, she could speak no other language than German.

With that one word spoken, she heard the unmistakable metallic clicks of rifle bolts. Her mind went into top gear. There was no time to take chances. They were intrusive Russians.

Without a second thought, she fired at the burning cigarette ends, in a spraying action. She had no notion of the number of men in the group, but the cigarettes went out and a scream split the night air like a flash of lightning.

The volley of small arms fire that followed her first strafing revealed their gun flashes. They were being aimed into the middle of the river. She opened fire a second time at them, while pressing her body low in her canoe.

Elsa pushed off into the middle of the river, just as a

soldier—perhaps the only survivor—clambered crazily over the timbers of the jetty, rocking them as he ran, firing wildly at the dimly seen object out on the water.

Elsa calmly switched her gun to single shot, took aim, and felled him into the river. She collected her wits, muttering to herself.

'This time surprise was on my side. I have always been told it is the main advantage to give you the upper hand.'

Her time was up. The delay had occupied only a little over a minute, but she had to paddle furiously to reach the rendezvous point by the appointed hour of midnight.

The Dombrücke had a distinctive shape. It was impossible to mistake the bridge. Its superstructure was concentrated in the centre of the bridge, supported by a huge stone pillar in the middle of the river. Built in 1889, it had long been festooned with the love-locks of countless lovers. It was the ideal place to meet strange people for a risky mission.

The waiting army personnel were fully alert, scanning the surface of the river by the time Elsa approached. She was guided to the river bank by shielded torches, where a welcoming party awaited her.

'I am Major Zimmermann, aide to Oberst Beck, commander of the garrison in Breslau. You have some documents for us?'

An attendant secured the canoe and helped Elsa to step onto solid land. She was cold and stiff, still trembling a little from her exchange of fire with the Russian patrol.

'Sir, Leutnant Bauer reporting. This was the best bridge to use for the purpose, Major,' was Elsa's first word of greeting.

'Indeed, it was,' he replied. 'There are over a hundred bridges in Breslau, so you might have got lost if any other had been chosen.'

'You have taken on a difficult and dangerous defence of the city,' Elsa said. 'But knowing the city so well and using the numerous waterways will be an advantage to you. When I lived here, I became conversant with the variegated mixture of water and bridges.'

'We certainly are up against it,' he replied. 'There used to be over six hundred thousand people in the city. It was swollen to nearly a million by the addition of prisoners of war and forced labour in the factories. Now it's down to under two hundred thousand people. Over forty thousand have been killed. Most have fled westwards to cities like Dresden.'

While the major was speaking, Elsa was stripping several layers of her winter garments. She finally removed the sealed and waterproof wallet from her skin, where it had been strapped against her body.

'I'm glad to say this package has escaped the water and the soviets on the way, sir, but at least it is still dry and warm.'

'What do you mean by the soviets, Leutnant?'

'I had to check my route and time when I reached the outskirts about a mile north of here. I pulled in to a flat wooden structure jutting out from the north bank. To my surprise, I stumbled on a small patrol of Russians. They seemed to have been resting.

'When they called out in German, I replied in German. When I heard them cock their rifles, I anticipated them with a burst from this gun. They fired too high. I was at water level. I fired again. One of them survived and fired madly into the night near my canoe. His firing only provided me with a good target for a single shot, which put him in the water.'

'You put down a soviet patrol to get yourself here? That

must merit an award,' he said, 'I will see to it.'

'Oh, it's nothing, sir, my job is to get the engineer back safely to Peenemünde. Have you got him all right?'

'Yes, as agreed. He is resting. We have had a job to protect him from the cold. It's going to be a tough job for you on the return leg, as I don't think he will be up to wielding a paddle.'

'At least I have the downstream current to help me,' Elsa said. 'I never thought I would ever be back here. I was at the university, just before the war, but I put the city behind me when I left.'

'One never knows when the past will catch up with us,' he joked.

A couple of infantrymen fetched the engineer from a nearby makeshift shelter and helped him into his rear seat in the canoe, while another two held the craft still. After that it was time for Elsa to say her farewells to the major and the memory of her years in Breslau at university. She felt exulted.

'Give my love to Königsplatz, Zwingerstrasse, Tauentzienstrasse, and Krullstrasse—and don't forget Großer Ring zu Breslau, that wonderful Market Square, incorporating nearly four hectares. They tell me it's the biggest in the world.'

'That it is. I hope you will come back to it all one day,' was the major's parting shot, as Elsa slowly eased the canoe out to midstream, leaving those on the shore fading into invisibility in the dark.

16

Elsa was unaccustomed to paddle with so much weight on board, but glad that she had endured extended practice with the bricks two days before. She soon felt the benefit of the downstream flow of the river. Within minutes she had come to the conclusion that even if her host did not participate in the paddling, she would make the return journey in the appointed time.

The man didn't speak. If he had spoken, Elsa would scarcely have been able to discern his words. Her head was covered in woollens and a helmet. The temperature had continued dropping.

Soon she heard something in the water strike her canoe, but she was speeding at too fast a rate to identify the object. A moment later it happened again—and again.

Suddenly the reality of it dawned on her.

The river is freezing, she said to herself. *It will be slowly now, but faster later. I'm glad I chose midnight for the rendezvous and not the early hours of the morning. By four o'clock this river will become impassable for a canoe with its extra weight.*

She cherished the hope that the further north she went, the wider and deeper the river bed would be. With every mile she paddled, the water was less likely to be icebound than it was already fast becoming in its higher reaches. Icing was a deficit she had not considered in planning the mission.

The advantage of paddling downstream was being squandered by the amount of ice that she had to paddle through. The possible freeze up of the river troubled her. While she pondered on the likelihood of the handicap the ice would cause, another more serious situation demanded her attention.

She felt the canoe was slightly listing to the right. That could only mean her passenger was lacking the ability to hold himself erect on the centre line. She tried calling out to him to no avail. The list became worse. It endangered her steering. A solution just had to be found.

She allowed the list, aided by her paddle strokes, to take the canoe into the right-hand bank, arriving at a watery point offering some access to rushes and a flatter bank wall. Just as she came to a rest, her passenger finally lost consciousness and keeled over, leaning almost out of the canoe.

Using all her strength, Elsa pushed his upper body back over the canoe structure. She then took hold of his two feet and dragged him down, as far as the room in the bowels of the canoe allowed, leaving part of his torso sprawled back over his seat.

From her top overalls, she retrieved a lanyard and lashed his body in the centre of his seat, adjusting his clothing and headgear as she did so. She felt his pulse and declared to herself. *He is not dead. But then, I do not want him to be killed by frostbite.*

It was touch and go. *Canoeing will be more difficult now,* she thought.

Getting back in her seat she nearly turned the canoe over, but the craft floated well when it reached clear water again.

The ice had become more ubiquitous during those few minutes of forced delay. Nevertheless, she set off with renewed energy, and resolve.

She estimated there were three miles to go to her second rendezvous that night. Every time she plunged the paddle into the water, she counted down from one hundred slowly in reverse.

Her life and destiny seemed to hang in the balance. She was approaching a state of exhaustion.

Mindless, in the sense that she had concentrated only on the countdown to the exclusion of all else, Elsa was eventually shaken from her riveted mental task by lights on the water ahead of her.

In her languorous state, she stopped counting and steered into her left, the western bank, where ever-eager hands recovered her, the passenger, and the canoe.

Little was said.

The waiting shock troops, the feldwebel and driver had been frozen to the marrow, waiting around with nothing to do to keep them active and warm. The impetus that drove them on was the thought of a woman in a canoe on the river, at night, in below freezing temperatures.

Elsa was spent. She scarcely had the energy or the time to reflect on the absence of Franz.

With no more ado, the truck made a fast return to Liegnitz, first, direct to the military hospital to save the engineer from further suffering, and then to the barracks where Elsa and the troops plunged into their welcome beds.

It was on waking the following morning that Elsa experienced the first reactions to her ordeal. Her body was aching and tired.

Her first duty was to enquire about the state of health of her passenger. It would be ironic if she had secured his return from the potential custody of the Russians, only to lose him to the coldness of the night.

She found him in his hospital bed. He was still rather quiet and suffering from the strenuous night he had spent. He had been given oxygen and medication to support his enfeebled health.

The medical staff members were variously adamant that he should not be moved that day. Their united front presented Elsa with a dilemma.

'He should be able to travel tomorrow, provided he doesn't have a relapse,' the doctor told Elsa. 'He has had an infection which left him very weak. It would have been better if his journey could have been postponed for another week.'

'That was just not a possibility,' Elsa replied. 'The Russians are already around the corner. They are going to encircle Breslau and press on westwards. You will be next in line.'

'It's a thought I cannot cope with,' he said.

'But you will have to move the military patients pretty soon. They are shooting everything military and abusing the civilian population as they come. If you say he will be ready to fly tomorrow, I will, of course, remain with him.'

'Surely, the time may have come, with what you say, for you to save yourself,' the doctor suggested.

'Not a bit of it. I was ordered to bring him back safely and that I shall do. But I do not know whether the aircraft can wait for him or not.'

Elsa was glad about the man's health but dismayed about his delayed departure. It was then that the full force of the loss of Franz hit her. He was no longer there for discussion and making a decision.

She contacted the army commander of the garrison force, meeting him in his office.

'Sir, as you know, Kapitäleutnant Weber was killed on our way to the start point to launch the canoe to fetch the Peenemünde engineer before the Russians could grab him. He was my boss.

'A problem has cropped up over our continued withdraw. The doctor and staff in the military hospital have insisted that he remains another day for treatment but is likely to be ready to move at the earliest tomorrow. As far as I am concerned if the man stays, I stay with him.'

'That is correct, Leutnant. Tell me. Did the Kapitäleutnant have an appointed deputy in the office?'

'No, sir.'

'The solution is obvious. You are appointed officer in charge of the unit from now. I will sign an emergency promotion note to that position for you right away and raise your rank to Oberleutnant zur See.'

'Sir,' she said, saluting. She dare not make any subjective remarks. They were out of order. He had used his position as commander of the garrison of Liegnitz to make emergency orders for all services when under his control in the city.

Elsa went straight to the airfield to meet the hauptmann, captain of the shock troops, and the pilot, co-pilot, navigator, and wireless operator flying the Junkers 52. The shock troops and members of the aircrew had ensconced themselves in the reception area, trying to take advantage of the little warmth that the building offered.

Elsa singled out the pilot immediately.

'I hope you had a comfortable night. The hospital has decided to keep the engineer another day under medical treatment. They hope he will be fit enough to travel tomorrow. I assume there is no chance the aircraft can wait here for twenty-four hours.'

'Correct. It would be a sitting duck for Russian fighters now that daylight has returned. The men were released only for the overnight period. I shall have to get permission to take off at once. It really is too risky to stay here a minute longer than necessary.'

He turned as if to find a responsible officer to agree the decision.

'There is no need,' said Elsa. 'The authority has been given to me. See this,' she said, handing him the official document from the commander of the garrison.

'I am now in charge in place of Kapitäleutnant Weber. I agree that the aircraft should return to Peenemünde. I will be in touch as necessary for any arrangements involving you.

'Thank you for the safe delivery of the party and good luck on your return flight. Please explain to the authorities at Peenemünde what has happened.'

She went out on the tarmac still talking to the pilot. When he went aboard the shock troops walked across the hard apron, led by their officer. Elsa stopped them at the foot of the ladder into the fuselage.

'I thank you all for what you have done. It was sad to lose my boss and the oberleutnant driving the truck, but you saved the rest of us and enabled the mission to go ahead to completion as planned. I shall give the fullest account of your remarkable performance in my report.'

She saluted the hauptmann. 'You are the real hero, ma'am,' he said. 'We have nothing but admiration for the way you have conducted this operation.'

Within minutes the Junkers 52 had left the ground, climbing away in a northerly direction on its way to Peenemünde.

Elsa returned to the city. She first had some enquiries to make with the army before visiting her canoe passenger again. She had formulated a proposition she wanted to test out on the man in the bed.

Since it was aimed at his good, she expected he would be reluctant to accept it, but would probably do so on the grounds that he had no choice.

Later that morning, she arrived at his bedside. The few hours that had elapsed since she had earlier called to see him at first light, had brought a wan smile to his face and a more cheerful choice of words to his conversation.

Elsa was more relaxed on that second visit. Perhaps it showed on her face and in her manner.

'Since the hospital has refused to let you go today, I have had to dismiss the Junkers 52, which was waiting here to take you all the way to Peenemünde, together with the shock troops who have been such stalwarts and saved us from a Russian patrol on the way to pick you up.'

'I didn't know about that. Can you tell me exactly what happened?'

Elsa declined. 'It can wait until later.'

She pointed out the risks the aircraft took in being parked on the ground, with marauding Russian fighters constantly supporting their ground forces ahead of their front line, glad to find any target worthy of their firepower.

It leaves us with the dilemma over how you and I will be able to catch up on the others.

Just at the moment they were engaged in earnest

conversation about a variety of alternative solutions, an orderly walked into the room.

'I'm looking for an officer called Elsa Bauer in the Women's Naval Service. I believe she came from Gotenhaven.'

'That is me,' Elsa called to her. She handed Elsa a message.

It was brief, readable in seconds.

The Junkers 52 en route from Liegnitz to Peenemünde was shot down by Russian fighters one hour after leaving Liegnitz. Everyone lost.

Elsa was flabbergasted. Her support team was dead. It was unlikely she would be able to call on the services of another Junkers 52. She and the engineer were not yet home.

They would have to recourse to unusual means to achieve their return to complete the mission.

'Bad news,' the man in the bed murmured.

'Yes. The Junkers 52 on its way home was shot down. Everybody on board has been killed. Do you realise what an escape from death you and I have just had? This is the third mishap this mission has suffered. By the way, I was never given your name, and I never asked what you were called.'

'It's Kurt. And yours?'

'I am Elsa Bauer. I am an Oberleutnant zur See in the Women's Naval Service based at Gotenhaven.'

'I think I have seen you before.'

'That's impossible. I have never been to Peenemünde.'

'But didn't you once have a friend with an interest in aeronautical design work?'

'As a matter of fact, I did, but that was in university days.'

'Where was that?'

'Breslau. I was in metallurgy. I did know a student called Kurt.'

'And I knew a student called Elsa,' he replied.

He immediately elaborated. 'It was that night out on the town. You were new and wide-eyed. We took you to the Market Square. I was a third-year student in metallurgy.'

'You got involved in devastating a Jewish business and I grabbed you and pulled you away from it, but never had any thanks for saving you from yourself. I remember. You are Kurt Neumann.'

'Yes. I had my family in Breslau. I have been continuously engaged at Peenemünde since leaving the university. I returned to see them before Christmas and became ill. You know the rest of the story. I have to thank you for getting me out. The reputation of the Russian armies has gone ahead of them. It is not good.'

'Well, now we are properly introduced, may I say that I have talked with the army. I have recently reconnoitred in Pomerania to assess the extent of the refugees, who have taken to the roads towards Gotenhaven.

'With my boss, I conducted it in an army motorcycle with sidecar. I think it is also an inconspicuous and ideal way for you and me to get away from here.

'We could head for Frankfort an der Oder, about a hundred miles, then to Stettin for another eighty. From there I might be able to get an airlift for you. If not, we would have to make another trip to Gotenhaven for a hundred and thirty miles.

'We have to keep in mind that the roads are now crowded, perhaps here and there, with refugees on foot, but no one knows the present extent of it. What do you think?'

'In itself it does not appeal to me, but it seems to be the

only solution.'

With that agreement, Elsa went back to the garrison commander to confirm the arrangement and permission to have the motorcycle, which would soon be redundant, they both realised, when the Russians arrived. She then rang Gotenhaven informing the office of her plans.

At the end of the day, she returned to the hospital to see if Kurt had improved. She consulted the doctor who confirmed that he could leave the next day.

17

The following morning, at a not unrespectable hour, Elsa drove the motorcycle and sidecar to the hospital. The staff had carefully clad Kurt Neumann in warm clothing for the ordeal of a long ride by road in the open sidecar.

Elsa had secured some reserve petrol in cans, strapped to the machine, and enough food for the day's drive. It was recent history repeating itself for her.

The time spent on the road in a similar machine with Franz had taught her about the wiles and idiosyncrasies of driving a motorcycle and sidecar. She adapted well to machinery. Had she not driven her father's ancient tractor and mastered its tortuous peculiarities?

'Have no fear, Kurt,' she light heartedly said to him, when she spied a look of apprehension on his face, as he was finally ensconced in the sidecar. 'Remember, it was I who studied metallurgy and a year or two helping to design the Type XXI.'

'I hope you will not be taking us into the water in this contraption,' he responded, with the first spontaneous laugh Elsa remembered Kurt making.

'You have just been in the water with me,' Elsa replied. 'What more do you want?'

They enjoyed a moment's reflection on the trip they had made by canoe coming back from Breslau. It reminded them of their good fortune, reinforced by the loss of the Junkers 52, on which they should have been passengers. They were still alive.

'So where are we setting off to now?'

'I told you it would be via Frankfort am der Oder and Stettin, but I have since ascertained that the way is open all the way to Gotenhaven via Lesnia, Poznan, and Bydgoszcz.

'It will cut our journey time significantly down to two hundred and fifty miles. There is a possibility we could make it in the day, but it depends on the roads. Military traffic west to east and refugees east to west do not make it a pleasant or convenient combination for driving.

'The main point to our advantage is that going north cuts across both those streams of traffic for the most part, so let's hope it will be better than expected.'

'Why will you be carrying that gun, then?'

'It's part of me. And my shoulder is the most comfortable place to keep it. I just hope I don't have to use it again.'

'Why are you saying that? Have you already used it? But not on this trip, I hope.'

'Never you mind, Kurt. We are safe so far.'

He was not to be deterred.

'But you have not used it on this trip, surely.'

'If you must know, we lost two men before we got the canoe anywhere near the water. Our escort wiped out the Russian patrol, which attacked the first truck we had sent ahead. On the way, just before midnight, I had a brush with a Russian patrol, when I stopped to check my timing. I just had to wipe them out to preserve the secrecy of my mission. Now let's forget it.'

Kurt lapsed into silence. Leaving at eight o'clock, they roared off down the road, the noise of their engine removing any point in trying to talk. They had an uninterrupted journey to Poznan. They stopped to top up the fuel tank of the motorbike—and themselves, with hot ersatz coffee from a flask.

'Poznan has been designated as a festung city, to be defended at all costs, if the Russians get this far,' Elsa remarked.

'I fear there is not much of a chance that they will not reach this far,' Kurt replied. 'The numbers on each side do not permit it.'

Elsa shrugged her shoulders, offering no further comment. Surprisingly, the road to Bydgoszcz was also passable in normal time.

When they paused in the city, they noted the quiet turmoil that possessed many streets and roads. An unusual number of people, heavily clad in winter clothing, were either leaving their homes or carrying a series of chattels from inside their houses or premises to be loaded on carts, some drawn with animals for empowerment, some clearly reserved for the arduous task of human effort.

'This is ominous, Kurt. It conforms to the survey I did eastwards from Gotenhaven, just before coming on this trip. All the signs of a substantial exodus of citizens fleeing westwards are in evidence. It means that they will attempt to walk northwards towards Gotenhaven, adding to the growing flood from the east.'

'In case you are right, we had better not delay. The going from here could get rough,' Kurt suggested.

'Agreed,' Elsa said, 'it's already late afternoon. Darkness is not far away. I wonder what the refugees will do when night falls. People cannot walk on forever. They must rest. I wonder if it would be to our advantage to travel after sundown.'

'Let's push on now and see if your prediction comes true,' Kurt said persuasively. 'We have nothing to lose.'

They motored out to the road to the north with a direct route alongside the River Oder to Danzig Bay and Gotenhaven. The further they went, they realised that they would be reduced to a slow speed, probably for the rest of the entire journey.

Elsa had exhausted herself. Frequently changing gear, she then had to speed up, only to have to brake again suddenly. So many people were using the road, many with carts, that a motorized vehicle had no chance of forging an easy passage through them.

Going north, they reached the west side of Graudenz, a town to their right. To their dismay, they saw another main road from the east of the town joining the road they were on, adding more refugees and making their freedom of movement worse.

Stopping to assess their plight, Elsa suggested to Kurt that if they diverted eastwards to their right, they could find a secondary road that would offer a better, if more circuitous, route to Gotenhaven.

'This machine remember is built to be driven over country land away from roads. If we have to, we can find our way by one means or another to complete our journey.'

'That would depend on being able to see your way,' Kurt said.

'We have headlights,' Elsa replied, 'we could unmask them if necessary. There are no fighter-bombers around after dark.'

'But think of our stomachs,' Kurt countered.

'If we have to do it, we will have to do it,' Elsa said with a touch of finality. 'I will not complete my mission until I have you safely back at Peenemünde,' she added resolutely. 'You are still important for the war effort.'

All went well on that road until they reached Marienburg.

More refugees were joining the throngs slowly wending their way westwards. Elsa stopped again to take stock of their chances.

'I think all roads now will be increasingly impossible to use without the slow, stop, wait, rev up, and move round a few more people syndrome.

'I know there is a local, secondary railway which turns off north and runs up to the Danzig to Elbing main road. It will soon be dark.

'If we are lucky, we can negotiate the railway line before night makes it a more difficult option. If we can then join the flow of refugees, I am sure will be crowding up that road, we shall reach the river Oder.

'I reckon we could then leave the road and use the river bank for a fast but bumpy ride by following the river towards Danzig. We can turn right before hitting the city and drive the twelve miles into Gotenhaven. How does that sound to you?'

'It's your area. You know it. I don't. We have made better progress than expected, so let's give it a big try. Nothing to lose except the crowds on the roads that bring us to a standstill, and possibly our stomachs. Before we go again, let us finish off the coffee. It has lasted better than the petrol and tastes better.'

'Whenever did you drink petrol to know that fact?' she asked, with a cynical smile on her face.

'I'm not used to drinking petrol. It was only my way of protesting the foul aroma and taste of the coffee,' he replied.

'But beggars can't be choosers. We should be thankful.'

Elsa noted Kurt's rising morale. She summoned up her reserves for the last leg of the journey. What a contrast it would be from her departure by air, if they made it into Gotenhaven in a motorcycle and sidecar, in spite of the crowded roads.

It would seem like an ignominious end to the most demanding job she had ever undertaken. But nevertheless, she would have fulfilled it.

They found the branch railway line going northwards and began the drive of a few miles along the rail-side space. It was quite smooth in places, but equally bumpy in others.

The weeds and trees intervening in their passage were all overcome. Driving on the right side of the permanent way, Elsa gave Kurt the agonizing job of sweeping away those impediments to their progress as they went, the unmasked headlight of the motorbike lighting up their passage as the darkness closed in.

Elsa took the opportunity to remove the sub-machine gun from her shoulder and stow it deep in the canoe. She was now in home territory. The gun became a hindrance. It kept being in the way of the tree branches and weeds that plagued the life out of them in certain parts of the railway line.

In the end it was worth the trouble they had taken on themselves. Covering the distance in record time, they were relieved to reach the east to west main road.

Turning westwards, there followed a struggle to go a distance of seven miles, necessitating horn-sounding and shouting to give them a frustratingly—at the end of a tiring day—slow movement progressing along the main Elbing to Danzig Road.

It was slow only in the sense that people were dominating

the tarmac instead of speeding motor vehicles. Their own speed in the bike was as fast as they could manage. The Russians, they spared the thought, might not be far behind.

Gratefully, they pulled off the bridge over the Oder, racing over the rough pasture of the bank side fields on the river's left-hand, western, slopes. It was a thoughtful choice, not by chance, that Elsa had chosen the left, as opposed to the right bank of the river. It might be difficult to cross later on with a motorbike and its sidecar.

Unimpeded, she drove madly on the flats and recklessly on the intervening rough ground. Kurt was in two minds about jumping out for his life.

His adrenalin was not pumping in anticipation of his full recovery, but for the immediate crisis it was preparing him for losing his life. His destiny seemed bound up with rivers and the perils they could bestow on him.

Their ride to freedom, however, was rudely arrested.

They ran headlong into a military installation.

Elsa knew nothing of it. She braked when lights were suddenly switched on and voices were raised.

She soon heard the imperative command. 'Halt.'

Elsa guessed they had run into a defensive site. Having already expected the word halt would be levelled at them, she immediately arrested the cavorting-like motorcycle and sidecar on the river bank, just in time to stop a warning shot coming their way.

It was the ignominious nature of their being stopped and the suppositions which followed, that gave them an experience contrasting so vividly with what she expected would have greeted her in Gotenhaven.

Several well-armed troops surrounded the motorcycle and

sidecar. In the dim light of the evening night, the soldiers expressed their displeasure at stopping a runaway woman with her man friend joy-riding off the public road in a stolen military vehicle.

There would be hell to pay.

At first, Elsa thought they were joking. Kurt thought so, too. It was only their persisting manner and order to both people to get away from the vehicle at the point of their guns that disabused the two motorcyclists of their confidence.

They had run into a serious situation.

Elsa first tried to correct their mistake. 'I am a Women's Naval Service officer.'

'And I am an engineer from Peenemünde,' Kurt added.

With that they all burst out laughing.

'It's the best one I have ever heard,' one of the men said to the others.

'Take them into the guard room,' the NCO ordered his men.

'It's too cold out here but I can prove it inside in the warmth,' Elsa said.

At gunpoint, Elsa and Kurt were led away to the guardroom.

Once inside, the soldiers saw two scruffy and travel-warn intruders. Their first assumption that they were local joy riders began to weaken. Both had twigs embedded in their woollen headgear, and a rent or two in their clothing.

As people they betrayed a demeanour suggesting anything but irresponsible tearaways.

Elsa began to strip off her clothes, a couple of the men faintly jeering and making ribald noises, suggesting in effect that she was trying to seduce her way out of a nasty fix.

After two layers of clothing were removed, she came to her uniform with its officer's insignia plain for all to see.

The silence was devastating.

At last, the NCO broke the impasse.

'Ma'am, we have committed an offence against you. Who is this man?'

'He is Kurt Neumann, one of Germany's top engineers working at Peenemünde on the V1 flying bomb and V2 rocket.'

'Well, ma'am, I am totally perplexed as to why you two were on this riverside in this vehicle in the dark. May I ask if you both have had an affair and were whooping it up. If so, we would understand.'

'You may not. That would be far from the truth,' Elsa replied. 'You may ask but be surprised at the true explanation.'

She then addressed the NCO in an official manner. She showed him the document issued by the commander of the garrison in Liegnitz.

'I am in the investigation department of the navy at Gotenhaven. I received a commission to rescue this man from Breslau in circumstances that do not concern you. The Russians are already investing the city. We could not let him fall into their hands. He has been ill and had to be hospitalised in Liegnitz.

'The Junkers 52 that took us down there and waited to bring us back had to leave. It was a sitting target for Russian fighter-bombers. The commandant helpfully set us up to drive this bike, but we have been held up by the number of refugees everywhere. We wanted to make it home by tonight.'

Elsa watched their faces as she related the story briefly. The soldiers were transformed from a state of triumphalism to one of humility in less than five minutes.

'I don't know what Kurt Neumann thinks about all this, or if he will take any further steps. But as far as I am concerned you were doing your job, and I will do nothing about it whatsoever.'

Kurt joined her in the disclaimer. 'There is nothing more to be said.'

The NCO whispered something to one of his men, handing him the document Elsa had proffered in her defence from the commandant at Liegnitz, sending him away.

'I hope you will let us recompense you for interrupting your progress. Would you like a more comfortable ride to Gotenhaven if I can arrange it?' he asked.

The man despatched returned quickly from his mission.

'We would like to assign our kübelwagen with its driver. Our CO has given permission for it to be used for this purpose.'

'Thank you, but that will not be necessary. You will soon need all the petrol you can use. You would then have an unproductive return journey, and I will need to get the motorbike home as well. I hope you can fill up its small tank instead.'

Within minutes a figure entered the guardroom. Elsa saw he was a hauptmann, a captain, and assumed he was the CO in question. She saluted. His soldiers stood to attention.

'I can't let you go on without a goodwill gesture, Oberleutnant. Can you spare a few minutes to have a drink and bite to eat? You must be starving.'

His friendly manner took the sting out of the atmosphere. Elsa looked at Kurt.

'Are you game?'

'Of course, I am. Thank you, sir. We can spare half an hour.' The captain led the way to a small officers' mess.

Inside was a junior officer having a meal.

He introduced the guests who had invited themselves unknowingly into their world, and offered them schnapps, coffee, and freshly baked pastries.

'You've had some adventures, I understand. Would you care to tell us about them?'

'Not really, but I can give you the bare bones of my mission.'

She repeated word for word her explanation to the NCO she had given previously in the guardroom.

'Well, that takes the biscuit as they say.'

'You were lucky not to run into any Russians.'

'That's another story,' Elsa responded, smilingly. 'But I have not made my report yet, so save me the embarrassment of having to decline any details.'

The hauptmann escorted them to their motorcycle that would carry them on the final leg of their long drive to Gotenhaven.

Elsa thanked him for the repast and top up of petrol. He saluted them as they drove away.

Making good time, in spite of some crowding of refugees on the roads, diminished in numbers by the fall of night, they completed their journey within the day to Elsa's home port.

Neither she nor Kurt Neumann had any stomach for doing anything except heading straight for bed. But Elsa could not resist calling in what was intended to be a brief visit to her office. There might be confirmation of her emergency appointment as the successor to Franz.

A skeleton staff was sustaining night duty when she

arrived. Ingrid, one of the staff on duty gave her a salute and called out.

'Welcome back, Oberleutnant zur See, did it all go as planned?'

Elsa noted with satisfaction that she had been addressed by her newly promoted rank. There was no need to enquire if the news of Franz's demise and her installation as his successor had been received in the office. The bureaucratic expertise of the country was still working well, even if some things had gone asunder.

'I have managed to bring the man back,' Elsa said. 'That was my instruction, but it did not fit into the plan quite as well as I had hoped.'

'Oh, well, it's not the impediments that matter. What counts is the result—and you have succeeded. It's good news for the office and for all of us who have been involved in it.' Ingrid smiled at Elsa.

It was a smile that warmed her heart after a trying journey that took so much out of her.

'Thank you for saying that. It has made the day for me.'

'Now there is an urgent message awaiting you. It's from Peenemünde.'

Ingrid handed Elsa a piece of paper scribbled with the message, hand written, but starkly illuminating.

'Can you read it to me?' Elsa asked. 'I have run out of energy, but my hearing is still good.'

They laughed together before Ingrid read out the message.

In view of the rapidly deteriorating military situation, the engineers engaged in the rocket developments at Peenemünde are to be moved westwards. Therefore, there is no need to arrange for the repatriation of Kurt Neumann to the

Peenemünde base. A party will be joining you shortly to be embarked on the Hans Frayling for transfer to Kiel. He has been informed separately of the arrangements. I would be glad if you could take care of his welfare until the twenty-ninth of January when the party will be arriving for embarkation. Your loyal and determined efforts to bring Kurt Neumann away from Breslau are greatly appreciated. Congratulations on a job well done.

'It was transmitted by a secretary direct from Wernher von Braun, the engineer director of the Peenemünde research station. He is a famous man,' Ingrid added.

All that remained for Elsa's attention that day was to ask Astrid if she could find a cabin for Kurt Neumann as she had been instructed to do. Everything else was banished to the fires of never-never land, while she and Astrid buried themselves in each other's arms.

18

After the strenuous and sometimes reckless driving of the previous day, Elsa woke up at a late hour the following morning. Her first thought was the responsibility of running the office in place of Franz. She tried to expunge his memory from her mind, not from disregard, but from the need that, with the fortunes of war closing in adversely for her, she had to give all the attention and energy she could muster to her job. A serious crisis was looming.

She went to see the civil authorities about their usage of the advanced warning of the arrivals of the refugees. Her visit only added to her confusion. The military had taken over the administration of the growing problem.

When Elsa had awakened that morning, Astrid was nowhere to be seen. It was time to find her. She might be able to shed some light on what was happening.

Elsa went back to the *Hans Frayling*. She headed first into the bowels of the ship to see if Astrid was in their shared cabin. As she hurried on her mission, she bumped into her friend walking in the opposite direction.

'There you are, darling,' Astrid cried. 'I was hoping to meet you as soon as possible.'

'I was just on my way down to our cabin to see if you had returned.'

'You've been lucky. I'm on my way out again and won't be back before nightfall. Have you heard the news?'

'What news?' replied Elsa. 'I've had no time to hear any news. It was late when I arrived home last night, and I have drawn a blank this morning, when trying to contact the local authorities.'

'Come with me, Elsa. Let's go to the visitors' lounge. This is shocking and stupendous news. You ought to sit down when you hear it. I'll get you a cup of coffee.'

Elsa was taken aback by Astrid's manner. It was unlike her to be overcome with what seemed to be the painful information she was about to impart.

'She returned with two cups of ersatz, with the same haunting visage about her to match the conundrum that passed for coffee in the cups.'

'Now tell me,' Elsa demanded. 'All I can say is that it does not look like good news.'

'How right you are!' replied Astrid. 'The refugee numbers have swollen so much, the place is overwhelmed, as you must have seen in going into the town and then back to the port.'

'Then don't spare me any of the details.'

'The navy has taken over the evacuation responsibility,' Astrid began. 'Several large liners will be used. They will include the *Hans Frayling*. The training programme has been cancelled. The ship will sail westwards, on the last day but one of the month. Gangs have already set about stripping the barracks, mess rooms, lecture rooms, and everything else occupying space, to make room for the masses of refugees it will take on board. Engineers are busily preparing the ship for going to sea after its long sojourn at a waterside pier.'

'What will happen to you?' Elsa asked.

'Of course, as a member of the permanent crew, I shall be sailing in the ship when it leaves.'

'That is the worst bit of the news you have for me,' Elsa said. 'I seem to be fated. You slip through my grasp, time and time again.'

'I wonder what will happen to you, Elsa. Surely, the naval intelligence office will have to join in the exodus. Nothing will be able to withstand the Russian onslaught.'

As if by a cue from the theatre pit for an aberrant member of the cast who forgot her lines, a thunderous roar assailed their ears.

'What on earth is that?' Elsa spat out the question. 'It sounds like heavy gunfire. Have the Russians suddenly appeared on our doorstep, while we had no inkling they were anywhere near us yet?'

'No. That is gunfire unleashed nearby. I saw yesterday that the *Prinz Eugen* had come out of the shipyards. It could be its guns we heard firing, but I have no idea whether in anger or in practice.'

'It cannot be in anger,' Elsa said. 'Its guns have a huge range, but I cannot believe their range is that far to reach the Russians.'

Elsa was correct. The *Prinz Eugen* was not firing in anger but testing its newly bored guns before crossing the Bay of Danzig to attempt to delay, and perhaps to prevent, the nearest Russian spearhead investing the far side of the huge bay.

While the *Prinz Eugen* had been returning to Gotenhaven in the middle of October, three months before, the battle cruiser had inadvertently rammed the light cruiser *Leipzig* amidships, north of Hela, during heavy fog. Struck amidships, the *Leipzig* was nearly cut in half, the two ships remaining wedged together for the best part of a day.

The *Prinz Eugen* was taken to Gotenhaven, where repairs

remarkably were completed within a month, enabling sea trials to begin in the following month, November.

Towards the end of that month, the ship supported German troops on the Sworbe Peninsula by firing five hundred rounds of the ship's main eight-inch guns. *Prinz Eugen* then returned to Gotenhaven for resupply and to have the worn-out main gun barrels re-bored.

The ship was ready for action by mid-January for renewed action. Its survival, announced by the firing of its main armaments, was that which had suddenly aroused Astrid, Elsa, and the population of Gotenhaven.

The ship then sailed for a short distance, eastwards, to carry out a bombardment of soviet forces advancing in Samland. The ship fired nearly nine hundred rounds of ammunition at the enemy advancing on the German bridgehead at Cranz, designed to protect the city of Königsberg.

Later that day, Elsa was informed that her findings from her reconnoitre to assess the eastwards refugee situation, as they might impinge on Gotenhaven, had been overtaken and were already being incorporated in the frantic preparations being fulfilled to mount a huge evacuation from the port.

The next day she herself was turned into a refugee.

She was surprised and displeased to receive a message from the commander of the Women's Naval Service that all members of the service should be ready to abandon their current work. The entire contingent was to be evacuated. They should assemble at the quayside of the *Hans Frayling* in a few days' time, on the twenty-ninth of the month.

Elsa informed Astrid of the instruction.

'All military personnel are being moved out. You are not

exceptional,' she replied.

'I'm lucky, I already have a berth on the ship,' Elsa said.

'Don't count your luck yet. It isn't known how many people the ship will take on board. It's bound to be a vast number.'

'You mean something in excess of our Strength through Joy trip we made together?' Elsa queried.

'I really do mean that. How many times that modest number will be exceeded is anyone's guess.'

'With several large liners, it should be possible to take all the refugees and those local inhabitants who want to leave.'

Their combined assessment of the potential dimensions of the evacuation, were soon thrown into disarray by the hordes of people who poured into the port area during the next two days. The message had evidently travelled far and wide among the refugees on the roads that liners were being prepared to carry everyone to safety.

'Are you scared about what is happening?' Elsa asked Astrid. She had sensed a novel disturbance in her friend.

'Yes and no,' Astrid answered. 'I shall be overwhelmed in my job if the potential of what I can see, actually materialises. People are so desperate to get away from the Russians. We might run out of controlling the passengers if too many embark.'

'I can see that it will not be easy for the crew to do their customary jobs. The captain will face a mountain of problems if we are forced to crowd the ship too much,' Elsa said, with understanding.

'I am very uneasy about it. The captain has remained in nominal command of the ship, but the navy has made all the important decisions. Now the word is that a navy captain will take the ship out to sea, in effect overruling the long-standing captain.'

'That sounds like a recipe for trouble,' Elsa commented. 'How can he know the characteristics of the ship, its propensities and idiosyncrasies, especially if the ship is overloaded?'

'That is exactly my question,' Astrid agreed. 'The navy man might be overbearing and presumptuous. I know our captain well enough to recognise a possible road of conflict may be in the making.

'It will be made doubly difficult by the fact that a sizeable proportion of the people on board will be naval, amid the mass of local citizens. Our captain will claim to be responsible for the ordinary people. The navy man will feel the same for the naval personnel and also claim precedence in view of the crisis in wartime.'

The next day Elsa rose early.

All gangways were heavily guarded by armed navy police.

She walked down one of the gangways to the quayside and had to elbow her way through the throngs of people standing, sitting, talking, or silent, with children running around everywhere. Most people had retained at least some of their chattels. She ran into another member of her contingent of the Women's Naval Service.

'Hello there, Frieda,' Elsa called to her.

Frieda turned with a smile on her face, fresh, and anything but careworn.

'It's good to see you again Elsa. I see you have been promoted. Congratulations. What on earth do you make of all this? It's a mad world we are in. Are they really going to take all these people on board that ship?'

'I don't know about that, but we are all supposed to be going aboard, either tomorrow or the next day,' Elsa said.

She had lost her grip on what was taking place. The sudden swelling of the refugee influx and being deprived of her job as replacement for Franz had thrown her into a vacuum of bewilderment.

'The day after tomorrow,' Frieda confirmed. 'I hope they leave some room for us. The odd double suite would be quite nice for the two of us, would it not?'

'I think it will be safest to add in another twenty people,' Elsa jibbed. 'Perhaps even more.'

While she surveyed the scene, including the human element in it—people pregnant with fear, expectation, and hope—she saw a column of naval personnel approaching.

Their determined marching step carved a way through the scattered men, women, and children on the quayside.

They marched to a particular gangway of the ship and were brought to a halt by a chief petty officer, whose voice was more than adequate to command attention on the barrack square but could hardly be heard by the men under his command on the overcrowded quayside. Most men heard it and obeyed the order, but some, perhaps lost in thought, or half asleep, tried to make a further step onwards only to collide with the men in front of them.

The arrival of the navy men turned out to be only the first of four columns of sailors that arrived during the next hour.

The two women on the quayside watched with everyone else as the men filed up the gangway, envious of their priority embarkation.

'They are men involved in training for the submarine

service,' Elsa said.

'I suppose they have to escape to fight another day,' Frieda added, when the last column had gone aboard.

'How many navy men who came in first before them do you reckon there were altogether?' Elsa asked, hoping to add up the numbers.

'In total it must run to hundreds. Who did you think they were to deserve such priority treatment?' Frieda asked. 'Many of them seemed so young.'

'Oh, there is no doubt about it,' Elsa answered. 'They are new recruits to the submarine service. They are going to have a prior place on board. Altogether the navy has embarked all their submariners in various stages of training. There must have been a thousand of them. It seems it is intended to carry on training them elsewhere.'

'Do you think it is still worth it? The war is getting closer.' Frieda threw caution to the winds in framing such a question.

'I have to say, of course, it is worth it. It would be treason to say otherwise,' Elsa made the politically correct reply. But in her heart, she could have repeated the hopelessness of the situation.

The air was disturbed by the sound of bells. For the next forty minutes, they watched while a succession of ambulances arrived, carrying soldiers wounded from the Russian front, who had been moved back behind the lines, which themselves had in a flash become unsafe. There were eighty or more stretcher cases. Trucks followed behind them loaded with wounded but walking soldiers.

Frieda considered herself a good judge of estimating numbers.

'I reckon we are seeing nearly two hundred soldiers

loaded on the ship, while we have been standing here.'

'There is also the ship's crew of nearly two hundred, as well,' Elsa added.

At that moment, the entire concourse of people on the quayside of the *Hans Frayling*—and, as far as one could see on the surrounding quaysides—was suddenly startled to hear the air raid sirens. Even before they had finished their mournful howl, the sound of low flying aircraft could be heard, terrifying those on the ground.

Some people began the fruitless act of trying to leave the quayside, while others sought to find cover. But candidly, their efforts were worse than useless. There was nowhere to go other than to more open spaces at a distance and crowds of people.

Two aircraft made a pass before turning.

'They look like fighter aircraft protecting the port,' Frieda said.

'Let's step inside here,' Elsa said to Frieda, 'just in case they are not ours. Be quick. You have only seconds.'

Forming a grandstand view of the quayside and the loading of the ship, Elsa and Frieda secured a position with their backs to the huge dockside shed.

The building completely lacked the properties of an air raid shelter, but that deficiency depended on the type of armaments the attacking aircraft used, as to whether it offered any protection at all.

The vast majority of people, mostly refugees from other parts, had nowhere to go. They were so confused by the diversion.

But the cry of 'Down, down, on the ground' radiated like wild fire among the throng. With a huge rippling effect, hundreds of people copied those with the presence of mind to do the only defence they had left to them. They dropped prostrate on the spot where they had been standing.

Someone nearby shouted out. 'They are Bell American fighters.'

Another protested. 'They can't be. It's too far for them to fly this far east.'

Others asserted, 'They are soviets.'

Someone actually said, 'I saw the Russian markings on them as they went past. But we shall soon know because here they come again.'

The two aircraft flew the length of the quayside. Everybody waited with bated breath for the inevitable sounds of machine gun and cannon fire.

It was all over in seconds. The panic had been unnecessary. They did not deliver the death warrant that everyone expected. The planes flew on and away.

'Well, that was a disaster that never was,' Frieda exclaimed.

'I wonder if that was a reconnaissance mission, just to see what was happening in the port and what was likely to happen,' Elsa contemplated. 'Let's hope the communications between their different services are as chaotic as ours locally are becoming.'

The one unforeseen outcome of the dummy visit of the Russian aircraft was the effect on the people who had feared their lives were at risk. People had been waiting patiently for orders they expected would be honourably delivered to them to be able to board the ship and be saved.

The scare of the soviet visit changed them from being passive to being aggressive. They gathered round the gangways demanding a place on the ship. The guards were hard pressed to prevent them forcing their way up the gangways.

With another day to go, the combined pressure on the authorities and security staff grew to unbearable proportions.

A group of specialist dockyard engineers arrived next, followed by another select but small body of rocket engineers from the Baltic secret ranges, who had assembled the day before, joined by Kurt Neumann.

Within the same day, the commandant of the Women's Naval Service contingent, who had circulated all her members to report to the quayside, chose to embark a day earlier than planned. They feared that the reserved accommodation for them would be seized and overwhelmed by the thousands who were milling around and expecting to secure a passage to freedom.

Astrid had been exempted from the commandant's injunction to discontinue her job and await the order to embark. She was already part of the ship and intended to retain it. She realised that her powers of management of the accommodation were withering by the hour.

She foresaw that by the time the ship sailed all rhyme and reason would be out of the window. There really was a chance that control of the outcomes would be lost.

Elsa and Frieda simply stayed put, awaiting the arrival of the other members, numbering well over three hundred. They gathered in dribs and drabs until the full complement of the Women's Navy Service personnel had been reached. Astrid turned up to lead them aboard, apologising for their unappetising accommodation in a former navy barrack room in the bowels of the ship.

'This is not the gift of the gods, but it is the best I can do. You will have a certain amount of privacy here but, believe me, soon we are going to be overwhelmed by the mass of refugees who are anticipating coming aboard.

'It's a question of having a comfortable ride, seated in an overcrowded bus, as opposed to travelling standing up with everyone else in an equally crowded cattle truck.'

Astrid and Elsa managed to extricate themselves from the concourse of women to flee to Astrid's cabin.

Astrid was fatigued by attending to her various responsibilities of the day.

Elsa, released from her secondment, had become preoccupied with the prospect of sailing on the ship and the unknown outcome it would entail.

19

The morrow, the day before the *Hans Frayling* was scheduled to sail, brought nothing less than utter chaos, and nothing less than the despair of those who had to witness it, trying to mitigate and regulate it into a controllable enterprise.

When the word was spread that the ship was about to leave the port, half the population of the refugee exodus in the area converged onto the quayside.

Astrid and other staff had been working all through the night to document the names of all the service personnel already aboard.

As daylight came, adults with children were added to the passenger list. The somewhat leisurely way that this process took, led to a growing resentment in the hundreds of people milling around and waiting to secure a place.

By the afternoon patience had been exhausted. It may have been the case that some men or women, with a radical determination and a keen eye for opportunity, had sized up a way to break through the guards on the gangways. They certainly could have assumed that the guards would not shoot their own kith and kin from around the region.

But to force the issue was the undoing of the crowd's conduct that day. At last, those attempting to control the embarkation were compelled to stand aside while the patient, but desperate civilians seized the chance to take to the sea.

By nightfall, an unimaginable number of passengers had

forced themselves onto the ship. During the night that number was stretched into the realm of the bizarre. Cabins, corridors, alleyways, and all the larger rooms for both private and public use were full of people. People actually joined the spaces reserved for the various groups of service personnel.

When it became obvious that the ship was bloated chaotically with men, women, and children, even more people clamoured to join them.

It was impossible for members of the crew to make a passage from one point to another to regulate the influx. The flood tide of passengers in the corridors and companionways forbade the crew's access, making attempted journeys from one part of the ship to another in the normal way impossible to achieve.

Inevitably, people were hurt but they could not be taken to the ship's medical centre. It, too, was full, overwhelming the staff and preventing them from conducting their usual services.

The injured had to be comforted and, where necessary, treated on the same spot where their injury occurred by anyone with the slightest medical knowledge.

Cases of maternal instinct and self-sacrifice were witnessed among the people on the quayside unable to join the passengers on the overcrowded liner. The point of final frantic panic had been reached. It drove some people out of their minds and into the realm of unreality.

When, eventually, the gangways were closed and disconnected, distraught mothers threw babies from their arms to the outstretched hands of sympathetic people on board.

More than one infant was lost between ship and shore, drowned before they could be rescued: another was crushed by the gentle but inexorable movements of the ship against the quayside wall.

One of the more creative mothers found rope long enough to throw one end of it suitably weighted to those waiting with helpful hands, on board. Tying her infant to the other end, she lowered the child down towards the water as far as she could reach, while the man holding the other end tried to save the screaming baby from hitting the water. He successfully hauled the infant up to the warm embrace of a stranger with welcoming, unknown, but safe arms.

With the entire ship loaded and no longer reachable from the shore, the *Hans Frayling* was eased away from the quayside by releasing its remaining retaining ropes. It left Gotenhaven in the afternoon on the last day but one of January in the last year of the war.

It left on the quayside a small knot of mothers, shocked and grief-stricken by their last-minute attempts to give their infants a future life, even as an orphan, by depositing them one way or another on the departing liner.

The only solace left to them was the shared fear and desperation of the residual masses of refugees, still waiting forlornly for another ship to remove them from the impending savagery of the invading armies.

The *Hans Frayling* set a course, westwards, escorted only by a small navy auxiliary ship. On board, the long-standing captain was at odds with the assumptions of the navy captain, who had been put in charge to take the ship to safety.

They were soon in dispute about the course the ship should take in its perilous passage.

The navy captain argued that a course as close to the coast as possible would be the best prevention of attacks from

Russian submarines.

The resident captain thought the best course would be well out to sea, where the chances of meeting an enemy submarine were reduced by the massive expanse of the waters of the Baltic.

Captain Hofmann, the navy captain, put his case succinctly.

'My knowledge of this coast will put an enemy submarine at a disadvantage. We should sail without lights.

'The Russians are not noted for using impeccably accurate sea maps. If we sail close to the coast, enemy submarines will be so preoccupied with avoiding one underwater rock deposit after another, that their attacks would be ineffective.

'They will find it too forbidding and retire. Being on the coast also gives us the benefit of any coastal guns and Luftwaffe patrols.'

Captain Richter's counter argument stated that the challenge of the hazards would be enough to tempt a submarine captain to be a hero.

'The open sea is the best deterrent. You might be unlucky, but the chances are that the statistical odds of avoiding an enemy are better at sea where the ship can be zig-zagged.

'On the coast you have to follow a predictable course, which could be an easy target for a submarine captain.

'Above all, we could run into mines shed by Russian submarines or surface ships. We know that a mine-free passage in the open sea exists, and we should follow it.'

In the event, against the powerful arguments for keeping near the coast, the ship took a deep-sea course, westwards, using the remaining daylight hours to make good progress.

The outward appearance of the liner gave no indication of

the ships inside condition, and the suffering that was soon overtaking everyone on board.

Astrid and Elsa took stock of the scene. It was impossible to transit the ship end to end to make an assessment of the picture.

They could only infer from their immediate surround what the successive conditions yard by yard throughout the ship would constitute. Astrid mentioned some of the first factors that occurred to her.

'To start with, how can anybody move far enough to visit the toilets? The state of the toilets must be unimaginable. I can see that there are bound to be accidents—by chance or deliberate, by choice—when people want to urinate or defecate.

'We shall be at sea at least until tomorrow morning, so the prospects are nothing short of unmentionable chaos. The only mitigating thing is that there is no food or drink, except that which people have brought aboard on their person.'

'If anybody needs medical attention, nothing can be done,' Elsa added, remembering her previous observation on the quayside.

'Can you just imagine it,' Astrid continued. 'We took in around two thousand official passengers at first. That itself was in excess of the total passenger list the liner was originally designed to carry.

'Then we were overwhelmed. At a guess there must be ten thousand people on board altogether, five times the normal capacity of the ship, when all its facilities and services are working properly—catering, sleeping, and medical.'

'Your graphic summary has triggered an idea in my mind,' Elsa broke Astrid's train of thought.

'Just supposing, but it's only a distant possibility I know, that we were torpedoed. The hole in the ship caused by the explosion would drown any number you could mention. It would scarcely permit people to fight their way out.

'The hundreds in the bulk of the ship would be unable to move far enough and perhaps quickly enough to save themselves from becoming confined in a coffin that would take them to the bottom.'

'I am one step ahead of you, now,' Astrid interrupted. 'We ought to reserve a spot that would give us a good chance of survival in that event.'

'Quite so,' Elsa commented. 'If the ship remained upright, the main deck would be a good place to be. Even if the ship turned turtle, it would still be the best location for saving yourself.'

Astrid shuddered. 'It doesn't bear thinking about. Fortunately, it should only take twenty-four hours to reach Kiel. The closer we get to it, the more protection there will be.'

As darkness fell, the anxiety of the passengers rose. No internal lights on board were permitted. In the crowded cabins and corridors, it was impossible for people to recognise their neighbours. A familiar face alongside a passenger one minute, could be replaced by a stranger in the next.

Total darkness was not without its local risks, as Elsa pointed out to Astrid.

'This is now a golden opportunity for light-fingered and unscrupulous individuals to take advantage of the utter confusion, or perhaps just to amuse themselves. I'll bet a few wallets will disappear on this voyage.'

'Let's hope no erstwhile baby snatchers have come aboard,' Astrid quipped, 'but they couldn't get very far, what with the congestion and the yells of the infant.'

Astrid made a journey to the bridge. She found the First Officer and reported.

'I can say that as far as I have been able to ascertain, the passengers everywhere are herded in like cattle in a wagon on their way to market. They are not happy but glad to pay the price of acute inconvenience—and in some cases suffering—to escape to safety.

'But that is only after a part of the journey has been completed. By the time of arrival, we shall be confronted with medical cases, perhaps heart attacks, and other symptoms of the extreme conditions.'

'Thank you, Astrid. We are stuck with an imponderable problem. We have to hope for the best, which will be fulfilled if we get through unscathed, whatever chaos occurs on the ship.'

Elsa and Astrid pushed and struggled their way to the nearest deck on the port side, which happened to be the lifeboat deck. They were bent on finding a spot offering the best chance of finding a jumping pad into the sea.

'We have our lifejackets on,' Astrid said. 'I notice that about half the people who were wearing them have discarded them, some of which have been snatched up by others.

'It must be awful to be crammed into the cabins and passageways with lifejackets on. Just think, the protrusion of lifejackets must delete about ten per cent of the standing space on the floor.

'Did you know that the majority of those who stormed the ship before leaving port never received a lifejacket, simply because the supply had long since given out?'

'Yes, I noticed that. It was an inevitable outcome, given

the numbers. This is a good place to be,' Elsa declared. 'Very few are camping out on or near the lifeboats. This one is furthest from the bows in case we hit a mine.'

The two women tried to accommodate themselves among the lifeboat rigging.

'We shall never survive hitched up here,' said Astrid. 'It's so cold. The waters of the Baltic are usually five degrees in winter, but at the moment they are not far off freezing. Anyone who drops into that water will soon die if not rescued within a few minutes.'

Elsa ruminated on the gloomy prospect painted by her friend.

She added her own frightful prognostication to cheer Astrid up and to vent her own fears.

'It would be just our fate if a torpedo struck the ship on the side at the point just where we are standing. We would know nothing about it. If it was near but far enough away not to kill us, we could be thrown into the water. There have been many survivals of people that way. We could be lucky.'

The many people on the main and four other decks had opted to use the only space on board to secure their passage.

They were wearing every stitch of clothing they possessed to withstand the freezing cold and were not short of huddling together like a flock of starlings at night sharing their warmth with each other in a tree.

After an hour at their new post, Astrid was itching to go below, lured by her call of duty in spite of the impossibility of being able to discharge it.

'You need to forget it, darling,' Elsa said gently to her. 'There is literally nothing you can do. The captains and senior officers are ensconced on the bridge, glad to have the immunisation of that sacred place to themselves, away from the madding crowd and remaining protected from interference by armed guards.'

'It's hard for me to sign off on my own ship,' Astrid replied, close to tears. 'Excuse me, darling. You have never seen me cry.'

'It's the bitter weather,' Elsa hugged her. 'It's shrivelling all of us into something less than our normal selves.'

'Perhaps I could go to get the latest information about our prospects,' Astrid said, struggling to come to terms with the hopeless paradox of her position on board.

'I will come part of the way with you to get some shelter from the cold. But this is where I shall now be and where I hope to stay,' Elsa said. 'It's our choice of the chance of survival. It's the last lifeboat from the bows on the port side. Don't forget. If anything, untoward happens, come back here.'

Astrid came back within a few minutes.

'Darling, some good news. We have had a message from a mysterious source to say that a group of minesweepers is sailing against us in an easterly direction to ensure that a broad channel is free from mines, hopefully all the way to Kiel.

'The captains are delighted with the news and have decided to light up the ship with its identification signals and to turn on limited on-board lighting throughout the ship.'

'That will be advertising ourselves to the ocean,' Elsa protested. 'You say the message had a mysterious source. Suppose the Russians have cooked up the story to prevent the evacuation. I bet their submarines are waiting for their prey.'

Elsa suddenly regretted there had been no time to vet the refugees in Gotenhaven for opportunistic spies who could communicate the departure of ships westwards.

'Well, we shall soon see,' Astrid said. 'This could save us a lot of trouble on board.'

It could run us into disaster as well, Elsa thought, but did not voice it.

Nightfall had come early in mid-winter. By eight o'clock the ship had defied the darkness of the night and enemy advances for about four hours.

Those on board in the know, were all looking westwards for the expected minesweeping ships of the Kriegsmarine that had been notified but not confirmed.

With the encouraging news delivered to Elsa, Astrid turned on her heels and went to enquire if the medical quarters could use the lighting to establish some kind of service for the expected sick and injured people among the passengers.

They would have to be rescued from the dense throngs occupying the ship in all the obvious and unexpected places.

About an hour later, when Elsa had forlornly retrieved her shared slot in the rigging of the eleventh lifeboat, waiting for Astrid to return, the still of the night, the rhythmic throb of the ship's engines, and her private thoughts were obliterated.

An explosion a long way forward near the bows of the liner was felt and heard.

With the passing of only a few seconds, a second explosion of equal force, registered itself in the same general area, but a little closer than the first.

Elsa had no time to react, to ask herself what she had heard, when a third occurred amidships, not far from her station where she had been patiently waiting for Astrid.

Simultaneously with the third explosion, which she hardly heard or saw, she sensed that she was flying through the air, half conscious and mentally stunned by the force and nearness of it. A wild thought shot momentarily through her head.

This could completely change my view of life.

In the crazy world she had been ushered into, she felt she had to justify such an unreasonable thought. Her answer surprisingly had a strain of logic accumulating in her brain, realising she was going to die.

That can only be torpedo hits. One hit on a liner of the Hans Frayling's size might be survivable, but three were bound to spell disaster. All three had hit the port side and were patently fired from between the ship and the German coast. It was goodbye to everyone and everything.

The seconds occupied by her unwelcome and repugnant flight through the air of a freezing night seemed to last for an interminable time.

She had been caught in the violent upward draught of the explosion. *Am I concussed?* was a thought passing through her mind. *Am I about to die?* followed immediately.

At the last moment, her presence of mind returned to tell her she was about to be enveloped in the ice-forming waters of the Baltic Sea.

Nothing was alight, she noted. How could that be? None of the three torpedoes had started a fire on board the ship. The night was adamantly dark, but not as dark as those deep waters into which she crashed.

The sudden, icy-cold ocean dragged her downwards. She was momentarily glad to have dressed in skin-tight thermal underwear encased in watertight material.

She had secured that protective underwear from the members of the diving team attached to the naval intelligence in Gotenhaven when she wanted something to withstand her chilly expedition to Breslau.

It did not save her from the shock of the cold water, but it mitigated its effects for long enough for her to swim to the surface and collect her wits.

The shock of the explosion, her high dive, and the frightful impact of the collision of her body with the water, had put her brain into automatic self-preservation, but she was practically unconscious.

Her body was carried away from the scene by the natural movement of the ocean and the movement of the ship. With returning consciousness, her eyes became accustomed to the night. She saw wreckage around her and people calling, some screaming.

With the explosions of the torpedoes a thing of the past, everything was about to be buried in the ocean. At that moment, the current scene was otherwise incredibly quiet.

The ship was engulfed in total blackness. The only sound she discerned was human.

Elsa was floating buoyantly in her lifejacket, wondering what to do next. She could feel the cold penetrating her body and knew she would have little time left to live if she could not escape immediately from the excruciating waters.

Like the best of choreographies, she cried out in exultation on seeing at a distance, but close enough to make a guess at their recognition, some little ships approaching.

They were the minesweeping flotilla Astrid had told her was on the way towards the fleeing ship. They had already reached the sinking liner. Accepting they had encountered a monumental disaster, they were scattering around the crippled *Hans Frayling*.

Elsa could see the liner was beginning to list to port and was already slightly down by the bows. *If Astrid is able to make her way back to our jumping point, she will find me and the lifeboat missing*, was the muddled thought that passed through Elsa's brain.

'Astrid,' she shouted, 'Astrid, Astrid.'

She knew it was useless to waste the use of her lungs, but it eased her acute feelings of guilt. She suddenly felt she needed to assuage the fact that she was in the water and her best friend was still on the ship that looked as if it was sinking.

Elsa was swimming in spite of her lifejacket towards the approaching little ships. The one nearest to her switched a shielded light onto the water and sprayed it around. It stopped when it found a body. She saw crewmen hauling it onto their vessel, but the body never moved to help them.

It was dead.

Elsa shouted at the top of her voice, exerting her last few reserves of energy as the small vessel drew near.

She actually heard one of the men call out. 'There's another, over there, look, it's moving.'

She prayed he meant her. She raised her voice for a last call for help. She could see that the vessel was small. It had no lifeboat or auxiliary boat on board. The little ship itself had to move towards her.

Eager hands grasped her with the energy of strong seafaring men. They hauled her on board with a final welcome surge of effort. Her salvation was complete.

'My God, it's a woman, and she's survived,' one man cried.

'But she's frozen to the marrow,' his mate added frantically. 'You can see. Look at her lips. They are blue. She is practically unconscious. Get her below and strip her clothing.'

They tore off her sodden outer clothing and found her uniform underneath. 'She's an officer in the Women's Naval Service. I wonder how many more there are on the ship?' said another crewmember, who added himself to the rescue process.

He dried her with a warm towel, putting some of his own clothes on her, and a tot of brandy down between her lips, straight from the bottle that he himself had been drinking from as a defence against the intense coldness of the night.

Elsa soon stirred from her trauma and found she could still speak. 'Where am I?' was the first words she said. 'And who are you?'

'You are safe now. You are on *Torpedofangboot TF21*, torpedo recovery boat, of the Kriegsmarine. We were helping with the minesweeper operation and coming your way. Just in time for you, ma'am. I am Obermechaniker, chief petty officer. My name is Peter Voigt. I am in charge of the engines. We are happy to have saved you.'

'Thanks, would not nearly be enough, Obermechaniker, but what are the chances for the thousands on board the liner?'

'There is no knowing at the moment. As far as we are concerned, we have to keep looking for survivors like you.

'We were the first ship to arrive so we shall press on searching where the torpedoes evidently have struck, to pick up any passengers evicted by the blast as you were.'

'I am truly stuck with you,' Elsa declared. 'But I shall be able to help in any way I can. You must have had a challenging time rehabilitating a drowning woman rescued from the deep.'

They both managed a restrained laugh at her implications.

'Would it be any different if a woman did the same for an otherwise dying man?' he asked.

'No, of course not. I shall be able to take over down here if you find any more survivors.'

'Thanks, and let's hope we do.'

'You are in charge of the engines,' Elsa stated, rather than asked. 'How many men do you carry?'

'Normally ten, but we have had to do with only eight lately,' he said. 'It has meant I have only two engineers to share the watches round the clock, as necessary.'

Just at that moment, someone was shouting out on the deck outside, distracting the obermechaniker. He went to answer the call, muttering, 'I hope the captain is not having trouble with our engines.'

He came back almost immediately.

'We have found an engineer from the ship. The third torpedo hit amidships. It must have been the one that threw you into the ocean. It's unusual for engineers to escape from torpedo attacks. They are almost always the earliest victims.'

Four crewmen dragged and carried a drenched man into the crew room of the *TF21*. He was young and conscious.

Elsa established her opportunistic authority.

'Leave him to me. Get back for the others,' she ordered.

Turning to the man she asked him, 'What is your name?'

'Michael Fischer, engineer, and what is yours?'

'I'm Elsa Bauer, Women's Naval Service. I was on the ship and had a lucky escape as you have had.'

She gave the rescued man the same treatment that had been given to her. She kept a record of his name and job on the ship. He had been sucked out in a torrent of water, dazed by the explosion but miraculously not impaired by it.

He soon gave her the bad news. The third torpedo had destroyed the engine room and all heating and lighting facilities throughout the ship. Of course, he had not seen the outcomes of that disastrous blow to the ship, but together they inferred the terrible effects it must be having.

Elsa exclaimed the horrifying possibilities.

'Those in the crowded cabins and companionways will have no means of direction. Any blockages holding up the progress of escape will defy successful clearance. Children and elderly people will be trampled underneath other people falling over them. The rampant cold of the icy ocean will gradually permeate the ship, freezing people to death before it drowns them.'

'I fear the majority of the passengers and crew will perish. Only those like you and me who had no part in what happened to us will survive,' the crewman said. 'Heaven help the crew in the bows which is already under the water. The automatic doors will have closed locking them in.'

Neither had more time to contemplate the potentially catastrophic results in the ship that was still sitting on the water, dimly visible, if majestic in size, only a short distance from them.

Another cry from above heralded the sighting of another person in the water. The *TF21* was expertly steered to the latest discovery. The survivor was clinging to wooden wreckage and evidently still alive but seemingly not moving.

Whoever it was paid no part in helping the rescuers to deny the deep to another victim. Two men were leaning off their own vessel and trying to grasp the person's clothing. The exuberance of one of them was his undoing.

He slipped and plunged into the freezing waters, drifting a few metres away from the passenger he was anxious to save. Making the most of his mishap, he bravely struck out towards the stricken person.

When only an arm's length away, the body he was trying to salvage slipped off the floating wooden supports. He had to go under water for a short depth to prevent the person drowning.

The *TF21* came alongside him for four crewmen to pull both bodies out of the water. Their journey to the crew room on the ship was the shortest possible. They were given the utmost, generous treatment. The crewman was stripped of his clothes instantly. The passenger was covered in oil but identified as a woman. Elsa declared that the latest survivor was a member of the Women's Naval Services and was unconscious.

The one member of the *TF21*'s crew delegated for such medical services as could be afforded for such a small ship, together with Elsa, who had incorporated first aid in her training, worked to rid the woman of the water she had swallowed, to bring her back to consciousness, and to remove the oily mess from her body.

It took an hour's hard labour to achieve only a modicum of success. Elsa was determined they would not fail. For a further hour they laboured on.

The *TF21* was not privileged to rescue any more survivors. But six other and larger vessels in the minesweeping flotilla were engaged frantically in trying to mitigate an appalling disaster.

Taking a break from the care of her service colleague, Elsa went to the bridge to meet the captain, a young leutnant.

'I can't say I'm glad to meet you,' was his first words to her. 'But I'm glad you are safe.'

'Thanks to you and your crew,' she responded. 'We are

witnessing what must be one of the worst tragedies ever on the high seas. What has been happening up here while we have been so preoccupied down below?'

'The *Hans Frayling* took nearly an hour to sink. At first its battered bows drew in the water to cause its stern to rise and the ship to list to port. The total damage from three torpedo hits on the port side exacerbated the inclination of the ship to fall into an almost full port broadside posture flat on the ocean.'

'Talk about a prison ship,' Elsa commented. 'They had no chance.'

'It is something one has to close one's mind to,' he said. 'When the ship was almost lying flat on its port side, we could see that most of the lifeboats on the starboard side were smashed on the side of the ship when they tried to launch them.'

'Was it not possible to launch any of them?'

'Possibly one or two. I am getting the count on my radio from the larger ships which carried on searching, so I will be able to give you the score before long.'

'You have managed to save three survivors,' Elsa said.

'How is that woman doing now?' he asked.

'I think she is going to make it,' Elsa replied. 'I think she will not be able to tell us much, but it depends on how she managed to escape.'

'It looks as if the first torpedo hit the liner's crew quarters in the extreme bow. The second was a direct hit on the accommodation of hundreds of women of your own unit.

'So, we have to hope for the best. The third put the engines and lighting out of action. It could not have been a worse place to hit.'

'I must get back down below,' Elsa said, soberly.

She had felt a pang of grief. She dared not be concerned about Astrid. 'I will see you later.'

And then, as she turned to go down below, for the first time she remembered that Kurt Neumann, the engineer, whom she had struggled to fetch and safeguard only a few days before, had embarked on the liner with other colleagues from Peenemünde. He, too, would have been lost.

So much for the economy of warfare. My own life was at risk. Franz and the local army oberleutnant lost their lives and then all the people on board the Junkers 52 died in saving him, she thought to herself. *And the Russian soldiers I had to kill should be added in. It makes no sense. But then, in war, sense is a foreign body and becomes irrelevant.*

20

On returning to the crew cabin, she was heartened to see that her sister member of the Women's Naval Services had recovered consciousness. Elsa rushed to her side, laying a hand on her head with tender strokes.

'You are safe. What is your name?'

'Gina Lange,' she whispered. 'Whatever happened to me?'

'Our ship was torpedoed. You and I are survivors. Do not worry about it. When you have pulled yourself together, we can talk,' Elsa gently said to her. 'We are safe on a naval ship going to Kiel.'

Obermechaniker Peter Voigt came in to join them. 'Is she recovered yet?' he asked.

'She is talking a bit. I think in another hour, with some food and a drop more brandy, she will be able to talk to us with some sense.'

Gina Lange had been in the water for no more than ten minutes. The shock and cold water had worked their detrimental effects on her, but she was young and had the benefit of military training. It might have killed an elderly person, but she sported the advantages of being in the prime of life.

It could have been the tested clothing that Elsa had worn that enabled her to recover so quickly from her own plunge into the sea. But Gina had nothing comparable to protect her.

In addition, she had been washed in oil.

As soon as Gina was able to talk coherently, she and Elsa exchanged identities. It soon became clear why she had been so comparatively worse off than Elsa.

'You were thrown into the air!' Gina repeated what Elsa had told her about her short but dangerous journey from the lifeboat perch to the crew cabin of the *TF21*.

'My lot was to be gouged out by a torrent of water and spewed into the ocean. It was terribly cold. I never thought I could have survived it. I was sitting on the floor in the very corner of the former swimming pool, which had been allocated to the entire detachment.

'The explosion happened at the opposite end of the pool, and of course lower down. It had been drained and given over to the women for their living quarters. It was, as you can imagine, excessively crowded.

'Many women had to occupy the spectator areas around the pool, joined by the last-minute passengers who crowded into any space they found.

'Momentarily, I saw the tiles of the pool being violently detached and given flight. I saw nothing further.

'There were over four hundred people down there, being bombarded by flying tiles and in the direct line of the explosion, which came from below.

'I knew nothing more apart from that split second glimpse. The side of the ship was evidently destroyed, and a torrent of water must have sucked me out and away from the ship. The rest you know about.'

Elsa listened in awe to her story, as she tried to tell the rest that happened to her.

'What an unimaginable disaster!' Elsa said. 'It means that

many women were injured, perhaps killed, by the explosion and its effects. They would have had no chance to save themselves anyway.

'We shall know what their fate happened to be as soon as we know the extent of the operation achieved by the rescue bid. We are three survivors on this ship.

'The first to be picked up was a member of the crew, but he was dead. I saw his rescue. Then they saw me and picked me up.

'The next survivor is a crewman. He is an engineer who, like you, was washed out by a freak wave from the explosion of the third torpedo that hit the engines and generators, which put paid to the ship's lighting systems. It put a fatal handicap on those on the ship who might have been able to join those outside on the five decks, who jumped overboard.'

Peter Voigt listened in silence.

Elsa asked him if the rescue had been terminated.

'Not quite yet. The ship has gone down for an hour now. I think one of the navy ships will remain in case anyone is still able to break free and come to the surface.'

'How many ships were here in the minesweeping flotilla?' Elsa queried.

'Seven navy ships altogether—three minesweepers, two torpedo boats, a patrol boat, and ourselves, as a torpedo recovery boat. We were joined by a freighter and a steamer on the way, making nine rescue ships in all.'

'Do we have any idea what the number of survivors is?' Elsa asked.

'Not yet. But don't put your hopes up too high. It's bound to be a disappointing figure in the end. The commander of the flotilla is computing the numbers at the moment. They will radio the details to all the ships that have contributed to the rescue.'

'We are also waiting for orders. We were on the way to meeting you, to complete a mine-free passage to Kiel. We don't know yet if we are expected to continue eastwards to Gotenhaven to help other ships to escape or whether we have to return to base.'

'The fortuitous rescue of the survivors will make a difference to your orders, I suppose. None will want to return to Gotenhaven,' Elsa suggested.

'True enough. We will know soon,' he said. 'How is Gina looking, now?' He walked over to her. 'Do you feel fit enough to transfer ships if you have to?'

'I think so,' she replied, 'but not by sea.'

Gina's quip after her ordeal was a welcome sign that she was feeling a lot stronger. Seeing her progress with pleasure, added to the implicit humour of her remark, made all three force a quiet laugh for the first time.

It was a sign of impending hope and acceptance of the horrors of war that could ensnare so many at one time and yet deliver others, though only a few, to live another day.

The radio-man poked his head around the corner of the cabin.

'The captain says I should give you this message. Just decoded, sir,' he said.

Obermechaniker Peter Voigt took the sheet of paper from his outstretched hand and read it silently.

This is from the commodore to all captains in the flotilla for the information of their crews. The Hans Frayling has settled in the deep. May God take care of the souls who have perished with the ship. The seven ships of our flotilla, together with the freighter and steamer that joined us in the hour of dire need, have between them saved just under a thousand people.

I pay tribute to the staunch efforts made by all captains and their crews who have made this rescue an extraordinarily successful outcome. The fact that the figure represents only ten percent of the passengers and crew believed to be on board the Hans Frayling, should not detract from the laborious efforts made at risk to save as many people who escaped from the ship, or who had been removed unwittingly from it by the forces of nature.

The captain of the freighter, Captain Klaus Engelhard, and of the steamer, Captain Günter Trautmann, the ships both steaming eastwards, have agreed to reverse their passage.

They will take on board the entire body of survivors between them for delivery at Kiel. This will enable the flotilla's seven ships to complete its mission to make a mine-free passage to Gotenhaven for the aid of other ships taking part in the evacuation from there.

Apologies to all survivors, but this operation has to be done. Under my command, the seven naval ships will transfer their passengers to either the freighter or the steamer. The majority of the survivors have already been taken by navy auxiliary and long boats to these two ships during the rescue operation. It remains to transfer the rest of the survivors, forty-five people to the freighter, and fifty-six to the steamer. This will be accomplished by long boat to both ships.

We all hope that this will be accomplished without mishap. God be with you all.

He read it again for the benefit of the three survivors, not expecting any notable reactions from any of them.

Elsa spoke first. 'I have a gut feeling that I have lost my best friend. She was a member of the crew. She left our jumping off point trying to pursue her duty.'

'You have to steel yourself, ma'am,' Peter Voigt gently advised her. 'This war is taking a terrible toll out of all of us. It will leave some of us alive. You are one of them. Be brave.'

'That transfer will not be an easy operation in the dark,' Michael Fischer, the surviving engineer chimed in, hoping to take Elsa's mind away from her anguish. 'But I expect they will use searchlights from the freighter and the steamer while the vessel discharging its survivors moves in between them for the sea boats to be loaded.'

'What sort of boats will they be?' Elsa asked.

'They might be powered or with a rowing crew. I expect the latter. These old vessels normally do not have propeller driven engines on their auxiliary boats,' he replied.

'I am certainly not looking forward to it,' Gina Lange commented. And then she added a further thought. 'In spite of being in the Women's Naval Service.'

'Well, it's a chance at last to get your sea legs,' Elsa quipped.

They all three chuckled at the forced humour. It relieved the gloomy prospect, if only for a few minutes.

They could hear a change of sounds on their small ship.

The engine revs rose, and orders were being shouted among the crew members.

Elsa went up to the deck to see what was taking place. She used her status to stand near the captain, who was instructing the coxswain to move the ship into position.

The freighter and steamer had moved side by side with a

distance of around a hundred metres between them, into which gap a minesweeper was slowly approaching.

The ships were flooding the channel between them with the beams from searchlight lamps. She could see two large rowing boats, with what appeared to be more than two rowers in each.

'It's a miracle the sea is so calm,' she said to the captain.

'That's the benefit of having a starlit night and icy cold conditions,' he replied. 'There could be a gale blowing and that would make it unthinkable to undertake such an operation.'

They watched the small boats, one each side of the minesweeper, disembarking all the survivors remaining to be transferred. Apparently, a single trip by the rowing teams was enough to transfer them to the two commercial ships.

Elsa could see the rising and falling of the ocean swell, sometimes in concert with, but often in contradistinction to, the movement of the waters between a large ship and a small boat.

It put a premium on compelling the transferees to obey the orders of their boat crewmen.

Evidently, many of the rescued people were ignorant of the fact that when standing on two disparately moving platforms one's feet are moving in two directions, such as between two boats at sea or in an earthquake. It took a cool head and a spritely response to leave one sure footing for the other.

The boatmen leant into their oars, rowing as one, the boat on the navy ship's port side setting off to the freighter, the other to the steamer, where, in both cases, their passengers embarked through hull-side doors into a safe haven.

At the very first opportunity, the minesweeper slowly

moved forwards, drawing ahead of the transfer scene into the night, followed at once by the second minesweeper.

The crew of the second ship was anxious only to repeat the success of the first in the transfer of their passengers. The two minesweepers were followed by the third, with repeated success.

Next, it was the turn of *TF21* with Elsa aboard. She had had time to express her heartfelt thanks to the captain and crew for her rescue and treatment.

'It is something I shall never get over. You will be in my heart forever,' she promised them. 'Make sure you, too, survive the war.'

With only three surviving passengers to collect from the *TF21*, only one of the two transferring rowing boats waited for it, transferring them to the freighter.

Meanwhile, the first of the two torpedo boats also shed its passengers quickly. They were transferred to the steamer.

The crew of Elsa's transfer boat, having delivered their survivors and not to be outdone, redoubled their efforts, returning to meet the second torpedo boat and the patrol boat, the last of the seven navy ships in the minesweeping flotilla.

Perhaps because it was another smaller vessel, the boatmen had difficulty transferring the few passengers it carried. Perhaps it was because the boatmen were tired by then and not quite as sharp as they had been.

While their boat was manoeuvred alongside the torpedo boat to retrieve the survivors for transfer to the larger vessel, a young woman and an older man misjudged their steps and lost their balance.

Perhaps they did not strictly obey the orders of the boatmen.

They fell into the sea. The woman was immediately in danger of being crushed between the rising and falling of the long boat and the second torpedo boat alongside each other.

Trying to prevent that happening, the older man struggled to recover her body. It was a fruitless effort. The woman disappeared, while the man drifted away.

The boatmen saw no option but to give chase, while they could still see the man in the floodlights. Given the surge of adrenalin the situation demanded, the oarsmen laid into their oars with a will, following the man still being swept away for a distance of fifty metres.

They succeeded in reaching him but found dragging him into their boat from the sea, turning choppy, was far from being an easy task. He was not a lightweight. It required strength and persistence to haul him on board.

The sailor in charge of the boat called out to the other survivors to move to the opposite side of the boat to counteract the physical exertions of the sailors who were engaged in the recovery. It was an unwelcome and unpleasant distraction, but fully effective.

'He's unconscious and very cold,' one sailor announced.

The boatmen had to row about twice the distance to the freighter than had been their custom for the transfer operations. On board the freighter that would take them to Kiel, Elsa and Gina rose to the occasion. The ship had over four hundred passengers on board, rescued from the *Hans Frayling*. Fortunately, a member of the ship's regular crew had some considerable medical experience.

With the greater freedom of passengers to move around the ship, the call went out for any qualified nurses and, or doctors, to report to a certain point, which acted as a rendezvous for individuals needing medical help.

Elsa's first thought was for the poor man who had been swept away and rescued for the second time from the ocean. She and Gina took one look at him in his hypothermic state.

'There's only one thing we can do for this man, Gina.'

'I think I know what you are going to say,' she said. 'Give him the Luftwaffe sandwich treatment.'

'Absolutely. The air force has used it commonly for the recovery of downed airmen from the ocean who have passed into a frozen state,' she added.

Elsa negotiated one of the very few cabins the freighter carried for what she had in mind. One of the ship's officers responded warmly to her representation of the problem and her suggested solution.

The man was taken, still unconscious, to the cabin and stripped of all his clothing. He was also joined by Elsa and Gina, who stripped off their clothing to their bare skins.

The three bodies were then buried, one woman on each side of the frozen man, under as much bedding as they could find, supplemented by a supply of blankets the officer had already contributed.

It was not a sinecure undertaking and far from being an enjoyable experience. They cuddled the inert man as closely as possible, turning their bodies as frequently as needed to dispel the coldness from the injured man, all with the view to injecting further warmth into his unrecovered parts.

It took nearly two hours of patient and persistent treatment before the man showed any signs of life.

Gina was the first to detect a ripple of movement in his body.

'It's there all right,' she said. 'If he recovers fully, what are we going to say to him? Suppose he thinks we have taken advantage of him?' They were no more than rhetorical questions.

'I should think that if he suddenly becomes aware of his bed companions, the shock will drag him completely out of his trauma in one swell swoop,' Elsa said, with a touch of humour not lost on Gina.

'Let's hope, then, that his recovery will be neither rapid nor violent enough to cause him to take advantage of us,' Gina responded.

'It will be a unique occasion to be involved with three people in a bed, one of whom had to be warmed up first,' Elsa quipped.

'Tell that to the girls in the women's air force service who have often performed this over the war years,' Gina added.

'If that happened to us, I would have to leap out first and leave him to your tender mercies, Gina,' Elsa said.

'I am here promising I don't want to make a habit of this,' Gina laughed.

The man was glad to recover consciousness.

He awoke to see two, well dressed women giving him the best nursing treatment he could have expected, but in ignorance of what it had entailed.

'I think I ought to be going,' he said simply.

'But you can't be fit enough yet to look after yourself,' Gina observed. 'I can give you the rendezvous point on the ship for any medical help you now need. Perhaps you have family with you.'

'That would be nice,' he said. 'I came with my wife. I will look for her. She must know I was not missing in the end. And thank you both for all you have done.'

He looked as if he could stand. Elsa called for someone to help him on his way. He was glad of that helping hand, as he passed out of the cabin door.

Gina locked the cabin door as he left, putting the key in her pocket. Her action suddenly sent a shot of adrenalin through Elsa's body. She waited for Gina to turn.

She did not turn. Still facing the door, she straightened up. Elsa's heartbeat quickened.

Without a sound, Gina began to undress.

The implication of her conduct accelerated Elsa's blood circulation.

Had their merciful handiwork with the man who had just left awakened more than a satisfaction in those who had administered it? *I don't think so,* Elsa said to herself. *This has only presented the opportunity to capitalise on it. It was there all the time. And I'm to be the happy beneficiary of it.*

Without a word, Elsa sidled forward. With tender hands she carried on the work on Gina's clothing that the wearer had already started.

It was during that sequence that Gina slowly turned to face Elsa. Her face portrayed a sparkling, ruthless, passion, the like of which Elsa had never seen on anyone's face before.

'Darling,' Elsa gasped. There was nothing more to say.

So, this is what I saved you for, Elsa thought.

As if echoing that thought, Gina whispered to Elsa, the most seductive words that could have been formed.

'This is what you saved me for. I fell in love with you in Gotenhaven. We never knew each other, nor came into contact at work. But I knew you had a lover. The fortunes of war can work for the advantage as well as the disadvantage. How could the wheels of fortune turn so minutely as to bring us to this very moment?'

'I am breathless with my own body,' Elsa whispered in reply. 'Your passion has stirred me to the limit. When succouring you on the little ship I could have forgotten myself time after time. I had to keep my distance. The time has surely come.'

While Elsa was speaking, Gina slowly began to undress her companion.

'It is a reward for a job well done,' she said. 'Those air force girls knew what they volunteered for. We have nothing to hide. The undress rehearsal has already been done.'

21

Still clinging to each other as if the ship was about to plunge into the deep, the hours passed with absolute satisfaction. Little was said, but their bonding had been enough to promise a lasting commitment.

They exchanged the basic details of family and biography.

'Where were you brought up, darling?' Gina asked.

'In the wilds of Pomerania, not far from the Polish frontier. My family was in farming. At the moment, I do not know how far the Russians have reached in that area. But I know that they have overrun my family's home.

'It has cost my family everything. They have become refugees. My siblings are all grown up and serving in the forces. I do not know where. I had a letter from my father in Gotenhaven to say my mother and he have fled westwards. They are staying with family in Dresden.'

'In Dresden,' Gina echoed. 'That's where I come from. It's where I shall be heading when we reach land.'

'I would like to travel with you. I must see them after all this time. It is several years since I last went home. Would that be convenient?'

'Not just convenient, imperative,' Gina said immediately.

'We might as well hang on to this cabin for as long as possible,' Elsa said. 'The officer who fixed it up has probably forgotten what he did for us. We are unknown on the ship, so there is no one to call us to account.'

'It was meant to be. A little recompense for our tribulations,' Gina added. 'If he comes back, shall we seduce him?'

Elsa was surprised at her suggestion but understood the reasons for it.

Later, an unexpected knock on the door put them on the alert.

'Do nothing. Whoever it is will think we have left,' Gina said. They kept quiet.

Suddenly they heard a key being inserted in the lock from outside.

The officer strode into the room before they could take any aversive action. You two are still here. He had remembered and counted his chances.

'Please close the door,' Gina asked.

He took one look at them and closed the door from the inside.

It was wartime. The disastrous end was near. He could not afford to let an opportunity pass to indulge the games they invited him to play.

It was the means, apart from other reasons, for keeping the cabin to themselves all the way to Kiel. Both women felt a pang of conscience about it, but they had both endured a dangerous exit from the torpedoed liner and had laboured to revive another survivor from passing through death's door.

Their latest guest could not stay long. His absence would have been noticed, but he stayed long enough to rejoin his duties on board with a lighter heart and greater energy than he had expected to take into Kiel.

All the bureaucratic procedures imaginable were extended as

a welcome for the rescued passengers when the freighter docked in Kiel.

It took an infuriating time for the ship to tie up, after negotiating a fog that had greeted the daylight. The fog was only a precursor to the many questions the officials levelled at the survivors. Most had no identification. They felt like aliens attempting to access a foreign country illegally.

An officer from the Women's Naval Service was among those waiting for the people to disembark. Elsa was apprehensive. She realised she would have catastrophic news to tell her.

Seeing the woman's uniform, she and Gina made tracks towards her. They noted her rank, kapitän zur see, a captain, a relatively high rank for a woman.

The waiting officer was somewhat startled when the two women, dressed in the oddest combination of clothing she could imagine, came boldly in front of her and came to attention.

Elsa spoke first.

'I am Oberleutnant zur See Elsa Bauer.'

'I am Leutnant zur See Gina Lange.'

'As far as we know, ma'am, we are the only two survivors from the contingent of between three and four hundred women from the service who embarked on the *Hans Frayling* in Gotenhaven.'

'I am Kapitän zur See Erika Möller, commander of the detachment in Kiel. I am speechless. This is a disaster of unimaginable proportions.

'In view of the hiatus that has overtaken us, I can still extend a welcome to you both to join this detachment. I shall not expect you to be duty fit immediately, so I can give you one week's leave, returning on 7 February.

'Come with me now. I can arrange a decent meal, re-kit you out, and show you your quarters. It will take me a while to absorb the shocking news you have brought. To think that the detachment sent to Gotenhaven has been wiped out is something I could never have imagined. I will try to answer any questions you may have. We could do that over lunch.'

She sounds so dispassionate, Elsa thought. *Or was her manner and what she said merely the cover of a wartime leader, used to facing the unthinkable? She really could not be expected to weep at the loss of so many women who were coming to her command.*

She by-passed the bureaucrats waiting to process the survivors, except to say to the principal teller that she would file a direct report by the next day.

'I am taking away the only two survivors from the contingent of Women's Naval Service that was on board. The report will have details of the loss of the Women's Naval Service members in the sinking that I expect to gather from them and the official records I hope I will have already received by then.'

Outside the port offices and sheds, she took them to a parked kübelwagen, an officer's runabout car, and drove them to the naval officers' mess in the port—but only after calling at the Women's Naval Service warehouse, where the two bedraggled survivors could shed all their clothes in a last act of throwing off the terrible nightmare at sea. They also called in to the captain's office to collect two rail passes to Dresden with their leave certificates for one week.

The brief rehabilitation and resumption of normal activity induced a certain amount of rejuvenation in Elsa and Gina.

It overcame the inherent fatigue they were both feeling, simmering tardily under the surface. They had to put a bold face on it in front of their new commanding officer.

At lunch, Erika Möller laid aside the rather formal and distant demeanour she had presented to the survivors on their first meeting. She actually portrayed herself as a caring and fair-dealing commander.

Perhaps she had had time to weigh up the two strangers she had met and had decided they were genuine and trustworthy. She had been able to confirm their ranks from her records.

The food was unusually varied and of good quality.

'The menu is remarkably good for this time in the war, ma'am,' Gina said. 'It's no worse than peacetime.'

'I'll let you into a well-known secret in these parts,' was the reply. 'We are getting a lot of supplies brought over from Sweden. It's a sort of black market, or, if you like, a local contraband system we have developed during the war.

'The locals here take all the risks, and we derive the benefit. One doesn't talk about it and the higher authorities don't know about it, or if they do, they prefer not to mention it, let alone take action against it.'

'At Kiel, you find one place with heaven on earth while everything around it is struggling in hell,' Elsa said.

'Be careful. That could be interpreted as defeatist talk. It's punishable by death. You never know who your friends are around here.'

'Thanks for the warning. I forgot, ma'am.'

'Please drop the ma'am. I'm Erika. May I call you Elsa? And you are Gina. You will be interested to know that you are the only members of the Women's Naval Service that I command.'

'What on earth has happened to the large detachment that was based at Kiel, busy in the shipyards, company offices, as well as the whole range of naval services,' Gina responded.

'The detachment at Kiel had already in fact shrunk badly during the last few months. Many were killed in the bombing. Many more were injured. A few have deserted. The remainder were sent away to other postings. They needed a rest, away from the bombings.

'It was thought that the contingent from Gotenhaven coming here, as fresh as any of us can become these days, and with a lot of skills and in a well organised condition, would replace them under my command.'

'Then the news we gave you on the quayside that it had been wiped out completely was a double shock for you, Erika,' Elsa said.

'It was something you hid from us so well,' Gina said.

'It was an unthinkable stunner for me,' Erika said. 'It was like a sea captain watching while his ship went down. So now, I am without a job. But I have been told to await further orders if they ever come through. With every day passing now the timing, detachment, precision, and integrity of orders have been dwindling.'

'It was a unique experience to suffer,' Elsa sympathised.

'Where will you both be spending your few days' leave?' Erika asked.

'In Dresden,' Elsa said. 'It was only on the rescue ship, where Gina and I met for the first time, that she told me she came from Dresden. I was overjoyed to hear that because my parents had already been driven out of Pomerania and had made their way to Dresden to dad's brother's farm. I haven't seen them for over three years, so I am looking forward to a reunion with them.'

'You two did not know each other until then?' Erika questioned. 'That's hard to believe since you were in the same detachment.'

'It's true,' Gina said, 'although we must have set eyes on each other at some time during our work in Gotenhaven, but Elsa never joined the get-togethers of the detachment members. She went almost privately from the design department of Blohm and Voss in Hamburg to Gotenhaven, to be attached to the naval intelligence servicing the port.'

'It just had to happen that way,' Elsa added. 'It was prudent to be isolated for security reasons. Just as well in the event. I had to investigate some widespread supplementary but illegal victualling of U-boats, from stocks managed by some of our members.'

'Sounds like an interesting story to tell,' Erika conceded. 'Some other time, perhaps.'

Gina gave her apologies for leaving the table to visit the ladies' cloakroom.

'Shout if you go to sleep,' Elsa advised her, laughing.

'If I do, don't leave me while I'm gone,' Gina warned, 'I don't know my way around Kiel, and I need to find the railway station.'

Erika used Gina's absence to query Elsa's intentions further.

'Do you have a partner to go to?' Erika asked.

'No,' she replied.

'You mean you have no love life at all?' The look on Erika's face supported the disbelief implicit in her question.

'I have always kept it in the service,' was Elsa's enigmatic reply.

'And now it has been wiped out,' Erika commented.

'It's symptomatic of the shrinkage of life around here at large,' Elsa added. 'Even the best things are disappearing.'

Elsa began to wonder where their conversation would have gone if Gina had not returned to their table at that moment. Elsa noted Erika had warmed to the exchange. At one point, the expression on her face was nothing if not voluptuous.

She had been contemplating returning the question of her affiliations to Erika. She was a beautiful woman. Her tailor-made uniform was a perfect fit around a body carved in flesh that mirrored the dream-like perfection artists the world over had made into idols.

Unknown to Elsa, the strange conjunction of their conversation and Gina's return led to Erika's same calibre of assessment of Elsa's body. But she had put a proviso on her observation. Above all else, it was Elsa's scintillating personality that captivated her. She had become riveted to it.

22

Erika ushered them out of the officers' mess to a neighbouring wing of the building where they could buy a few desirables to take with them on their journey to Dresden, a distance of over two hundred and fifty miles. With darkness falling late in the afternoon, they had planned the only sensible decision possible, to travel after dark to escape the likelihood of fighter-bomber attacks.

'Trains are so vulnerable in daylight. They are tending to run only at night-time on the tracks that are still intact. But I must say the railway workers have worked wonders, day after day to repair railway lines that have been damaged,' Erika said.

'Unfortunately, the same cannot be said about the railway station. It has been obliterated. The lines and railway foundations have been torn up beyond immediate repair. We have to go out to the edge of the city to catch the train.'

'That is a touch of ingenuity in the face of impossibility,' Elsa declared. 'Let's hope it is working for us.'

When the train came into the area in reverse, the two women had to climb up from ground level, but only after having saluted their captain and thanking her for the thoughtful treatment she had afforded them during the day.

'I shall look forward to your return on 7 February,' Erika called out. 'By then, perhaps, I hope to have some news about what is expected of us.'

Their train journey was surprisingly uneventful. The train

was far from being crowded. It seemed that no one wanted to travel from west to east any more.

The train carried no refreshment facilities. It travelled slowly, stopping an inordinate number of times, but covered the two hundred and fifty miles or so in eight hours.

'An average speed of thirty miles an hour these days can't be too bad,' Elsa remarked to Gina.

'I think it would be impossible to do it in daylight. If a train manages to cover the same journey at all, it will take a lot longer,' Gina said. 'Let's hope our return will be as good.'

Arriving at Dresden, they were awestruck on finding the station, located on the north-west side of the city, undamaged. It was midnight. No one met them, simply because their families in Dresden had not been informed they would be coming.

Walking out of the station, they were impressed by the streets and buildings. They were still intact. Dresden had been lucky.

'What a surprise!' Elsa said. 'This is the first time I have been to Dresden but have always been aware of the historic fame of the city. It will be nice to walk around in daylight to see its glorious parks and remarkable architecture.'

'That's something we can do together in a day or two's time,' Gina promised. 'I will be able to leave my parents to get on with their lives later this week, after they have vented their excitement at seeing me again after so long.

'It's very late, Elsa. I think it will be impossible to get out to your uncle's farm at this time of night. No buses are running. Taxis are out of the question. Give it up for the night. Come with me. You can go out to the farm tomorrow morning at your leisure.'

'Why did we not think of the problem before leaving?' Elsa asked the question, not expecting an answer.

'There is a reason for the omission,' Gina said. 'We did not know that a train could carry us to Dresden or the amount of time it would take.'

'Your suggestion is very convenient and acceptable. I don't feel like walking six miles or more right at this moment,' Elsa conceded.

Even so, the two women had to walk for nearly half an hour to Gina's parents' home.

They thought it would be necessary to knock up the Lange home, Gina's parents having long since retired to bed.

At the last minute they became apprehensive about waking them at something like one o'clock, in the beginning of an icy winter's February night. In any case the front door was locked.

Gina racked her memory to recall where her mother used to hide the front door house key. She felt under an exterior matting square in front of the door. On finding the key, she sighed with relief, when remembering the long-standing custom of the past age, that locking the doors of one's house was regarded as a prohibitive social act her parents had always eschewed.

'Let's go to the kitchen first,' Gina suggested. 'We need to get some food and drinks to take up to my room. I forgot to ask you if you would mind sharing my room. It is always left ready for me to use whenever I could come home.'

'Not if you promise not to seduce me,' Elsa giggled. 'It makes me feel I have been picked up on the streets and will spend a wakeful night.'

'It could be possible,' Gina said. 'But we may have run

out of steam.'

'I cannot see that happening,' Elsa said. 'Think of the lost opportunities you have endured in life. I am sure we shall rise to the occasion.'

'You say such nice things, Elsa,' Gina laughed. 'It turns me on. Even if you are nasty, I still love you. It makes me wish we had met earlier and in better circumstances.'

'The time for talking about it is over.'

They hungrily consumed some food and a glass of wine, before tumbling into bed.

'What will happen in the morning?' Elsa asked. 'Are your parents early risers?'

'I think they will be tomorrow. I left a note on the kitchen table saying we had arrived and that you plan to move on without more ado.'

The morning was colder than ever. They had managed about six hours' sleep. Gina went up to her parents' bedroom.

Elsa could hear the shock of seeing their daughter in her dressing gown. She heard her explanation for having a friend with her. They had not yet seen the message on the kitchen table.

Breakfast that morning was the celebration of Gina's homecoming and Elsa's introduction to her parents.

'I think it will be hello and goodbye,' Elsa declared. 'My parents do not know I am on my way to see them. We haven't been together for over three years. They have been driven out of their farm by the Russians. They seem to have fled with only the goods they can carry with them. I do not know how they managed to get here.

'I'm hoping to come into town in a couple of days to join Gina for a look around the city. Perhaps, I can see you again then.'

'You will be most welcome,' her mother said.

Gina's father gave Elsa instructions for going to her uncle's farm. It involved a bus ride and then a long walk. She postponed leaving until later in the day to spend more time with Gina.

She anticipated an evening with her parents in their sitting room. It was time to finish talking over with them what had happened over their expulsion from Pomerania and Elsa's own adventures in the service of her country.

23

Obviously, the infamous reputation of the Russians had unrolled ahead of their front lines. Without waiting to see if they could be a benign occupier of newly conquered territory, Elsa's parents had taken to the roads as common refugees, together with scores of their neighbours.

Elsa was keener to squeeze their story out of them than she was to labour through her own story, chapter by chapter, after taking up the secondment at Blohm and Voss.

She was finally saved from telling her own story, when her enjoyable homecoming, sitting by the fireside in the middle of the evening, was brought to a sudden halt by the sound of air raid sirens.

'That's unusual,' her uncle said. 'We have escaped the fate of so many cities and consider ourselves lucky.'

'Do you think it may have something to do with the advances the Russians have made? They seem to be unstoppable,' Elsa's father ventured a reason. 'Is it going to get worse for towns in the path of their invasion of the fatherland?'

'We have to assume that nothing is now sacred,' his brother replied. 'Cities were first subjected to strategic bombing, but it has now changed to tactical bombing.

'The enemy wants the communications of towns ahead of their forward moving army to be blunted—road, railways, and electricity. They want their enemy's reserves to be disrupted, terrified, and put into disorganisation.'

'The Russians would rather capture a town intact for their own use and ease of movement than to stop to clear streets from rubble. Widespread damage destroys living quarters. It provides the means for prolonged resistance by stragglers and ambushes by shock troops.'

'The population of Dresden must be swollen,' Elsa said. 'When I was in Breslau a few days ago, I was told the city population was down to a hundred and fifty thousand. Nearly half a million had left or been killed. It was widely believed that many thousands of them had headed for Dresden.

'Then you have to add the prisoners of war and forced labour recruits working in the factories. In the absence of public shelters, the casualty rate will be high if the bombing is the kind of attack we had in Hamburg.'

'What were you doing in Breslau? Did you say only a few days ago? It has been surrounded by Russians since the end of December,' her father asked.

'Sorry, Dad, I cannot say,' she replied.

'That air raid siren has interrupted our get-together,' her father reluctantly concluded. 'We might never be able to know what you have been up to now.'

'Only if we are all wiped out,' Elsa sniggered.

Her father deplored the turn of events. 'We came all this way to escape them and now they are catching us up.'

Even as he spoke bombs began falling.

'This sounds like an unprecedented attack on the city,' Elsa's uncle proclaimed. 'I have never heard such an anti-aircraft barrage before. Only stray bombers have dropped bombs before in or near the city.'

'What do you do when bombs are falling?' Elsa asked.

'We have never had to worry before about that. Being

outside the city we haven't exactly felt inured from bombing, but the city has been declared a festung, a prohibited target owing to its historic and cultural status, like Paris and Breslau.'

'But not London,' Elsa broke in. 'It was originally agreed, like Berlin. But all the agreements and promises have been broken in the war, which has changed us all for the worse.'

'That sounds like treasonable talk, Elsa,' her uncle said.

'Oh, I am simply stating the facts. Perhaps you didn't know them.'

Before he could think of anything more to say, loud explosions suddenly cascaded into their lives. They happened in the darkness—outside in the fields, in the countryside, and some of them, very near.

'Extinguish all lights,' Elsa urged.

Her uncle did so, but they continued to sit around their sitting room, overcome with the cacophony that never seemed to end.

'This is entering into the devil's kitchen,' her father expostulated. 'The raid has been coming and going for at least an hour. It must soon be over.'

Elsa's aunt had left the room when the talking became a little heated.

She apparently came back, but no one could see her.

'The whole sky is red over the city. I will pull open the blinds. The fire is bright enough to light up the rooms,' she declared.

They finally admitted they were witnessing an epic attack.

'What a pity it is in support of the Russian interests,' someone said.

'We are freezing, now I have doused the fire,' Elsa's uncle said. 'But look in the city, they are roasting alive in the firestorm. I cannot believe what I am seeing. It is unthinkable.'

Elsa suddenly spoke.

'I am going to walk away from the house, deeper into the country. Will anyone come with me?' she asked. 'This is the start of a night of terror suffered by so many cities in our land and others throughout the war. I appeal to you all to save yourselves.'

She hastily dressed in her warmest clothes and gave a last-minute appeal to her parents and her uncle and aunt.

'It's too risky to be so close to the bombing on this scale. Just remember that bombs released at the height these bombers are flying at are subject to fine tuning, but any small error on release can cause the bombs to miss a target by a big margin.'

They all declined her offer. The farm was isolated. It was a relatively safe haven. There was no serious precedent for the event.

Elsa was relieved to get out of the house. In it, she felt vulnerable. Perhaps it was the very first enemy bombing her parents and their in-laws had experienced, close at hand and in such volume. They had a certain vain hope that their relative isolation would be their best protection. Elsa was not so sure.

She struck off away from the city into the dark to find the river Elbe flowing north-west from Dresden. Her uncle's property, which he described as a farm—but she had concluded was best described as a market garden—was one of many adjacent to one another.

It had survived and derived its prosperity, among the many other enterprises scattered around the flattish land surrounding Dresden, from supplying the large regular market the city demanded.

Elsa decided her walking was easy on her feet. She soon

found the river, already flowing fast and with a substantial width. At that point it had all the promise of becoming what it ultimately became, one of the most massive rivers in the whole of Europe.

On seeing the swiftly running waters for the first time, her recent memories of her midnight expedition on the river Oder swept through her mind.

She consciously and suddenly terminated her increasing reminiscence, by turning to witness the attack on Dresden. The bombing still continued. The fires were even larger. She grieved for the treasures of architecture and culture going up in flames. But more than that, her heart was torn for Gina and her family.

I can do nothing for them, she said to herself. *If I dwell on their plight, I shall lose my own impetus to survive. How can fate be so arbitrary, sudden, unexpected, and ruthless as this?*

Alongside the river were more farms, as her uncle described them, interspersed with sporting properties for soccer and hockey.

At that time of the early morning, she was surprised to see a few private boats on the river, as if people—with the liberty to do so—had taken to the river to get away from the sustained bombing that was destroying the city.

After a few more minutes' walking, she was overjoyed to see a navy flag waving. Moored to the bank was a fast river patrol boat. Her heart and her head were both turned upside down as she contemplated the implications and possibilities of what she could see.

She kept walking towards that particular building, not daring to waste time. But her mind was going into full revolutions.

This is a God-sent opportunity, she thought. *But have I the courage to seize it?* she asked herself. *I am not an impetuous person,* she mused. *But I really have to weigh up the pros and cons of what this offers.*

It looks as if the small navy crew has already left or is preparing to move away in their vessel. I must find out if reality is as close to appearances as it seems.

'Hello, there,' she called into the simple building that resembled a boating house for a rowing club, 'can I come in?'

There was a disturbance somewhere at the back of the building. Footsteps were followed by the appearance of a man in his forties, in the uniform of a naval lieutenant, a leutnant in the Kriegsmarine.

'Hello,' she said. Elsa tried to sound as relaxed and casual as she could manage in the small hours of the morning, with the bombing continuing, and her anxiety over her parents looming as large as ever.

'What do you want? You are not allowed in here. Leave at once.' The leutnant brusquely called to her once he saw the owner of the first hello. He clearly had no expectation of an answer to his question.

'I nearly said good morning to you, leutnant. Then thought better of it. So, I thought it best to be as friendly as possible.'

'Who are you? I thought I ordered you to leave these premises immediately,' he replied.

'Perhaps you don't think I look the part, but underneath all these clothes I have the uniform of an officer in the Women's Naval Service. I am Oberleutnant Elsa Bauer.'

On hearing her identity, he strode forward and saluted.

'You have to be so careful,' he said. 'With the bombing

we have to be on our guard against looters. And there is always the chance of an allied airman shot down and looking for a hideaway. But may I ask why you are here in the middle of the night and a serious bombing attack?'

'My parents are living just a mile or two away with their in-laws. They were farmers, escaping from the Russians in Pomerania. They became common refugees and ended up here. I only arrived two days ago for a visit. I think I may have misjudged the timing of it pretty badly. I came out of the house for my own safety. The others all refused my warning. I just hope they are still alive. I see you have a boat tied up. But where are the crew?'

'We have two river patrol boats, one for working south and up-river, the other working north and down-river. When the unprecedented bombing started, I sent one boat down river away from the city with the crew for safety. They have a hiding place about four miles away under a belt of overhanging trees.

'These boats are big enough to be a likely target, especially in the glow of the fireball that has hit the city. A few more fires along the riverside and the second boat will become vulnerable. I have been pondering taking it away as well, with its crew, but it would leave all our equipment and belongings exposed to theft.'

Even as he spoke, the bombing ceased as sharply as it had begun. It had lasted for an hour and a half. The all-clear sirens confirmed their impressions.

'I think it is time to marshal the crew of the boat we have left to patrol the city stretch,' he said. 'We need to assess the chaos and the use made of the river after that deluge.'

'Do you think I could join the crew for the trip?' Elsa asked.

'Yes, of course, we are short-handed anyway, but I suppose you have never been on the water as a service job, so I shall not ask you to do anything.'

Elsa gave him a wry grin. 'You would be surprised,' she told him.

'Now you have got me guessing,' he said.

The crew were alerted to the decision. They were in an adjacent hut, some asleep, others playing cards, or writing home. The leutnant would be captain for this trip. He had sent the other boat downstream in the charge of his second-in-command, an oberfähnrich zur see, sub-lieutenant.

The second crew would consist, after the captain, of the obermaat, the chief petty officer for the entire unit, an elderly man; an unterofficiere ohne portepee, a junior non-commissioned officer; two matroses, ordinary seamen, and not forgetting the key member of the crew, the bootsmann, or boatswain. The last named steered the boat on the river with the experience of knowing the perils under the water as well as those on it.

They assembled in the crew room, where the leutnant introduced Oberleutnant Elsa Bauer of the Women's Naval Service. 'I have only just met the oberleutnant. She came to us on seeing the Kriegsmarine flag. Her parents live in the vicinity.'

It was Elsa's turn to say a word. 'I'm glad your commander mentioned why I have appeared out of the blue. Mostly, I'm glad because I can assure you, I am not a Russian spy. It is not for me to explain who I am by telling you what I have been up to, but I was sent on leave—after some arduous experiences during January—to see my parents who have become refugees from Pomerania. It will be an honour to join you tonight in what you have to do.'

'It's our privilege to have you with us,' the chief petty officer said.

They locked the premises and boarded the moored boat.

The diesel engines started without a fuss, while the seamen released the ropes tying the boat to the river shore.

As soon as they slowly eased into the middle of the river, all eyes were focused on the conflagration of the city. As they reduced the distance southwards to the part of the river contiguous with the heartland of the city, the light and heat became palpable.

*There cannot be many people alive in the middle of that confl*agration was the thought of everyone on board. No one dared voice it aloud.

Someone said, 'Do you realise that bombing raid only lasted for just under one and a half hours? They have perfected bombing from a random and wasteful operation to a precision, clinical instrument of warfare.'

How were they to know that over seven hundred aircraft had delivered their bomb loads in that short space of time?

The further the river patrol boat went up-stream in a southward direction, the more acute the bombing of the central city seemed to be. Scores of fire hoses had been thrown into the river. The fire engines were only occasionally seen as they drew on a free supply of water that, bountiful as it was, could patently make little difference to the surging fires that burned out of control.

The roar of the burning city obscured the sound of the air raid sirens for the second time that night. It was just after one o'clock, about three hours after the initial raid, which all and sundry thought would last the city not only for the war but for a lifetime.

The timing of the second attack was deliberate.

Those on the river patrol boat heard nothing until a cascade of bombs fell randomly among the inferno to spread the fire still further.

It was the captain who suddenly put two and two together to realise the purpose of the second major attack in the same night.

He ordered the boatswain to reverse the boat's direction, and the engineers to increase the boat's speed.

While sailing northwards in the reverse direction downstream towards their point of departure, the bombing once again stopped.

It had lasted for half an hour.

Over five hundred aircraft had bombed the city again.

Some had agitated the damage to the central city, but a majority had extended the total area of attack.

Riverside and market garden properties, suburban districts, parks, and residential flats had been pummelled, not with the same intensity as delivered to the central city but severely enough to inflict widespread damage and casualties.

The crew were clearly taken aback when they surveyed the scene at their home base. Their silence extended to discharging the order by the captain to tie up the river pilot boat on an available capstan.

Elsa asked the captain what he expected the next step would have to be. 'The authorities will take a day or two to pull themselves together, but what will you do meantime?'

'Who knows,' he breathed, as much to himself as to her. 'I wonder how far the Russians are away from Dresden at the moment.'

'I happen to know not too far.' Elsa replied.

'How do you know what we don't know, ma'am? Excuse my asking.'

'They were around one hundred and twenty-five miles a week ago,' she replied. 'Don't ask me how I know. I observed a Russian patrol being wiped out by a small party of shock troops with me after the patrol tried to stop me from discharging my mission. During the mission I had a contretemps with another patrol. I know I had the better of them, killing four and perhaps a fifth.'

'You did what? Are you pulling my leg, ma'am?'

'No, of course not. You asked a question and I happened to know the answer.'

'In that case I expect my command headquarters will soon order us to withdraw to a safer location.'

'Can you promise me that you will not leave without me?' Elsa asked. 'It looks as if I have lost my friend and my family. But I will check it out first, and report back to you, as soon as it is daylight.'

She assisted the crew to recover whatever intact and useful equipment and personal belongings they could find among the damaged naval properties. The only sleep they enjoyed that night consisted of catnaps in the early hours of the morning.

Elsa had discovered a bicycle she would use to go the mile or two to her uncle's farm. She went at daybreak but could not find it. Sticks of high explosive had been dropped in many parts of the market gardening area, as if in a deliberate attempt to deny the population of its food supply.

She finally identified the ruins of the farmhouse. Any life in it had been obliterated. While she was surveying the shocking scene, the air raid sirens of the city sounded for the third time.

That must be a false alarm after the night we have had, she thought.

They won't come all this way in broad daylight.

But they did return, many hundreds of them. This time American aircraft poured their bomb loads into the same extended target area that the two night attacks had observed.

As soon as she heard the approaching aircraft, Elsa fled back to the river, abandoning any further investigation of the whereabouts of her family, but reluctantly concluding with the worst possible explanation.

Did the allies hate her country's regime so much that they would go to such lengths to support the Soviet interests? was the returning dominant question in her head as she pedalled her way through the only loophole left for her escape.

The captain of the remaining vessel, and naval commander of the tiny detachment based at Dresden, had kept his word. Preparations for leaving were well advanced. They had found some food among the rubble. But they had not left.

The latest attack, which had materialised while Elsa had been away only an hour before, must have strained the captain's resolution, she thought.

Hot and flustered from her frantic return ride, she made straight for the boat, still being loaded with bits and pieces from their desolate site.

'Any hope?' he asked, still disengaged enough to show an interest in her family.

'No, I have to say, absolutely not,' she replied. 'The bike came in handy. Have you any room to take it with us?'

'Throw it in the rescue skiff,' he called out to her. 'Be

sharp, we are going right now.'

The twin diesels rumbled into life as the seamen hastily undid the knots of the fastenings by which the vessel had been locked to the river bank.

Elsa joined the captain at his side. He was suddenly looking very concerned. 'This is a very heavy raid. In broad daylight we shall be seen from the air. I can see a bomb or two hitting the river bank and one falling in the river itself behind us. Fortunately, every mile we cover to the north will be drawing away from the danger.'

'I'm sorry, I didn't ask your name when we first met?'

'It's Leutnant zur See Otto Schumacher,' he announced.

'I shall always be indebted to you for saving my life,' Elsa said.

'That is putting an extreme description on it,' he said.

'I don't think so,' she replied. 'If I had not discovered the navy flag and roused you from your sleep, or whatever you were doing at the back of the building, I would have had to go back to my uncle's house, and we know now with what results.'

'In that case I have to say how pleased I am to have been of service. It was created by the enemy, but even the enemy can sometimes do some good.'

They both enjoyed a laugh at that assertion.

'Are we going to pick up the other boat?' she asked him.

'I hope not. I ordered them to move north after the second night raid. We will catch up with them and hand over their belongings. I had a message from Hamburg ordering us to vacate the post entirely. The Russians will possibly breakthrough in this area.'

'Do you have much trouble from Russian fighter-bombers

in daytime?'

'Not yet. The trouble is that their activity is so uneven. In some places they are operating westwards far ahead of their armies than in other parts of the front line. As soon as they conquer territory, they establish landing fields for their aircraft to harry us.'

'We shall have to be sharp on the lookout for them during daylight. I see the vessel is well-equipped with anti-aircraft defence,' Elsa observed.

'True enough, but it is not easy to defend yourself against low flying aircraft, which can drop a bomb or strafe you by surprise. It depends on the kind of land the river is running through at the time.'

'So, you are returning to Hamburg?' Elsa asked.

'Yes, our headquarters are there. I have no idea what lies in store for us. Just anything goes, I suppose.'

'Where will you be heading, then?' he asked Elsa.

'I have to report back to Kiel by the seventh of the month. How long do you anticipate it will take to Hamburg?'

'If nothing goes wrong, about twelve hours continuous sailing. If we meet obstacles, it could take days.'

They had been under way for several hours, when, in the middle of the day, one of the crew came to the captain to report that he had seen smoke on the horizon, well ahead of their own vessel.

'Thank you,' he said to the crewman, acknowledging the report. 'Keep an eye open now to the river and let me have an explanation as soon as possible.'

After another three quarters of an hour's journey, the lookout came back to the captain, with his binoculars around his neck.

'It's something on the river, sir. It has burned furiously and is still smoking. There appears to be nothing going on around it or nearby on the banks.'

'We will approach cautiously. Report as soon as you can identify the cause of it. Our other vessel was well ahead of us in leaving, so I hope they were clear of this area.'

After the lookout had gone back to his post, the captain detailed one member of the crew on each side of the vessel to scrutinise the river bank as carefully as possible for any sign of an ambush. He then turned to Elsa.

'This is ominous. I have a gut feeling that our other boat has run into trouble. Prepare for the worst.'

Before long, the lookout ran to the captain with the news that the burning wreck was their other ship.

'It's a complete write off, sir. But I can see a small number of people on the left bank of the river but cannot identify them yet.'

They approached cautiously. Passing the sinking river vessel, their crew responded to the waving of the people on the bank, on recognising they were members of the destroyed boat's crew.

The boatswain skilfully brought the riverboat as close to the bank as it was possible to reach without running aground.

The stranded crew members boarded their own skiff, which they had used to escape from their burning ship, to paddle out to their other boat arriving to save them.

The sub-leutnant, who had captained the lost boat, called out for a cheer from the survivors. On boarding the riverboat, he saluted the captain.

'Thank God, you made it safely, sir. We had no trouble in our hideaway but were surprised by two fighter-bombers from behind. We had no chance. One man was killed. Two others were injured, one of them badly, as you can see. We have not been in any danger on this left bank. I think the Russians are some way to the east, but we were vulnerable on the river to enemy aircraft.'

'Who is the other wounded man?' the captain asked his deputy.

'I have that honour, sir,' he replied.

'Then you had better get some treatment as soon as possible. It is not an honour, but if you have been hiding your injury, you have done more than your duty. Get below at once and await my announcement.'

The captain then spoke on the loudspeaker.

'To everyone. We are now a crowded ship. We have in effect the remains of two crews, and an awful lot of luggage. We are heading for Hamburg. Our two diesel engines will take us there without any problems. If we have to use the skiff before we get there, please take the bicycle out of it carefully and don't throw it in the water. It belongs to our guest on board, Oberleutnant Elsa Bauer of the Women's Naval Service. We shall never live it down if it gets damaged. I think she intends to cycle from Hamburg to Kiel.'

In spite of the stress and suffering represented in various ways on the vessel, the joke raised a laugh and a handclap.

The captain continued. *'The first priority is the wounded. We are lucky to have our guest. She has considerable experience in action of tending the wounded, and I am sure she will give us her best. Help her as much as possible. For the rest, crew duties will be arranged. Those rescued will be able to recover their property from the mass of luggage we were able to load from the ruins of our property in Dresden.'*

Elsa supervised moving the badly wounded crewman to as comfortable a bed as could be found. He had suffered a bullet wound to his left shoulder. He was still conscious, but clearly in pain and visibly distressed.

On examining the wound, Elsa concluded that the chances of removing the bullet from his body were good.

She then examined the sub-leutnant. His wound may have been more serious than the first man's. A bullet had ripped into his left side above the hipbone from the rear and exited the front of his stomach low down. It was still bleeding a little.

Assisted by the crewman responsible for first aid and medical supplies, Elsa gave the first man an anaesthetic. With sterilized instruments she probed his wound and extracted the bullet. He was given antiseptic treatment and temporary bandaging.

The second man was treated to stop the minimal blood flow, but Elsa was concerned for the general condition of the man himself. He had chosen to conceal his wound for several hours.

Consequently, his constitution had taken an enormous strain. The wound needed an x-ray to identify any complications.

After a couple of hours' work, Elsa felt exhausted. Her tiredness had been exaggerated by an almost entire lack of sleep through the previous night. She remembered the men were also under the same kind of disadvantage. But she knew she would carry on as if she had all the energy in the world.

She had made up her mind about the two wounded men. Reporting to the captain, she confronted him with the inevitable.

'I think it would be a good idea to take these two men to a hospital en route. I have done all I could competently do, including removing the bullet from a man's shoulder, and cleaning and sterilizing your deputy's wound, which might be more serious. It needs an x-ray.'

The captain glanced at his river map. 'I think Magdeburg is close enough to serve our purpose. It would be the best solution. It has a big hospital. I will ask the wireless operator to get a message to Magdeburg.'

To the relief of all the crew members and particularly Elsa, an ambulance was waiting at the pier when the riverboat reached the half-way point to Hamburg. No sooner had they tied up for the disembarkation of the wounded men, than the sound of low flying aircraft could be heard.

The captain called over the loudspeaker.

'Action stations everybody. There's no air raid alarm, but we can't take any more chances.'

Two Russian fighter-bombers screamed overhead to survey their targets, before turning and flying along the river at an impossibly low level.

The boat and vehicles on the quayside were hit. The two gunners crewing the anti-aircraft, heavy duty, double-barrelled machine gun were both killed, and several others injured.

'They are coming round again,' the captain called out.

Elsa heard his warning while still caring in the bowels of the boat for the wounded waiting to be discharged. She ran onto the deck and threw herself on the quayside, taking a ground firing position with a navy sub-machine gun, she had found and adopted on the boat.

The enemy aircraft made the mistake of repeating their run towards the quayside from the same direction and from the same angle, probably assuming the target area had been rendered into a soft option by their previous attack.

Their head-on approach presented Elsa with several

seconds of a fixed target. She aimed at the leading aircraft, bearing in mind that bullets take time to reach their target.

Calmly holding her finger on the firing trigger, she rejoiced to see she was hitting the aircraft. 'But I don't think I have been lethal to it,' she shouted out.

Both aircraft flew over their boat and the quayside, but only the second aircraft was seen to be still firing its guns.

Perhaps the first has jammed his weapons, she thought.

The noise from the aircraft faded.

The captain intervened in the events with renewed energy to unload the dead and wounded of his crew.

'The quicker we can get under way the better for us. They will be back to finish us off.'

Elsa reported to the ambulance crew that in addition to the two wounded men from the previous incident, they needed to provide for a further two wounded and two dead from the latest attack.

As soon as the on-shore medics had disembarked the wounded and dead, the captain ordered the ship-to-shore walkway to be heaved on board, together with the release of the ropes holding the boat to its moorings.

They were glad to be on the move. Two men were assigned as gunners to the anti-aircraft heavy machine gun.

'It looks as if your shooting at the last minute was enough to put them off their purpose. Another round from those two aircraft, and we might not be sailing away like this,' the captain told Elsa. 'I am wondering where you learned to shoot like that.'

'I got used to having a similar weapon as my constant companion, that's all,' she said. 'It's all behind me now, I'm glad to say.'

The resumption of their journey was conducted without

incident, the boat arriving at Hamburg, their home port, at nine o'clock on a dark winter's night, just as one of the many successive bombing raids had begun.

The crew and Elsa disembarked and went to the underground shelters. The raid was not another of the blockbuster raids delivered to Hamburg. They were in the past. The city and port area were so thoroughly destroyed that the only use Hamburg had for enemy bomber operations was as a diversionary target in support of a major onslaught on another city.

On the release of Hamburg from the bombing, Elsa and the remaining members of the crew spent what was left of the night in the makeshift naval barracks. It had been several times removed by bombing from the original pre-war permanent navy accommodation for its sailors.

Elsa had a sense of coming home.

24

Elsa was pleased to be in Hamburg but only as a jumping off point for reaching Kiel to the north. Her respect for duty and loyalty to the Women's Naval Service had been locked into the person of Kapitän zur See Erika Möller. Chaos and arbitrary conduct were gradually taking over the fatherland. She did not intend to contribute to the trend.

It was about sixty miles to Kiel. Since road traffic was almost at a standstill, buses could no longer be running. The railway was a doubtful proposition. As she mused over the matter of transport to Kiel, the thought humorously included in the captain's message to his crew on the riverboat came back to her.

Otto Schumacher had quipped that Elsa was keeping the bicycle for cycling from Hamburg to Kiel. He evidently did not believe it.

It was a challenge she would take up. Time was no problem. She had a spare day or two before the deadline to report back on the date assigned by Erika Möller.

With the return of daylight, Elsa marched with the rest of the crew to their berthed riverboat. The crew were all under orders.

She had nothing else to do than bid them all the best of luck. She had a special farewell thanks to give the captain, which he generously returned to her.

'As it happened, you were an inspiration to us. Your work

on the wounded was enough to prevent the deterioration of their wounds and your recommendation to hospitalise them, I am sure, will save their lives.'

He saluted Elsa, his superior in rank. She returned the salute and then did the unmentionable thing in front of subordinate ranks by giving him a heartfelt kiss, in contradiction to military decorum. It raised a salutary cheer from the gathered remainder of the crew.

A seaman retrieved her bike and placed it on the quayside. She had nothing else of her own to carry away. The little she had collected for the trip to Dresden had been lost.

She set her mind and heart on the sixty miles to Kiel.

There was no need to hurry, hold ups and impediments notwithstanding. The only, but important issue that she faced was where and how to find some accommodation overnight for two nights. She had only a pittance of money in her pocket.

After cycling all morning at a leisurely pace, she stopped at a wayside refreshment place for truck drivers, motorists, and any other persons like her, who, in winter and under the threat of wartime activities, had taken to the roads.

While musing at her table, she suddenly thought she should look at her leave pass to ascertain exactly what explicit or implicit instructions might be included in them.

The leave pass and her identity document were in an intact, waterproof cover fixed to her skin, where, she had always believed, it was best to carry precious items.

While she was foraging about with her clothes to extract them, some soldiers came in laughing and exuding a playful attitude to anyone in their environment as they passed.

Seeing Elsa attracted their attention.

'What have we here?' one of them asked a rhetorical

question.

One of the others answered, immediately, without thinking.

'She saw us coming and was preparing a welcome party.'

Elsa was heated up from her long cycle ride. Her first instinct was to label them five loud-mouthed layabouts. She restrained herself. They were soldiers. Their lot in prospect was not good. She decided to play along with them. She could always surprise them later.

'Not all of you, you halfwits,' she rejoined. 'Especially you.' She addressed the man who had made the ribald comment.

Her comment gave way to cheers and jeers, followed by gales of laughter. For soldiers, they were certainly in a good mood.

'Now, you boys, behave yourselves. The fatherland is watching,' she said. The remark curbed their ribaldry for the moment. They were thrown into uncertainty by the remark, wondering whether it was a warning or an out-of-date joke.

They queued up for a hot drink, sustaining the general atmosphere of good humour created by the interchange, returning one by one to Elsa to continue their banter.

Elsa began to revel in the exchange.

'Where are you men heading?' she asked them. 'I could do with a lift.'

That request brought a round of laughter from them and a series of suggestive comments that revealed what was most in their minds.

'Is that how you do it?'

'On the way!'

'And then dismount as if nothing ever happened?'

'That's a pretty smart way of operating!'

'Have you ever been caught?'

All five spoke at once, either as questions or exclamations, but all expressing their surprise and admiration for Elsa's imagined modus operandi.

They were anxious to return to their truck.

Elsa renewed her question. 'I asked where are you heading?'

'Now, miss,' one of their number replied in a serious voice. 'We are not allowed to pick up civilians, especially at this stage of the war.'

'It would be nice if you made me an exception today,' Elsa countered.

'Sorry, but it can't be done,' he answered.

There was a moment's silence.

Elsa stood up and started to peel off her top dungarees, woollen-lined, a style of dressing that had served her so well against the cold on various missions.

The soldiers at first were gobsmacked. Their second thought was to make their escape from a most compromising involvement. Their last thought was bewilderment, reducing them to silence.

On revealing her neat officer's uniform, Elsa was taken aback by the instantaneous reaction of all five of the soldiers, who leapt to their feet, as if they were one man. Everyone, having retained his hat on his head, saluted. Elsa responded.

The silence was remarkable.

'Please give an answer to my question, which way are you going?'

'We are going to Hamburg, ma'am,' their spokesman replied. 'I want to give you our apologies for what has happened. We are loyal soldiers and regret our conduct with you.'

'Let me tell you something. I was improperly dressed. You had no way of knowing otherwise. As far as I am concerned, the matter is closed. Put it down to experience. I have become used to wearing this outfit on a number of operations I have undertaken. By your uniform badges I can see you have been on the Russian front.'

'That is correct, ma'am. We are the only survivors from our whole battalion that was wiped out. They thought we needed a rest.'

'That is an understatement. I take my hat off to you. I have just returned from Dresden, where my friend in the service and her parents, and my parents, were all killed in the bombing. As I am going to Kiel, I must be on my way. It is a pity I have to go in the opposite direction to you.'

She strode out of the premises, accompanied by the soldiers, who lined up and saluted while she mounted her bicycle, desperately hoping she would not fall off it in front of them, and rode away.

She had still failed to look at her leave pass.

After an hour's ride, she stopped to look at it.

She was intrigued to read that leave was granted for such time in the period stated that the holder wished to be away from service. In her case the seventh of February was the final deadline date beyond which the holder became a deserter. All dates in between were optional for returning to duty.

I am fed up with messing around day after day, she said to herself. *I will report back as soon as I arrive. My excuse is self-evident. At least I can get cleaned up and put some personal things together again.*

Elsa despatched the remaining miles to Kiel, arriving late afternoon. She had needed no overnight accommodation between Hamburg and Kiel. The thought of it had been a miscalculation on her part.

She found the office of the Women's Naval Service. The building itself seemed empty. Before reporting, Elsa had arrived without having had the means to wash and brush up after her travel-stained journey from Dresden.

She propped her bicycle outside the office, went into the foyer, and followed the signs to the commandant's office.

Erika Möller was the sole occupant, sitting in her office, silent, and writing. Her impeccable appearance was the exact opposite from how Elsa felt. An impartial observer would have judged that Elsa's appearance matched her inner feelings. Her hair, attire, and unwashed face spoke of acute neglect.

'Oberleutnant zur See Elsa Bauer reporting, ma'am,' Elsa declared, saluting.

'Elsa!' Erika proclaimed. 'You are early. There must be a reason. But it is good to see you. It seems ages since you left, yet it's only days. You look the worse for wear.'

She surprised Elsa by getting up from her chair and coming around her desk to give Elsa a warm welcome hug. She gripped Elsa in a manner more familiar than would have been expected from an acquaintance, let alone a fellow officer.

Her smell had an intoxicating effect on the weary but heated up Elsa. Erika had been drinking but was far from being drunk.

The encounter gave Elsa a required lift. After losing friend and family, she had not yet had time to consider herself friendless, but she knew the thought was lurking at the back of her mind. This welcome was a tonic. It rejuvenated her, injecting new hope in her that the morrow would be a good day and today a worthy precursor to it.

'It's the end of my normal working day. I will clear up here. Where will you be staying until you report for service?'

'I have just this minute arrived. My transport is outside. I have absolutely nothing fixed, but I can soon arrange something, now I have seen you.'

'That need not be necessary,' Erika said. 'I have a good-sized house. I am alone in it. You will be welcome to stay there until you can be fixed up. Rest a day or so and take your time.'

'That is very generous of you. I don't know my way around Kiel yet, but it would help me to collect some personal effects together again. I have lost everything except what I am standing up in. So, it would be a great help.'

'That's settled then,' Erika said. 'We can move out while it's still daylight.'

Outside she asked Elsa how she had travelled to Kiel.

'It's a very long story, Erika. Can I tell you everything when we get to your home? But that bicycle is how I came from Hamburg to Kiel.'

'You did what!' she expostulated. 'My darling, it is not as if the bike is a special and reliable machine. It looks old and somewhat rusty. What an amazing feat of endurance you must have gone through. You could leave it where it is. My kübelwagon is around the corner.'

'I suppose the bike will come in useful sometimes. When you run out of petrol,' Elsa said rather lamely.

Erika's house was on the outskirts of Kiel. It had escaped the bombing, concentrated on the shipyards, dockyards, and industrial heart of the city. It suddenly seemed a peaceful place to be, set back from grassy mounds with a generous sprinkling of trees.

Elsa was beginning to look forward to a night between sheets. She suspected that before that could happen, Erika would demonstrate her wares as an old hand. She had no qualms about what to expect from this delightful officer, only just one step superior in rank to her.

Elsa gratefully paid a visit to the bathroom, aided by the cosmetics Erika gave her. A travel worn and dishevelled woman went in, a polished officer in the Women's Naval Service came out.

'Wow, what a transformation!' Erika remarked. 'You really are something from another world.'

'That makes two of us,' Elsa retorted.

'I've got a special present for you, darling,' Erika said.

'I can't imagine what that could be. There seems to be nothing around that's special any more. Perhaps you have it from a source in that other world you came from,' Elsa said with a smile on her face.

'This will surprise you, then. It is from another world. It came to our world before it was turned upside down.'

'Now you really have me guessing. It must be pretty old in that case.'

Erika went to another room. She had a small store of wines there. But she returned to the sitting room holding a bottle of genuine Scotch whisky.

'Good God, Erika, where on earth did you find that?'

'I've had it from before the war. When the war started, I kept it hidden, thinking I would open it when the war was over.'

'You could be opening it in a few months.'

'For the wrong reason. I was naturally expecting our

victory.'

'But you are not going to open it for me, are you?'

'I most certainly am about to do just that.'

She put the bottle on the table and ceremonially opened the select scotch, while Elsa watched in amazement.

'I must be dreaming. I could never have imagined what you are now doing. It's beyond the world of dreams.'

Two glasses appeared.

'One for you, one for me,' she said, pouring a generous tot in each. Handing one to Elsa, she picked up her own.

With a loving look on her face, she suggested a toast.

'To Elsa, from Erika. You are the most delectable and adorable woman I have ever met. Could we not put the clock back ten years while we enjoy each other for those lost years?'

Elsa's constitution rose to the occasion. Her secret admiration for the commandant had prepared her for the summit, which now opened up before her, but she was startled by Erika's words.

After drinking to Erika's toast, she raised her own glass.

'To Erika, from Elsa. You are the most untouchable beauty I have ever met. I was dying to get back to you. We are made for each other, you and I. It has been written up in heaven. Now it is a reality, my darling.'

'Did you call me my darling, Elsa?'

'Yes, I did.'

'No one has had the temerity to call me that before.'

'Your beauty must have paralysed them. I've been saving it for you.'

'But I have still wanted to be loved by someone I could love, too.' She renewed the generous tot in each of their glasses.

'Erika, I love you,' Elsa said, placing her glass on the table.

She slowly but firmly hugged Erika, closing their bodies seductively by wrapping her arms around her and placing a kiss, such as only she could deliver on her mouth. That was all.

She picked up her glass again, saying simply, 'To us. This war has brought us together. I wonder what it still has in store for us before it ends.'

Erika added a third tot to Elsa's glass and then her own. They were both stalwarts in the drinking game. They would see it through together.

'Did you know that Russian army generals eat some butter before they enjoy a drinking spree?'

Elsa thought Erika had not heard her say it.

After a pause, Erika said, 'They then only drink that wretched vodka stuff. It's enough to give a girl a headache.'

They laughed.

'This may put you under the table, but it won't give you a headache,' Elsa added.

'I hope you are right,' Erika said. 'I've never actually drunk a whole bottle of whisky, or shall I say, shared a bottle. But a bottle shared is a symbol of shared love. So, keep going.'

'I shall have no trouble in sharing my share,' Elsa stated.

'I think you got a word wrong in what you just said,' Erika laughed. 'How can you share a share?'

'I meant to say that I could share your share and you could share mine. Or did I mean I could have both shares?' Elsa responded.

'Only if I had a second bottle,' Erika spluttered.

'Now I have to say that we will get our words right if we

have another glass of whisky. It sharpens your aspirations,' Elsa declared.

'It could also do wonders for your aspirants, too,' Erika corrected Elsa's mistake. 'You will need another glass to get it right. I am amazed that I spotted that, but as I said, another glass does wonders for your asperitics.'

They both erupted in laughter as Erika ended on an errant note. Both women were standing.

Erika suddenly put her glass on the table.

She took one hungry look at Elsa and gave her a kiss, also on her mouth. 'I will put the food on to cook, while we finish off the bottle. We are still on our feet. If we have to sit down, let us do it together. It will be handy for reaching for the bottle.'

'I hope to finish it while I'm still standing,' Elsa said. 'Once I sit down, I shall not want to get up again. At least for a while.'

'You will then have to start on another bottle,' Erika warned her.

'Oh, I could manage that after a couple of hours if I have to,' Elsa said, fairly evenly. 'But it would have to be an ersatz whisky, not the real stuff from the highlands of Scotland. I would like to go there one day and see how they drink their own whisky.'

'As a matter of fact, which might not be too far away, by the course the war is taking at the moment,' Erika said.

'Shhh. That is defeatist talk. You are not supposed to be so objective. You could be shot as a middle-ranking officer for talking like that,' Elsa blurted out, in a mock state of shock that she didn't mean in the least, as Erika could see.

They burst out laughing.

'We need something to take our minds away from this bloody mess and hopeless outcome we are in,' Erika compounded her own misconduct a step further.

'What is going to happen to you and me? I can only see matters getting worse by the hour. If they forget us and where we are, you and I will have to think about what we can do to save ourselves and our sanity.'

'I have a solution to our problem,' Elsa said seriously.

'Then you must have been drinking,' Erika said quickly.

'Let's go to bed. We need a rest. The day is still young. We can get up again when the cooking is finished and have our meal,' Elsa suggested.

'What a good idea! Do you think we shall need a meal a bit later?' Erika asked, looking Elsa straight in the eye.

'There is a huge doubt about that!' Elsa replied.

'I wonder what we could do after eating a meal if we have to?' Erika asked a rhetorical question, delivered suggestively.

'Go back to bed,' Elsa chose to answer it, with an equal innuendo in her voice. 'I would be unable to wait.'

25

The following morning, they woke early. On their way to her office, Erika confessed to Elsa that she hoped to find a message had been left from the navy authorities that would keep them in employment, in spite of the pending disaster approaching from both the west and the east.

They were astonished to find that overnight Kiel had been attacked from the air yet again. They had slept so soundly that they had heard neither the air raid sirens nor the explosions from the bombs dropping. The raid had inflicted more damage on the residential areas of the city.

In one area, their way was blocked by streets littered with debris from half-destroyed buildings.

Erika was about to turn the kübelwagon around to find an alternative route, when she realised that the many buildings in a devastated state had no rescue teams working on them yet. Steam was thinly rising from one building, water spouting from another.

'Elsa, there must be people buried alive under that rubble. The rescue people have not yet arrived.'

'We should give it a look over to make sure,' Elsa replied.

They clambered out of the vehicle and ran to the worst building that had once been a block of flats.

'Oh, what a mess!' Erika exclaimed. 'Can you hear that crying?'

'Yes,' Elsa said. 'Where is it coming from?'

They climbed over the mounds of bricks, stone, steel, and timber. Erika suddenly went to her right and bent over.

'There's someone under here. Give me a hand.'

By the time Elsa reached her, Erika had scooped away several pieces of debris and had actually caught hold of a human arm. She was uttering soothing sounds to the owner of the arm.

'It's a child's arm. We are going to get you out of here immediately. Can you breathe? Can you feel your legs and arms?' she was asking, hoping for some answers.

Elsa noted that Erika had pursued her task without regard to her uniform, already covered in dust, or her hands, which were soon the worse for wear, dirty and bruised.

The two women tore into the surrounding pieces of debris together. They found a child had been partially shielded by a steel girder but was in danger from unstable masonry that would fall on her if it were disturbed.

With care they levered the child out of the hole they had made. She was a young girl, about seven years old.

They gave her a cursory examination at once for any signs or symptoms of injury. She was covered in thick dust and distraught, but her body seemed to be intact, except for her unimaginable trauma.

Erika gently took the child in her arms and repeated a string of assertions that the girl was now rescued, and that she would live.

Elsa was impressed by the tenderness and care Erika displayed.

Rescue people, too few of them, were supplementing those already arriving on the bombsite. Erika carried the girl to the kübelwagen.

Elsa had a word with the official in charge of the rescue operation.

'We will take her to the hospital and send you a report afterwards.'

Once in their vehicle, Erika chose not to go to the hospital but to the Women's Naval Service offices.

'Will this diversion get us into trouble, Erika?' Elsa asked.

'I was a trained senior nurse before the war,' she replied. 'I will give her a thorough check-up. Would you mind if we took her home with us until she can be looked after properly?'

'Of course not. While you are looking after her, I will go out and find some new clothes for her.' Elsa used her bicycle and revelled in the physical exercise it gave her.

While she was on her mission, the air raid sirens went again. It was yet another predatory sweep by fighter-bombers, from the allied forces closing in on the north German ports.

On eventually returning to the offices, Elsa was horrified to see that Erika's kübelwagon in the nearby car park had been completely destroyed. As a military vehicle, it was a choice target for a low-level daylight attack.

Inside the offices, Erika was comforting the rescued girl. She had established her name as Rita. She was six years old.

Elsa told Erika that she was going out again but would not be gone very long. She had had a brain wave but was unwilling to discuss it with Erika before she tested her idea.

During her search for clothing for Rita, she had noticed a car park shot up by the British aircraft. She was bent on purloining any surviving van she could find. Something less military looking than a kübelwagon fitted the bill.

She found plenty of vans that had escaped aerial attack.

One had been damaged and still had a supply of petrol in its tank. The key had been left in the ignition, a common practice by drivers anxious only for a swift escape from air attacks.

She stole it and drove it to Erika's offices.

'Erika, my darling, your precious kübelwagon has been destroyed. It is totally wrecked. But I have found a replacement vehicle. We can go home now.'

Erika carried Rita outside to their newly acquired van. Elsa drove them both home.

With a stranger in the house, the two women were acutely on edge. The fact was unspoken between them, but they were aware that they were technically kidnappers, whatever their intentions, as long as they had not notified an appointed authority.

Elsa had promised they would submit a report, but that was with the assumption that the child would have been returned to the rescue workers and into the system established for surviving children.

They were soon engulfed in conversation with what the presence of Rita engendered. The girl was in a remarkable state of recovery, considering the ordeal she had suffered during the past twenty-four hours. Her nasty bruises and lacerations would take a while to heal, under Erika's watchful eye and tireless attention.

'Considering we have no duties to undertake commensurate with our ranks, we are left as two responsible officers waiting for a commission,' Elsa said. 'If we are not in receipt of one from our higher authorities, we have only one option.'

She had been influenced in what she was about to say by Erika's amazing display of care and concern for the child of the night, who had awakened in the morning as an orphan.

The bombing was still bringing havoc to the population of Kiel.

'And what would that be?' Erika asked her. It was a genuine question.

She had no idea what Elsa's answer would be.

'We have to create our own commission,' Elsa declared.

She stopped, impeded by the questionable motives and dubious morality of herself and Erika, implicit in what was in her mind.

'Go on, then. Keep talking.' Erika urged her to divulge the latest thoughts of her partner. Being fresh from the upsetting and challenging experience they had just been through, Erika was suddenly afraid that Elsa would be deterred from staying with her.

'We should establish our own trust for saving orphaned girls.'

Elsa took a deep breath, having said it. She waited for Erika to pillory her idea as unworkable, irregular for serving navy officers, duplicating the work of the social services, and smacking of opportunistic objectives.

Instead, Erika took a large breath of relief. The idea had never occurred to her as an option to be undertaken, but it was in keeping with her own inner feelings and came as a liberating step to take.

'What a good idea, darling. We could call ourselves the E & E Fraulein Trust. It would be just for girls. But where would we find the children?'

'We could visit any further bombing incidents and take over any girls we spied as eligible. We could visit the various agencies and persuade them to part with any girl we wanted.

'We could house them in the Women's Naval Service offices. The excuse for using them could be the chaotic conditions of buildings and roads, and the dislocation of people.'

Elsa let her thoughts run riot, since Erika had given her a virtual carte blanche by her reaction.

'What if the authorities discover our activity?' Erika asked. 'What I am saying is, what will be our cover story?'

'It will not need a cover story in the sense that we can offer good care to a limited number of girls and a loving home,' Elsa responded. 'But we can always say we have to conserve the best of German females. We don't want anyone sending our people abroad, do we?'

'That sounds like the German habit of preserving racial purity. Do you remember the Strength through Joy movement pre-war?' Erika asked.

'I certainly do. I went on one trip in the *Hans Frayling*. It was a fraudulent trip to be near a member of the crew of the ship, later lost on its evacuation passage to Kiel. But our interests would be above board. We may have to pass the girls on eventually to a legitimate agency,' Elsa answered.

'But not if we could limit the number to those of a large family. We could raise them as our children,' Erika said suddenly.

'Erika, what you have just said is profoundly inspiring. What a sequel to our war service to have, say, ten orphaned girls aged between four and ten living with us. I think we could offer the love, discipline, orderly life, and economic terms that would do them the greatest service.'

'To secure the girls we need to build such a family… it might involve us in the charge of kidnapping,' Erika commented.

'But it would be governed by the best of motives. I am sure we could pull it off. It looks as if there will be an increasing collapse of order and discipline as Germany folds under the combined pressure of the attacks from west and east.

'If we hold our nerve and stay together, the girls would be safer with us than with the many agencies, some of which will collapse or be inundated with the huge numbers of parentless children they will accumulate by the end of hostilities.'

'I will go out in the van to find out what prospects actually exist,' Elsa said. 'Perhaps the various rescue services have not yet reached them all.'

She returned to the area bombed the previous night, where Rita had been found, walking around several streets of older houses in the port and docks area.

An elderly man was rummaging in the ruins of one house, and the fire brigade was wrestling with a gas escape in another, while rescue workers, such as they were, in small numbers, were concentrated on a large block of flats that had partially collapsed.

In a neighbouring street, Elsa found a young girl clutching a small girl in her arms, sitting silently and utterly forlorn on the debris of another block of flats. Elsa strode quickly to them.

'Hello,' she addressed them.

They did not reply and made no visible response.

Elsa knelt down bedside them, gently taking them into her own arms. They were surprisingly free from the dust that covered people in a bombed building that had collapsed. She concluded they had escaped the rigours of being buried in the adjacent building.

After a few minutes, Elsa told the older girl her own name and asked her for her name.

'Anita,' she whispered.

'That is a nice name,' Elsa whispered back. 'How old are you?' she asked.

'Eight,' she replied. 'I had my birthday only last week.'

'Is this your sister?' Elsa inquired.

'Yes, this is Sonja, she is five,' Anita replied.

'Why are you sitting here?' Elsa asked.

'We were staying with our friends in another street. When we came back this morning, they told us the worst had happened. We were told to stay here. Someone would come back for us.'

Her struggled statement was accompanied by a fresh burst of sobbing and a renewed hug of her younger sister, who looked too dazed to respond to any approach.

Elsa grasped the free hand of Sonja. For a moment, Anita refused to release Sonja from the hold she had on her younger sister, as if she had a duty to shelter her from the abyss.

Elsa held out her other hand to Anita, inviting her and Sonja to stand up. 'I will be a mother to you, both,' were the words coming from Elsa's lips.

She did not consciously intend to be so dramatic. She couldn't help saying them. They fell out of her mouth of their own accord.

With one child on each hand, Elsa took a circuitous track back to her van and drove straight home to Erika.

The two women spent the rest of the day rejuvenating the two newcomers and introducing them to Rita. They fastened on the reality that the three girls seemed to have an immediate distraction in their common suffering. Making a small group had its own advantages.

Erika remarked on the noticeable development.

'We are learning as we go, Elsa. We have to get them something to do. Probably something to make, rather than play things,' she said.

'I will go out and scout around to see what I can find,' Elsa responded.

'No, it's my turn. You've done your bit for the day. You could prepare some food for them if you wish.'

Erika drove the van to the naval seamen's favourite Lutheran Church to try her luck in the port area. It had not escaped the bombing.

Being half destroyed, it provided a focal point for homeless people. A few civilians were loitering there, waiting for a stroke of luck to satisfy whatever they had hoped to find.

She wandered in and met an older girl, standing with a nonchalant air. Erika thought she had not been a victim of the bombing.

'What are you doing in here?' she asked her. 'You seem to be unconcerned about what is going on around you.'

'My father taught me to look facts straight in the face. I cannot change anything. He was a soldier and is dead now. My mother and sister have been killed. I've been told to wait here until the people from the children's home come to fetch me. But I don't know what they would look like.'

Erika seized her opportunity. 'Well, here I am, at last. Let's get away as soon as we can. What is your name? You must be in your teens.'

'My name is Lisa. I'm sixteen.'

'You are tall for your age,' Erika told her, calmly walking her out of the front door and into the van.

'Where are you taking me?' she asked.

'Home,' Erika replied, 'but first I have to find some things for children to do. I am looking for games, play things, and some practical things to make.'

'Oh, I know a special place which has been collecting all that kind of thing from bombed damaged buildings. It's all in a small warehouse. You can collect as much as you like but I think you have to pay something towards the expenses.'

'Show me the way, then,' Erika demanded with relief.

Her luck had just turned her way. Lisa and she could indulge—and Lisa could direct—their choice of artefacts to keep the new family, at least in part, away from being preoccupied with their grievous loss of family members and destruction of their homes.

The aggregation of playthings and materials to make things had been assiduously collected over the past three years from the bombing of Kiel. The enthusiasm of the volunteers in charge of the enterprise had evidently roared ahead of the demand for their carefully collected salvage.

Perhaps the slowly descending numbers of the population who would normally have an interest in them were to blame for the lack of demand.

Consequently, they were able to help themselves to materials for painting and drawing, tapestry making, dressmaking, and embroidering, a plethora of reading books to suit all tastes, plus skipping ropes, and a variety of playtime vehicles including small, make-belief prams, baby cars, and proper bicycles of various sizes.

While they had been away, Elsa had been teaching Rita, Anita, and Sonja that moping was an alien language of behaviour. They each had to help in one small way or another, according to their talents, in running the house and preparing the food.

Erika's return to the house brought rejoicing over the bonanza. She directed the four helpers to unload the goods into a room she had set aside as a play store.

With a nice soft drink in the kitchen, Erika introduced Lisa to Elsa and the three incumbents. Lisa's height and age gave her a natural advantage over the family, but she had a kindly side to her as well to set beside her own self-discipline. She smiled at each of the three children and made a comforting remark about their joint suffering.

It was during those few minutes that Elsa felt that any more children they adopted should be younger. Afterwards, when comparing private notes, Erika declared she thought a total of eight would be the right limit.

The next day Elsa set out to complete the family. She took Lisa with her. The girl seemed to have a good knowledge of the ways and means by which the population of Kiel had exercised their manipulation of the officialdom that dominated this and every other city.

Lisa directed Elsa to follow the main railway lines out of the flattened railway station. They came to a series of bridges, carrying the lines over several main roads. Parking their van, Lisa explained to Elsa the reason for stopping in such a malodorous and clearly unattractive place.

'This is the area where the homeless from the bombing have been unofficially congregating. The authorities don't permit them to stay. They have a round up from time to time and take the children to the welfare centres. The adults are always women or old men. They are sent away on work gangs.'

Before they left the van, Elsa saw about two dozen children playing together, their mothers standing away from them in small groups, smoking and chatting. Many were from the poorer end of the population.

Elsa took off her officer's uniform jacket, replacing it with a woolly.

'Why are you doing that?' Lisa asked.

'I'll tell you later,' Elsa replied. 'Go and join the children who are on the left over there, playing on that wrecked lorry hit by air attack. Can you see that young girl about five years old, carrying a stone? You can see she has placed it on the ground. And look there, she is standing on it to climb inside the wreck.'

'Yes, of course I can see her. What do you want me to do?'

'Wander over to the site, as if you are just joining it. Talk to that little girl and take her by the hand. See if she is alone. Or see if she would like to come home with you, rather than go to a children's home.'

'You want me to use some charm, don't you!'

Elsa was a bit taken aback by Lisa's forthright remark. She had a precocity in advance of her age, or perhaps because of her upbringing.

'She would be better with us. If she is interested, bring her away from the adults and drift back over this way.'

Elsa watched Lisa taking her time but eventually getting close to the infant. Lisa bent her knees to adjust a second stone for the little girl to have an easier climb into the wreck.

She caught the girl by the waist and lowered her to the ground, giving her a charming smile. The child was so delighted with her perch that she gave Lisa an equally charming smile in return.

Elsa was pleased to see that happen. It confirmed her first sighting of the girl as a possible candidate for their family.

Lisa and the girl played on together for anther ten minutes.

Elsa saw Lisa stop to tell the girl something. It must have been important, she judged, by the rapt attention on the face of the latter.

Soon after, Elsa lost sight of them, until a knock on the van door told her that Lisa had returned to the van. But she could not be seen.

Elsa opened the van door to see the little girl alone, smiling, and holding out her arms. Elsa with a swift surge of passion picked her up and gave her a warm hug.

'What is your name, darling?'

'I am called Carla,' she said.

'And how old are you, Carla?'

'I am four, but nearly five,' she said.

'I am so happy that you have decided to come home with me,' Elsa said. 'You will be warm and be in a nice family.'

Just then there was a knock on the van door behind Elsa's back. She turned to see Lisa holding in her arms a very young girl—she guessed only three years old.

'This is Petra. She is only three. Carla's sister.'

'Where did you manage to find Petra, Lisa?'

'The officials have arrived over there to clear out the adults. They will come back soon for the children.'

'Carla told me she had a sister and pointed out her mother, who was carrying Petra in her arms.'

'I was talking with her mother when the officials arrived.'

Her mother took one look at them and said to me, 'Take Petra as well, I shall only lose them where I am going.'

Carla and Petra, muffled to their ears, ignored the

conversation, while they held on to each other's hand in the middle of the front seat of the van, but keeping a sharp eye on what went on around them.

'I discarded my uniform in case you come unstuck in your efforts,' Elsa told Lisa. 'I would have tried some other way of encouraging her to come with us. But you have done a good job. Thank you.'

'You are very beautiful, I wish I was as beautiful as you.'

Lisa surprised Elsa by the personal remark she uttered in reply.

'But you are beautiful, Lisa,' Elsa responded. 'Before the war, when I was your age, I was driving a tractor on my father's farm in Pomerania. I was a rough and tumble girl. You are a beautiful girl, Lisa, and you are now helping the war effort, or shall I say helping the tragic results of the war effort. We can do it together.'

Her words gave Lisa a feeling of being useful. Her morale rose to new levels. Since meeting her, she had wanted to know more about her adopted mother. Elsa seemed to be used to giving orders. She was so nice with it. *It's something I will find out one day*, she said to herself.

The two young children they took back to the house were warmly welcomed by the family. The oldest ones were only too pleased to have to look after a younger member they could call sister, once Petra's own real sister was willing to release her from the care and protection she had afforded her.

Erika and Elsa were surprised at the hardiness and emotional stability of the children so far in their care.

'Put it down to suffering. The long persistent bombing and the long dragging disappointment of the Russian campaign, but above all the toll the navy has paid in the oceans of the world have had their effect,' Erika said. 'The submarines have taken a huge loss rate that has shaken the northern ports more than anything else.'

'It is a good job you thought of limiting the number to eight,' Elsa said. 'We shall be running out of bed space.'

'Yes, it will be enough to manage a family of eight. By the way, it will be my job tomorrow to bring in the last of our family. I shall also be hunting for food. It was good fortune that we had the stores from the Women's Naval Service to fall back on. Food supply is getting worse by the day.'

26

Erika left on her mission in the middle of the next morning. Her destination was the clearing station for bombed out people. She wore her uniform and looked impressive as usual as she strolled around the depot.

Many older people were waiting for a solution to their homelessness.

The building had once belonged to the Heilsarmee, The Salvation Army, which the regime had permitted to operate before the war but, in common with other organisations of foreign origin, had received suspension notices when the war started.

She heard the shouts and screams of children at play. Walking to an open area, she found a dozen children playing together, exposed to the cold weather but in seeming ignorance of it. The group lacked supervision.

Watching them play, Erika was approached by several children for one purpose or another.

A three-year old delightful girl handed her a ball. Erika bounced it a few times, before rolling it towards the girl. This went on for several minutes. Erika gave her a sweet, eventually picking her up.

'What is your name, darling?' she asked.

'Margot,' she replied. 'I am three.'

'That's a nice name for a little girl. My name is Erika. Would you like to come with me to my house?'

'Yes, please. It is too cold out here. Can my sister come, too?'

'Who is your sister?'

'Angela, she is seven. That's her with the hat on, playing over there.'

Trying to look as casual as possible, Erika strolled over to the group at play. Angela ran to them when she saw Margot. Erika came straight to the point with the seven-year-old.

'Are you Angela? I would like to invite you and Margot to my house to join our family. It is a large, warm house with plenty to do. Would you like to give it a try?'

'If Margot goes, I will go, too,' she said.

They walked back to the van and drove away, straight to Erika's offices, to pillage the storeroom of foodstuffs that had been awaiting the arrival of the transferred Women's Naval Service contingent from Gotenhaven.

It included food that would soon deteriorate as well as long storage food, both that would never be eaten, as intended, by that entire contingent so tragically lost.

Angela and Margot actually helped Erika to carry the goods to the van.

On arriving home, Erika and Elsa called all eight children into the kitchen. They were served with hot drinks or cold drinks as they preferred, together with some wartime biscuits, courtesy of the Women's Naval Service.

Erika thought it time to pull their enterprise together. She spoke seriously and in plain language.

'Elsa and I are officers in the Women's Naval Service. We have recently lost all the women in a terrible disaster at sea. Elsa was one of only two who escaped. The other one has since been killed in the bombing of Dresden. They had been on their way to Kiel.

'We found ourselves wanting to do something useful instead. As far as we know, you have all been bombed out. Your dads and mums are far away or will be sent away. We have formed this family especially for you. Each of you will be a proper member of the family.

'Altogether, we are now a family of ten. We shall stay together until you are grown up. We shall always be together. We shall be happy together. We do not know what will happen in the war, but it will get worse. You will be our children. We will protect you and care for you and love you.

'We wanted you to know that we are choosing to do this because we cannot bear to see the children suffer. If anyone wants to ask a question, this is the time to ask it.'

Lisa was the only one who could frame a question.

'Do we live with you and what will you do if they try to take us away from you?'

Erika replied. 'We shall take steps to have each of you registered to be our family, to make it a legal undertaking. We have some influence as officers. No one knows at the moment how things will go if we lose the war and the allies take over, but we are determined to make our family a lasting one.'

From that day onwards, the two women slaved for the children, showing every sign of being loving and caring parents. They established meal times and going to bed at regular hours. Lisa was given special responsibilities alongside Erika and Elsa.

According to their ages, they were all subjected to formal learning, like being at school, which they would never have experienced if they had continued running loose, since systematic schooling had ceased in the badly damaged city.

They learned to cope with the squabbles in their newly founded family, and from homesickness that afflicted some of them in the early days.

The children learned to paint and draw, and to sew and embroider. Physical exercises at a certain time every day were established.

They had some free time each day, the school hours being only for a part of the day. They could go out on their own, when not scheduled for any household duty or learning time—for a maximum of two hours nearby outside the house, but for one hour only away from it.

After one month of the initial, trial-run schedule, the family had a conference to comment on the way the time had been spent, and how it could be improved.

Once started, the monthly conference grew on them into a regular institution for settling complaints and making adjustments.

During that month Elsa spent considerable time plaguing the officials in control of the available food rations being issued to the citizens, to provide new allowances for the eight children.

Erika similarly sought officials who could legitimize their adoption of the children. She was ready to accept any document that would fill the bill.

The months of March and April saw the steady and inevitable incursion of the Russians from the east and the allied forces from the west.

Erika and Elsa picked up items of news by hearsay during their efforts to sustain their family, while touring around the port and city.

'I think Kiel is going to be a prize in the race of both sides to take the remaining territory in these parts. The Russians are very close and appear to be letting nothing stop them from grabbing everything they want.'

Erika's comment was reinforced at the end of April, when the circulating rumours on balance suggested that the Russians would beat the allies to Kiel. It led to acute alarm and fear. If they invested Kiel, it would be in defiance of the agreement with the western allies at the conference held at Yalta.

Great was the joy that swept around the city on the first of May, therefore, when a British major, commanding over four hundred commando troops, appeared suddenly on the west side of Kiel, in contrast to the perceived train of events.

The force overcame any resistance by the remaining German garrison, which anyway was inclined to yield to the British as the better alternative to the Russians.

The British arrival secured the city and the state of Schleswig-Holstein. By implication, it probably prevented the Russians from overrunning Denmark, and possibly Norway.

The administration officers, who subsequently followed up the British takeover, were faced with a more than fifty percentage destruction of the central town and port.

All the pending ills, fell on their shoulders. In short, the controls and problems of a city without a normal administration of its own was theirs to derive order from ruin.

Elsa broke the news to Erika. She was hopeful of securing a confirmation of their family membership.

'We should wait a few days before we approach the British.'

Six days later, a cease-fire for the entire war was declared. Conflict had been finally terminated between Germany and the opposing allies.

When the message spread among the population that all their forces had to lay down their arms, Elsa and Erika quietly took off their officers' uniforms, replacing them with warm woollies.

All members of the armed forces were being caged in prisoner of war camps for screening. Some were released, only to be directed to work assignments. The majority remained in confinement for identification and investigation.

The two women escaped the incarceration. It was time to look forward. Erika and Elsa as Women's Naval Service officers had transformed themselves into two hard-working women, who had collected stray children, made orphans by the bombing, under the auspices of the E & E Fraulein Trust.

After a week or two, Elsa took Lisa to the British commandant's office. They were kept waiting an inordinate time in his outer reception area.

Eventually his aide-de-camp, Lieutenant James Robinson, of the Welsh Guards, told Elsa she was next to be interviewed. She noted he was speaking German to her. The young officer informed the commandant of his next interviewee but could not resist a comment.

'She is rather beautiful, sir. She has an equally beautiful young girl with her. I expect she has judged she can take advantage of her natural talents.'

'Show her in then, Robinson. We shall see if you are right.'

Elsa entered the office with all the presence she could muster. The major stood as a gentleman to welcome her and shake her hand.

'What can I do for you?' he said to her. Elsa was surprised that the officer, Major Ralph Williams, of the Welsh Guards, could speak German.

Elsa related the collection of the family from the bombing without stating any dates or other information about the details.

The major turned to Lisa.

'Please tell me how many children and their ages.'

'I'm sixteen, Anita is eight, Angela is seven, Rita is six, Sonja is five, Carla is four, Petra and Margot are both three.'

Addressing Elsa again, he asked, 'Your name and that of your partner?'

'I'm Elsa Bauer, my partner is Erika Möller, sir. We have been operating under the E & E Fraulein Trust.'

'Right. Come back in one week. Bring your partner and the other children. If I am satisfied with the prospects, I will have a document prepared for your legitimate care of the children. You will have to think about what you will do with the family in the future.'

'Thank you, sir.'

Elsa and Lisa took the good news back to their home. It was not a subject of interest or concern to the majority of the children, but Lisa could not restrain sharing it with Anita and Angela.

The others were variously curious about the excitement that had disturbed that particular day, but they were soon distracted by their pursuit of activities according to the regular schedule that Erika and Elsa had ruthlessly but kindly imposed.

They treated everything on a fun basis, encouraging the children to regard it as a game. There were penalties for lateness and rewards for exceptional effort in their studies, irrespective of the intrinsic merits of the product.

Naturally, when the day arrived for the visit to the office of the British commandant, Elsa and Erika wanted the children to be turned out at their best in a fitting demonstration of what devoted foster parents could do for orphaned or rejected war children.

The two mothers themselves were eager to emulate their children. Putting their minds to it, they knew how to add their undoubted impressive deportment with facial make-up and hairdos. Even the children had to reassess their view and appreciation of their parents when they finally saw the way they had prepared themselves that day.

With the two youngest in the front seat of the van with the two women, the others being in the back on seats they had installed, the family kept the appointment with the commandant.

All eyes in the reception area were glued on the group.

The aide-de-camp, Lieutenant James Robinson, announced their arrival to the major, who invited them in without delay.

'I have to congratulate you. You are looking splendid in spite of the hardship you must have felt. Unfortunately, I have bad news to tell you.'

His statement brought a deathly hush in the room. Even the youngest stopped shuffling their bodies.

In the ensuing silence, the proverbial pin could have been heard to drop.

'I have consulted with British and German officials. Private persons at the moment are not permitted to create families of homeless children as parents.'

With his announcement of the prohibition, a bubble of abject disappointment grew rampantly in the stomachs of Elsa and Erika. It was the nadir of their hopes. It carried them to a suffocating disillusion.

The major continued. 'The only exceptions to the rule would be in the case of persons who have a credible military background and show due diligence and competence.'

That was a shock addendum. If only they had known that fact, they could have worn their uniforms.

'Perhaps I should ask you again about yourselves. Who in fact are you? I have been in the military long enough to recognise that neither of you fills the bill for an ordinary woman citizen of Kiel. I must ask you to be frank with me.'

Erika spoke up first.

'I am Kapitän zur See Erika Möller, commander of the Women's Naval Service in Kiel. A contingent of nearly four hundred members at Gotenhaven were embarked on the *Hans Frayling*. They were returning to Kiel to be under my command. They were all drowned except two.' Erika produced her military name-tag and pay book.

'I am Oberleutnant zur See Elsa Bauer of the Women's Naval Service. I have served throughout the war in submarine design and on special duties. I am the sole survivor from the two members of the entire Women's Naval Service who perished in the *Hans Frayling*, sunk at the end of January. The other has since been killed in the bombing of Dresden.' Elsa produced her military name-tag and pay book.

There was an awkward silence after their declaration.

But then the major smiled. He said in the kindest voice, 'As the women's services have been disbanded, you are in the clear. I congratulate you on the handling of your lives amid the chaos of the past few months. I see no reason but to give you a document for the legitimate charge of the family you have congregated, in the hope that you will make a good life for them.'

The bubble of tragic reversal that had possessed Elsa and Erika suddenly burst. It was even for them a traumatic experience.

27

For many weeks after the cease-fire, chaos was the order of the day in the city, but under the British administration a semblance of respectability was gradually brought to it.

Streets were cleared of rubble, local and military police took control of the limited traffic, and local people were appointed to fill the leadership of various functions of the city that were vacant or neglected.

Food supplies were gradually restored. The supply of power, fuel, and building materials in some cases had to be established, and fresh chains of resources of domestic goods were painfully reintroduced.

Major Ralph Williams and Lieutenant James Robinson were the pivotal agents for getting things done. Their lives were a constant round of meetings with individuals, groups, and committees, representing and exercising the control of the occupying power.

But they were human and had to grasp whatever they could find to retain their sanity and sense of balance in their lives.

They never forgot the two women and eight children who had early on marched into their offices demanding a legitimization of their status as a family.

One day, out of the blue, a long time after meeting the family, the major recalled their existence to his aide.

'I wonder how that family is getting on. You remarked how beautiful the adoptive mother was and one of the children.'

'It has been over a year since they were in here,' his aide replied. 'They must have had a struggle to feed them. Presumably, they have been able to send them to the schools that opened up two or three months ago.'

'If you are out that way sometime, give them a call and see how they are getting on. Give them my regards as well. It would be nice to know that we made the right decision.'

Truth to tell, the family had slipped from the lieutenant's mind, preoccupied as he was with his job and a very full day's work every day. He chided himself with his lapse.

But Ralph has not forgotten, he mused. *He must have been impressed with those two women, but he never mentioned it again, until now. The oldest girl had the makings of a beauty, too, I recall. I shall have to take him up on his word. It was his way of giving a command, so I have no option.*

Early one evening of the following summer, Elsa had to be looking out from the sitting room window, when she saw a British army car stop a few houses away. It moved on after a moment, as if the numbers of houses were being checked.

It stopped right outside their house. No one alighted from it for about two minutes. *Are they weighing us up? Or is the driver sprucing himself up?* she asked herself.

One person opened the door of the car and stood outside looking at the house, before striding up to the front door.

Elsa recognized him immediately from her two visits to the office when they secured the legitimization for their family.

At the door, she said, 'Good evening, Lieutenant Robinson. It's nice to see you again. What can I do for you?'

The thoughts that coursed through his mind in answer to her question were quite different from what he actually voiced. He was too much of a gentleman to yield to expressing them.

She was a most attractive woman.

'The commandant asked me to call to see how you were coping with your large family. Over a year has passed since we last met.'

'There is no fear I shall ever forget our visit to your office. It was touch and go. But the result turned out as we wanted it to be. Come on in and see for yourself.'

'It's fortunately a big house to cope with a growing family,' he said. 'Did you already own it?'

'It belonged to Erika from before the war and as you see, it escaped damage from the bombing. We have managed with four bedrooms for the children. It was lucky we decided to limit our family to all girls. Lisa, who is seventeen, nearly eighteen now, has a room of her own. She has done well at school and wants to go to university. She and Erika have been out this afternoon and will be home soon. Come and see the other girls.'

Some were in one room, some were in another, scattered about the house. All seven were preoccupied, either reading or making something. Anita and Rita were reading, Angela was writing, Sonja was actually shelling peas, and Carla was sewing. Petra and Margot had come to the door with Elsa and were following her and the lieutenant around.

It was so quiet, it caused him to remark on it.

'It looks as if you have done wonders. They all seem busy. Do they give you any trouble?'

'Of course, they do. The usual thing, but we all learn to put it behind us.' Elsa offered the lieutenant a glass of wine or a cup of tea.

'Tea has been so scarce. A cup of tea would be nice.'

Erika and Lisa came in through the back door of the house, calling out to Elsa that they were home.

'What is that army car doing outside our house?' Lisa asked as she came into the room where Elsa and the lieutenant were seated.

On seeing the lieutenant, she stopped dead in her tracks.

He awkwardly stood up.

They were looking at each other. A moment of silence was followed by an indistinguishable murmur of embarrassment from Lisa.

'Oh, now I know who you are,' she said. 'You are the lieutenant aide-de-camp to the major, who gave us the right to exist as a family. I am pleased to see you again. It has been a long time.'

Erika shook hands with the lieutenant.

'I must get a cup of tea. What will you have Lisa?'

'Just the usual soft drink,' she said.

Elsa and Erika were party to this exchange of good fortune for Lisa. It was not difficult to see that the lieutenant was bowled over by Lisa's maturity.

While Erika was in the kitchen fixing the drinks, she called out to Elsa, who sensed she was making an excuse for leaving Lisa and the lieutenant alone for a few minutes.

'Elsa, can you come for a moment?'

'I hear your schooling is going well,' the lieutenant tried to start a conversation with her.

Lisa needed no enticement to engage in an exchange.

She immediately entered into a lucid account of the makeshift schools she had endured. 'I shall go for my abitur and somewhere to university,' she said.

'The army took me away from university,' he replied.

'To do what?' she asked.

'To command a troop of three tanks, landing in France, and fighting my way to Kiel. But if that had not happened, I would not be sitting here today,' he quipped. But Lisa was sharp enough to read his words as a hidden message for her, perhaps deliberately or inadvertently spoken.

Erika and Elsa returned.

'We hope you can give a satisfactory report on our family life, lieutenant, we have had a struggle, but we are still coping,' Erika said.

After he had gone, Lisa was left with a glow from the inner feelings the lieutenant's visit had created in her. She struggled to conceal her excitement, but her change of mood was not lost on either Elsa or Erika.

Soon after that visit, the lieutenant asked Erika and Elsa if it would be all right to invite Lisa to an officers' function, including a dinner and dance. It was relayed to Lisa for her decision. She jumped at the chance.

'It looks like the beginning of a romance,' Elsa said to Erika. 'She is of course, well past the age of consent, so we have to let her go.'

'She will know how to look after herself,' Erika commented. 'She is no fool. And I think she has secretly held back her love for him.'

As predicted, it was the start of a romance. He became a frequent visitor to the house. The children enjoyed having a man about the place. They rivalled each other to get his attention. The older ones inveigled him into playing games, the younger ones devoting their manufacturing endeavours to producing something acceptable to him as a special present.

A year later, when Erika was backing her van on a quayside in the port, the brakes failed on the aged vehicle. It went over the edge of the quay into the water, trapping Erika in the driving cab. Only one woman saw it happen. She raised the alarm, which took several minutes for any response to become active. By the time a man used to diving could be found, it was too late to save her.

Several hours elapsed before Elsa and Lisa received news of the accident. They decided not to tell the rest of the family until the following morning. Elsa and Lisa promised each other that nothing would change, but they agreed to notify the British Commandant's office. The communication brought Lieutenant Robinson for another visit to the house.

He and Lisa spent some time together talking about the crisis that had arisen from Erika's tragic accident. At the end of the morning, they asked Elsa to join them. She concealed the severe shock that Erika's death had brought to her.

Lisa spoke first.

'James has asked me to marry him, and I have said yes. He will be getting demobbed soon but will be staying in Kiel.'

It took Elsa's breath away.

James then interrupted.

'I want Lisa to go to university. We wondered if you would agree to our staying in this house to manage the children as our own family. In other words, I would replace Erika. Lisa is prepared to undertake her studies and still fulfil the work she has been doing so far with the family.'

'You have given me a huge shock,' Elsa said. 'I am at a loss with Erika's death. She has meant everything to me.

'Your suggestion has two major benefits from the family's point of view. You would be a father. They already know you well and have learned to love you.

'And Lisa has grown up to become a young mother to the youngest children. You would have to commit yourselves until the children melted away of their own accord. If you can guarantee that, I would welcome you to make this house your home.'

About a month later, Elsa received a message from a despatch rider. It came from the commandant's office. It was addressed to Elsa Bauer and simply read as follows.

Elsa Bauer

Could you spare time to call at this office when it is convenient for you.

Commandant's Office

Now I wonder what he wants from me this time, Elsa thought. *He must know about Erika's death. Perhaps he is concerned about the continuity of the family. But James Robertson must have told him about the arrangement we have made for the future. I wonder if he is opposed to the idea.*

She waited a week before notifying his office that she was free to come on a certain day. He replied with a time, which suited him.

She was not shown into his office but to another room where staff could break from their duties. He was relaxed and anything but the tense officer who had dealt with her problems earlier. Elsa herself had dressed and made-up to her usual high personal standard.

He welcomed her. After the first pleasantries, he led the way to a table, which had been prepared for tea, including a light repast. Casual conversation occupied their time until he seemed to manage to summon up something to say that had caused him some reticence.

'You must have guessed,' he said, 'that this is not a business meeting. The Welsh Guards are holding a special ball in a little over a month's time in Hamburg. Most of the regular officers who are married will be taking their wives, some coming over for the occasion from Britain.

'I wondered if you would be so kind as to accept my invitation to join me for a night at the ball. It will be an auspicious event. I would not imply any obligation on your part other than to come with me as a friend.'

'I cannot imagine what more a woman could expect in life that would bowl her over more than what you have just levelled at me,' she said.

'I naturally thought it would be a business appointment but coming into this room instantly disabused me of that. But the ball would be all British people and I would be the only German person there.'

'Not at all. German senior officers from the navy and army are jointly part of it, so you will be one of many from the Kriegsmarine and Werhmacht.'

'Would I be expected to wear my officer's uniform or come in civilian clothes? As far as I know the Women's Naval Service was disbanded on the cease-fire.'

'That was then. Officers have been formally reinstated. You would be eligible to wear it if you chose.'

'If I accepted your offer, which would you choose?'

'I am happy to leave that entirely to you.'

Elsa did some quick thinking. *If I wear civilian clothes people might assume I am his wife or fiancée. If I go in my uniform, I would pass for an acquaintance or associate in the administration. It would be a sort of protection if I didn't like the lie of the land.*

'Since it would be a military event, I would like to take advantage of my reinstated status and wear my uniform.'

'Are you saying yes to coming, then?'

'I am saying it now. Yes. I would love to come with you to the ball, particularly as it is a joint affair. But why can you not arrange for your wife to make the journey for it like other officers?'

'Because I have no wife. I am twenty-nine. I was a regular officer when the war broke out. I have had over six years of war and no time to marry.'

'So, I would be a wife substitute,' Elsa said.

'And I would be a husband substitute,' he rejoined at once. 'I gather you have never married.'

'You were quick on that one, major.' They laughed together. It broke the ice.

'My first name is Ralph. I would like you to use it.'

'And my name is Elsa. I think you have already used it. But that is my preference.'

'Thank you, Elsa. It will be my pleasure to do so.' Their good humour persisted. Two strong personalities had at last found a common footing. Each realised it at the same time.

Once found, Elsa mused, *I wonder if it will ever break.*

She will always haunt me, Ralph thought, *as she has done since I first set my eyes on her.*

A few silent minutes passed while both allowed their previous life experiences to cascade through their minds... ushered into the past in more sense than one. It seemed from that interchange that they were fast approaching making a commitment that life could only be with each other.

28

The date of the ball was several weeks away. Elsa arranged with Lisa and James that she would be away for three days from the house and family. News of the event sent them into gyrations of speculation.

'I didn't know the major had taken a liking to Elsa,' James told Lisa. 'I remember making a passing remark when the family first came to the office. When I announced her arrival, I said to him, "She is rather beautiful, sir. She has an equally beautiful young girl with her".'

'Oh, you are making that up,' Lisa protested.

'No, I am not. That was exactly what I said to him.'

'What did he reply?' she asked.

'Something like, "Show them in, we shall see". But he never mentioned it afterwards. It was as if he kept his impressions to himself. Of course, Elsa and Erika were together and in full flight soon after that visit.'

'It must have occurred to him not to travel over sacred ground,' Lisa said. 'With Erika's death the opportunity was eventually open for him.'

'Perhaps,' James said. 'Elsa is a tough nut to crack, but as the major said, "we shall see".'

Ralph and Elsa travelled by train to Hamburg. Although the tensions from the formal cease-fire and subsequent occupation had not died down completely, the aggressive attitude and political direction administered by the Russians in their sector of occupation threw the British and Germans closer together.

The ball was mounted in the best traditions of the British Army and German Wehrmacht, with high standards of cuisine, décor, conduct, and dancing.

It was preceded by a slightly intense cocktail party, designed to enable the evaporation of any reservations and nervousness among the diverse membership.

Elsa had secured a new uniform for the occasion. The excitement of the prospects she was harbouring secretly in her mind gave her face and body a lift into her healthiest condition.

The event evoked her greatest care in turning out to be the very best she could be.

When Ralph first saw her, he stopped in his tracks.

'You have to be the belle of the ball, if ever there was one,' he said.

Ralph introduced Elsa as Oberleutnant Elsa Bauer to his British officers and their wives. Elsa introduced Ralph as Major Ralph Williams to German officers, as necessary.

All went well for them. Then Elsa espied a figure she had forgotten. She had been the commandant-in-chief of the Women's Naval Service. The last time Elsa heard of her she was based in Hamburg. She was one of the very few German women officers present.

Inevitably their paths had to cross.

The commandant had no need for an introduction and did not wait for either Ralph or Elsa to speak.

'Elsa, it's you.' Her voice was pitched at an octave about the quiet hum of conversational talk going on among the many members to the ball.

'I thought you were dead. Welcome back to the living.'

Elsa suddenly realised that Erika had not notified her return from Gotenhaven. She had been evidently waiting for instructions and how she could keep Elsa in Kiel with her. They never came.

'Commandant Schmitt. It is good to see you again,' Elsa said. 'My partner is Major Ralph Williams of the Welsh Guards. He has been heading the administration in Kiel.'

'Pleased to meet you, Major,' she said. 'And I am surprised and astonished to see Elsa Bauer again. I thought she was lost. Headquarters completely lost track of her.'

'How do you mean?' he asked.

'Nearly four hundred women in my command were killed—or drowned if you prefer—in a ship bringing them and thousands of others from Gotenhaven to Kiel. It was torpedoed by a Russian submarine.'

'Only two survived from the contingent of the Women's Naval Service,' Elsa added. 'One other and me.' Elsa could not bring herself to mention her name. 'She and I went to Dresden where our families happened to be. She was killed on the night of the sixth of February, as were my parents.'

'That was a sad loss for you on top of your own escape from the ship. But now I have found you, there is something else. I am so pleased you have survived but mystified how we lost sight of you.'

'I just stayed with the commander at Kiel and waited for instructions. You mentioned something else.'

'It's all past now, but the other thing is not what I can tell you in front of your partner, unless you give me permission to do that.'

They all smiled.

'It all depends on what you are wanting to say, ma'am,'

Elsa said.

'You were awarded the Knight's Cross of the Iron Cross for military valour, when you rescued the key engineer from Breslau.'

'What!' Elsa exclaimed. 'That too is all in the past, now.'

'It may be, but the facts still have to speak for themselves,' the commandant said.

'But where does the valour part come into it, ma'am?' Ralph asked.

'I shall have to leave the full story to Elsa. Evidently, you don't know about it?' she asked, with a smile on her face.

'It's all behind me, now, ma'am,' Elsa said, coming to her own rescue.

'I hope you both enjoy this special evening. It has been a remarkable meeting for me to see you again. And congratulations.' Elsa remained embarrassed after she had passed on to talk to others.

'The commandant has whetted my appetite to know the whole story, Elsa. You are being what we call in English "being a dark horse",' Ralph said. 'Whatever did you do to merit a military valour award?'

'Oh, it's a bit of a story. I can't bring myself to recall it now. How about later? I promise to let you know.'

Elsa was surprised but elated by the news of the award.

The officer in Breslau who promised to action an award for her had evidently kept his word. She had ceased to think anything about what she had regarded as her duty. What had her millions of compatriots done in the defence of their homeland?

The rest of the evening was conducted in the best tradition of the Welsh Guards. There was a sense of relief that warfare had been put well behind them.

Tired from their long day, Elsa and Ralph retired thankfully to their rooms in a hotel on the outskirts of Hamburg. It had survived outright destruction, though it had been damaged but subsequently repaired.

'It has been a wonderful evening, Ralph. Thank you for inviting me.'

'The ball would not have been the same without you. I could say you brought charm and beauty to the floor. It was a proud moment for me when I embarked on that first dance.'

'And was I not so full of happiness to be dancing with such a handsome man? It put my past life in the shade. It was an entrance through the gates of paradise. I never believed I would ever regard any idea with such romance,' she replied.

'But it happens. We have a date at breakfast. A day to recover.' She kissed him on the cheek.

Meeting at breakfast, they both confessed their night's sleep had been rather more restless than usual.

'Let's hope our second night will be better,' Ralph said.

As he said it, he reflected on his disturbed state. He knew the previous day spent with Elsa, rounded off with the splendid ball, had resulted in his sleeplessness.

'Of course, it will be,' Elsa suggested. 'You have to get used to a new bed.'

Her comment was given in the manner of a courteous understanding. Her own wakefulness was the result of thinking that spending time with Ralph was having the effect of turning her whole life over.

'What shall we do today?' he asked her.

'I promised to tell you my story,' Elsa reminded him. 'I

shall be glad to get it off my chest, although it is now a chapter from my recent past.'

'I cannot understand why you received a combat award,' he said again.

She did not address his comment but began her story.

'Having achieved a degree in metallurgy, I spent the first part of the war in the design department of Blohm and Voss, working on the Type XX1, which was never combat ready, although four were made seaworthy.

'The bombing drove us all from Hamburg to Gotenhaven. I was taken off the office job and attached to the small, navy's port security office. My boss put me on a month's extra training, learning to use a canoe in the night as well as the day, firing various weapons, and regular physical training.

'I had to investigate a suspicion spreading around that, just before sailing, submarine crews were sneaking on board food and ammunition beyond their allocation. During my enquiries I witnessed extra torpedoes, shells, and food being clandestinely taken on submarines that sailed the next day.

'I established that the people responsible for the practice, which would have cost them severe punishments if they had been caught, were perpetrated by ex-navy submariners who were appalled at the way the renewal of supplies to U-boats had been implemented. They were in it for the love of their country. My boss and I turned a blind eye to it in the end.

'I then toured with my boss around the eastern regions near the front line where it was reported that Russian soldiers had abused women and children to the extent that the civilian population in advance of the Russian forces had become terrified of being overtaken as victims.

'People were taking to the roads, walking westwards. We

foresaw that thousands of people could appear as an avalanche in Gotenhaven and we would be overwhelmed.

'Buildings were requisitioned, and food was collected. But finally, it was decided that a number of liners should embark the refugees and transport them to Kiel.'

'That all makes sense to me,' Ralph said. 'But it doesn't account for the fact that you have been given a combat award, which implies direct contact with the enemy. When did that happen? You seem to have run out of time.'

'As soon as I returned from the survey, the decision to evacuate the refugees overshadowed everything. My boss barely had time to write a report. Our information about the numbers on the road and the confirmation we were able to make of the atrocities that had been committed, must have had an effect on the decision that evacuation was the only safe way to save the day.

'The boss was immediately ordered to find someone to go to Breslau to rescue a key engineer from Peenemünde who was trapped by the Russians. He knew that I had been at university there. He also knew that I had mastered the handling of a canoe in the night waters of the port. I had to volunteer. He told me he would personally supervise the arrangements.

'A small troop of shock troops turned up in the aircraft that called at Gotenhaven to pick him and me up, together with my canoe. The army was waiting at Liegnitz to take us eastwards to the front. On the way we were surprised by a Russian patrol that had crossed the river and was looking for our army.

'The first of our two trucks had been sent ahead as a decoy, but my boss chose to sit in the front with the driver. The enemy patrol shot the truck to pieces, killing both men.

'As soon as the noise of the firing was heard, the six shock troops in the second truck silently disappeared into the night. We waited in expectation that the mission would be thwarted.

'Suddenly all hell was let loose in the night. And then silence. The driver of my truck, the army guides from Liegnitz, and I, were frozen with fear as well as the cold.

'What was the outcome of the firing? It was the thought in everybody's mind. Shuffling footsteps were soon followed by the call of the captain in charge of the shock troops. "It's go again. We have cleared them out. We attacked them from behind. No loss to ourselves".'

'But that still did not involve you, did it?' Ralph said.

Elsa told him to wait for a moment.

'They put me in the water five or six miles from the north-west of Breslau. I had arranged through my boss that I would rendezvous at the Dombridge. I knew it so well. Its construction was singular enough to prevent my making mistakes over its identity.

'It was freezing cold at the end of January, but I was well padded up. I was sailing against the current. When I reached the outskirts of the city I saw a crude wooden jetty, dimly visible, protruding into the river by enough feet to be a berth for a private river craft of one of the nearby houses.

'At the same time, I suddenly sensed rather than saw a small collection of men on the bank near the end of the jetty.

'They were in complete darkness. What I really saw was dictated by the lighted cigarettes some of them were smoking. I saw at a glance that four were being smoked.

'I could hear the low sound of men talking. Coming in from midstream made me more visible the closer I came to the bank, on leaving the darkness of the river. It was in fact a starlit, bitterly cold night.

'The first intimation I had that they had seen me was when I heard the sliding of their rifle bolts and an injunction, spoken in German that I instantly interpreted was in a foreign accent.

'I had no other option. I carried around my shoulders a sub-machine gun, which I had used a lot on the ranges. It was my favourite weapon. I had kept the safety catch off once I set out in the canoe.

'In a single movement I sprayed the area twice where I had seen the red glows of cigarettes, immediately supplemented by their gun flashes, as a hail of bullets came my way. There were shouts.

'Keeping as low as I could on the water, I backtracked away from the jetty. As my firing stopped, a soldier charged down the jetty firing a light machine-gun into the middle of the river. With a quick flick of the single-shot button, I felled him into the water.'

Ralph interrupted her. 'You had the incredible advantage of complete surprise. They had reached the river, which is very wide.

'In the night it must have seemed to them like reaching a seashore. The last thing they could ever have dreamed about was being attacked from the water by a girl in a canoe. It could have been a unique experience on the Russian front. But Stalin didn't give medals for that.'

It was a break that generated a laugh, another drink, and a marked inclination to be physically close.

'My first reaction was to remember I had a mission. My fear was, apart from being hit myself, that the canoe would be holed under the water line. It would have ruined the entire mission.

'I could not stop for an inspection. I just had to paddle on, hoping for the best. Nothing must be allowed to delay me. A few swift strokes took the canoe fading into the darkness. I had planned to meet at twelve o'clock midnight and intended to keep it.

'My contacts were in place. They must have searched through their night glasses as I approached. They called out to me. I was relieved to pull in to the left bank. I had arrived carrying orders for the garrison of the city. The package was close to my skin.

'The engineer had been ill. He was wrapped up so well I could not recognise his face. Several soldiers in attendance wedged him in the second seat. The aide-de-camp of the commander took my delivery. I wished him well. The city was all but surrounded. The lot of the garrison was grim, indeed.

'I then had a passenger but was paddling with the flow of the river. We nearly turned the canoe over on the return trip when we ran into ice and the passenger slumped into unconsciousness. Nevertheless, we successfully completed the journey by the appointed time.

'Back at Liegnitz the engineer was too ill to return in the aircraft. He was kept in hospital. I stayed with him. His illness saved his life—and mine, too. The Junkers 52 carrying the shock troops was shot down by fighter-bombers from one side or the other. All on board were killed. That ends the combat bit of my story, but not quite.'

'And a credit it is to you, Elsa. If you were my wife, I would be so proud of you. What did the "not quite" bit mean?'

'I visited Dresden with the only other survivor of the Women's Naval Service from the sinking of the ship in the Baltic on the last day but one of January.

'She and her family were killed, as was my own family, who had escaped from Pomerania and walked all the way to

Dresden. When the bombing started, I pleaded with them to leave their farmhouse, but they refused.

'I just could not stay there. Finally, I escaped on a navy riverboat. On the way north to Hamburg, we stopped at Magdeburg to offload the wounded and dead from Russian fighter-bomber attacks on the unit's other boat, who we were able to rescue on the way.

'While we were berthed at the Magdeburg quayside, the low flying raiders found our own ship and came round twice to attack it. Our gunners were both killed during their first attack. When they appeared the second time I jumped onto the quayside and managed to get in a long burst of sub-machine fire at the first of the two aircraft as it approached. They didn't return.'

'I think I will change what I have just said. Although you are not my wife, may I call you, my friend? I am so proud of you.'

'If you were my wife, and I was your husband, I would be ashamed to tell it—now that the war is over. War is war. It makes us behave in a way that is unnatural to us and causes so much regret. Let's go into town. The Reeperbahn is still going strong. We could find some lunch and perhaps see a film.'

'That sounds like a good suggestion,' Ralph responded.

29

Their day was consumed with constant conversation about their respective families, origins, and former employment. Elsa had not realised until then, that British regular guards' officers tended to have high qualifying backgrounds, as had been the practice in Germany. It was not unusual for applicants to have titles in the peerage, or other societal orders linked with the crown, and were often members of families from landed estates.

Ralph was not one with a title, but he came from a historic family in Wales that maintained a property set in a substantial parkland reaching back over two hundred years.

Elsa had only a story of disaster to tell him about her own family. The farm, with all its historic potential for sharing the supply of food to the nation, had been seized by the Russians and given to the Poles.

'What will you ultimately do when the children are off your hands?' Ralph asked Elsa.

'I have partly bestowed the responsibility for them on Lisa and James, but the younger ones will not reach independence, of course, for another ten years.'

'There are ways for coping with that problem,' Ralph stated. 'For example, how would you feel about bringing the youngest to Wales, to my house, which is large enough to accommodate them comfortably.'

Elsa was shaken by his suggestion. She hid her inner

turbulence by saying something she didn't mean. 'But I would be a reluctant nanny. I shall possibly go back into the design and architectural field.'

'My parents are old. I shall inherit the house as the only son.'

'You will be a lucky man, then,'

'Possessions are a snare to the unwary, Elsa. I would become a decrepit old man, rattling around in that house, in a life of solitude and joyless isolation.'

'But you could rely on your memories of the war. You are in the prime of your life. There is nothing to stop you getting married and having your own family to bring life and joy to those sterile bricks and mortar that we call a house and a home.'

She presumed to be so personal since he had given her an opening to be so.

'How wise you are, Elsa,' he said. 'I wish I had taken more trouble to cultivate the friendship of women. They seem to bring a different perspective to personal problems.'

'Are you surprised? What is a women, other than a person?' she quipped, raising a laugh.

'But I don't want answers to my questions. I am surprised that you have said that. I should have thought that you had plenty of women running after you. You could have raised new perspectives on personal problems many times.'

'Opportunity, perhaps, but no time,' he replied. 'It amazes me that the war came as I graduated. I was posted to the Middle East in the first year of the war. It proved to be a long stay, lasting until the Italian surrender.

'Then back to Britain and the preparation for the invasion of France. And then I was given the job of administration officer in charge at Kiel. I just had no opportunities to cultivate girlfriends.'

'Perhaps you were short of potential,' Elsa said. 'We have lived through a transformation of thought and practice. Before the war, the customary ways of courtship and marriage still prevailed, particularly among certain classes of people.

'In seven or eight years, the restraints of the past have been side-lined. There is a pronounced expectation that people should be less inhibited. Life has been short, so people want to do what makes their life happy.'

'You have evidently come a long way in your thinking from the aristocratic influences of Pomerania where your family and your farm were located,' Ralph said. 'Say something which illustrates the point you are making.'

'Now you are tempting me. Yesterday was yesterday. Today, or what is left of it, is before us. So why not use the time we have to good purpose?

'Let us dispense with two bedrooms tonight. You can come to my room, or I will come to yours, if you prefer, and we can spend the night together. No strings on the face of it. I am unwilling to let slip the chance for the man I secretly love to go away without his knowing it.'

'I never expected you to be so frank. I am a man of plain words, but what you are thinking has always seemed so covert. You have foxed me since I first saw you. I fell in love with you the moment you came into my office.'

He looked Elsa straight in the eyes. 'This has been an eye-opener experience for me.'

'And me, too. I don't think life can be the same for us from this moment. I shall always love you Ralph, wherever you go.'

'Have no fear. I shall not be going far or for long in future without you.'

With the coming of the evening, Ralph did the gentlemanly thing. He moved into Elsa's room. To a man, her room seemed exquisite. Everything was in its proper place, everything scented.

It doesn't seem reasonable, he thought, *she had gunned down a Russian patrol and lives like this.*

Elsa had been studying him as he came into her room. She saw the pleasantly shocked look on his face. It must have contrasted from his own room. *Perhaps he misses his batman,* she thought.

She formally and ironically welcomed him.

'Welcome, sir, I am pleased you have arrived.'

He matched her play-acting.

'It's my pleasure to spend the night with you. May this be just the first!'

'It shall be as you wish, sir. There will be bountiful times ahead if you survive the first.'

Elsa slowly put her arms around his neck and drew his lips to hers. She felt his heart racing madly, reflecting on the novel experience for her. It gave her an internal lift of unprecedented pleasure that turned to passion for the man she had finally found.

Handsome man though he was, she thought he was inexperienced. It took all her artistic genius to overcome that disability, but by the recovery of daylight the following morning, she had achieved her unmitigated wishes.

Ralph had been ushered into a new world. He had no choice but to prefer it to the old.

She rejoiced over her conquest as he did, over winning

her. Elsa mused that she could have been described as a woman who had saved the men for last.

Her colleague at Blohm and Voss was killed in the bombing of Hamburg. He had been a suspected malcontent but turned out to be a friendly partner in the midst of the wartime onslaught against Hamburg.

A justifiable exception was the chief petty officer, destined to die in a U-boat on the oceans of the world. He had told her some of the secrets of the private practice of submarine crews to top up the supplies for their boats. It had won him a one-night stand. She was drunk at the time—but it served for the purpose of establishing the facts of the case in the fulfilment of her commission.

Both had been essentially opportunistic. Neither had the slightest grounds for permanence about it. Neither could have supplanted Erika. But Ralph was very special.

Ralph stayed in Germany for a further five years. It was sufficient time to enable Elsa to supervise the whole family until Lisa had completed her degree and the older girls to pass into the age of consent. Lisa and James married and continued to care for the young people, as they had promised. Elsa and Ralph lived together until he completed his military service.

He returned to Wales to administer his estate, both parents having died, but found adequate time to travel to Kiel to be alongside his partner and to fulfil their mutual passion for another two years.

Elsa made a number of trips to Wales, interlaced with Ralph's visits to Kiel.

She made her last trip to Wales to stay once the interests of all the family had been met. Erika had left her house to Elsa and the family. In turn, Elsa assigned the house to Lisa and James, who were finally free to raise their own family.

During that time, Carla and Petra, after being in the family for two years, rejoined their mother, who had survived forced labour. She had taken a while to trace them, but glad to recoup the motherhood she had thrown away as a precaution to protect her children.

Anita and Angela had both reached young adult status. Rita had reached thirteen, Sonja twelve, and Margot ten. All the latter three accepted a journey to Wales accompanied by Elsa to retain their membership of the original family.

When Elsa and Ralph married, they were in attendance as bridesmaids.

At a later date, the adopted children of the old family were ready to welcome their parents' first child into the new family. It was a daughter, born in 1955.

Her name was Helga.

30

Forty-four years later, Helga turned over in her early morning sleep. She had been dreaming wildly that she had slept with a man. Vernon, disturbed by her movement, put his arm around her.

'It's daylight. We have slept in. The night was to be only a view of the dancing and a story to follow…'

'It turned out to be a long story, with sex, sleep, and breakfast in bed,' Helga said, interrupting his train of thought. 'What a night! I can't fault it. Shall we do it again tonight?'

'But you won't have another story to tell. It was a remarkable account of your mother's career. What a wonderful woman she was. What a wonderful woman you are. I can see so much of what you have told me about her in you.'

'I don't know about that. Say something that will convince me.'

'You are like your mother in the way you tell a story. And taking the initiative in love-making is your speciality, as it was your mother's.'

'Is there anything wrong with that?'

'Absolutely not. It is so refreshing to meet a woman free from passivity.'

'It's part of life to be lively,' she stated quietly.

'I must say your stamina came to your aid last night. I never expected the story to be so long and so fulsome,' Vernon said.

'It was one way to get you into bed.'

'Then it must be an outstanding example of the seductive art.'

'It has never been practised by me until now,' she said, 'call it opportunism on my part, but you were designedly curious about the origin of my name, so it occurred to me that I would make an evening, or rather a night of it. I hope you have no regrets.'

'You have your mother's charm and powers of persuasion. Of course, I have no regrets, only that I didn't meet you long ago. I am staking my life on the years to come.'

'I will join you in that proposition,' she added. 'The day in Holyhead was a catalyst for both of us and a testimony to Elsa.'